Gator Queen

COVER DESIGN BY ALEXANDRA ALLEN

COVER IMAGES: SHUTTERSTOCK.COM

TYPESET BY TYPO-GLYPHIX

ISBN: 979-8-9893269-4-5

To the land of swamps, sunshine,
and suspicious characters.
Florida, you will always be
my problematic muse.

Chapter One

If alligators are the descendants of dinosaurs, this teeny reptile was disappointing millions of years of evolution.

The cute little two-footer paddled lazily in a backyard pool, circling a giant green alligator float. Maybe he thought the pool toy was his momma.

"Get a look at that beast. I can't believe this crap. What a way to start the new year." The homeowner was one of Wahoo's newest residents, if the moving boxes piled to the side of the salmon-colored stucco home were any indication. He ran a hand over his sweaty bald head and glanced at his preteen son, who was capturing the entire scene on his cell phone.

Northerners. They were so adorable. They always lost it over their first flying Florida cockroach and when they spotted that first alligator in the wild.

Or in their pool.

I set my duffel bag on a glass patio table, which was shaded by an umbrella the same hue as the house. "It's a baby. Not dangerous at all. Probably more afraid of us than we are of it. No need to panic."

"Oh, I'm plenty afraid of it, don't you worry. You don't see this kinda thing in Jersey. We've been here only ten days, and this monster shows up in our pool. Is trapping gonna take all day? I have some business to get to. First of the new year and all that shit. Gotta hustle, you know." The guy's thick New Jersey accent came out in one staccato string.

"Dad, you're a wuss, not a hustler," the kid chimed in. Both father and son sported baggy cargo shorts, potbellies, and fresh sunburns on their pale skin.

"Oh, I'm a hustler all right. But if your mother sees this, she's going to get on the next plane to Newark." The guy screwed up his face as he gestured toward the pool with a meaty hand. "My wife's in Orlando, doing some shopping. I want this thing gone before she comes home."

I shot him a reassuring smile. "Shouldn't take long to catch him. I could get in the pool and grab him, but I didn't bring my swimsuit."

The guy's jaw dropped and his eyes fell to my chest. Perv. He was in a tank top, and a downy pelt of hair covered his beefy shoulders.

"Kidding," I said. "You don't happen to have a pool net, do you?"

I had a snatch hook in the truck, but this gator was so small that a net would work just as well.

"Are you qualified to catch that thing? You look kinda young. What did you say your name was?" The man squinted at me in disbelief, probably because I was all of five-three and, at twenty-five, still routinely carded at bars.

"Maggie. Maggie Andrews." I unzipped my duffel and fished my laminated Florida gator permit out of a plastic zip-top bag. It declared that I was a certified trapper under the Statewide Nuisance Alligator Program, charmingly known as SNAP. I handed it to him.

His eyes flicked to the card, then he hastily gave it back. "OK, Maggie. I'll grab my pool skimmer."

"Mind if I take a photo?" I called out.

The guy stopped in his tracks and turned. "I don't want it out there publicly, like on social media. I'm a private person. Unlike this joker over here." He jerked a thumb toward his son, who stuck out his tongue.

"Oh, it's for my own records. I like to have photos of the critters I catch. So I can show future clients."

"Sure, go ahead."

He waved his hand at the tiny gator. It was now undulating through the water, using its tail to glide smoothly along the surface. When it reached one end of the pool, it did an Olympic-level turn underwater, as if it were doing laps. The January air was hot as Satan's wet fart, and I couldn't blame the little guy for wanting to take a dip.

The creature was probably having the best swim of its life. I was definitely jealous.

I stood at the edge of the pool and snapped a couple of photos on my phone while the guy hustled over to a white aluminum shed on the side of the property.

"For my records, what's your full name? I didn't quite catch it on the voicemail," I said.

"Bruce Doyle," he hollered. "That's my son, Brandon."

"Nice to meet you both." I returned to the table, rooting around in my large duffel. After I found my notebook, I jotted down Bruce's name and info. Then I attached a roll of duct tape to a clip on my belt and took out a bag of mini marshmallows.

The kid sidled up to me. "What are you doing with those?"

I went to open the package. "You want some?"

"Sure."

I used my Swiss Army knife to cut the plastic and extracted a few plump pillows of sugar, then deposited them in the kid's grubby hand. "Gators think they're eggs. When I throw one in the pool, it'll swim toward me, and I can catch it easier. But I have to warn you. Never, ever feed a gator yourself. This is only for professionals, and only for trapping purposes."

"Whoa. Epic." The kid popped the marshmallow in his mouth and swallowed it after a single bite. "My dad panicked when he saw the gator in the pool. He almost dropped his coffee cup. He's worried it's gonna eat our chihuahuas."

"That's a valid concern, my dude. Gators like to snack on small dogs, probably as much as you like those marshmallows." The kid stole another handful and shoved them in his mouth.

The dad lumbered over with the pool net and stared dubiously at the marshmallow package lying on the glass patio table. "You sure you know what you're doing?"

I fished two marshmallows out of the package and stood, motioning for him to hand me the net.

"It's no sweat, I've done this dozens of times. I'll get him out of here in no time. Y'all might want to stand back." I could probably grab the creature with my hands, but that would involve climbing into the water, and I didn't want to get my cute new Gator Queen T-shirt wet. I paused for dramatic effect and winked. "This could get a little rough."

"Sweet. I'm gonna post this online," the kid yelled while aiming his cell at me.

"For God's sakes, Brandon, don't get your arm chomped off. And for the millionth time, don't put our address on the interwebs. Christ, I knew there were alligators in Florida. I didn't think they'd end up in my pool. I was even gonna take a morning swim until this happened." The guy rambled on for a bit about the humidity.

"It's going to be a hot one all right," I said in a cheery voice. I'd been home all of six weeks and the warm weather had settled into my bones. And in my pores. And in crevices I'd forgotten about while living in Boston.

You could take the girl out of Florida, but you could never take Florida out of the girl.

Bruce stood there with his hands pressed into his hips, which only accentuated his fireplug-like body. "Where do you think the gator came from?"

"Well, there's that canal out back, and a swampy area, too. Plus a few small lakes. Gators are in almost every freshwater source in Florida." I took a few steps to the deep end of the pool. "There are about one-point-two-five million gators in the state, and some of them end up in backyards and pools. Sometimes they even knock on doors. I'd suggest getting a screened enclosure if you don't want this to happen again."

I didn't tell him that a large enough gator would rip through a pool enclosure like the Kool-Aid Man busting through a wall. A screen would probably deter the smaller critters like this one.

Maybe.

I tossed a marshmallow about eight feet into the water, a foot from the gator's snout. Within a few seconds, it floated over, opened its jaws, and snapped them shut around the candy. The kid let out a muffled squeal.

"Cool, right?" I said.

"Way cool," the kid responded.

"You need help?" the guy called out, from a safe distance. "Should we call for backup?"

"Nah, I've got this." Adrenaline surged through me. Even though this was only a small gator, I hadn't officially caught one here in Florida in a couple of years. The last time was when I'd come home from Boston and gone on a call with Dad. We'd nabbed a twelve-footer that day.

By my family's standards, that was what passed for a cherished memory.

With my toes at the edge of the pool, I dropped the second marshmallow into the water between me and the reptile.

"Come to momma, baby gator," I whispered.

The critter turned in my direction, aiming its snout right at the marshmallow. It was a cutie all right, with black and tan stripes on its tail and body, markings that would eventually fade to a menacing, leathery, dark gray in adulthood. It submerged everything but its gold-green eyes. Some people thought reptiles were gross. To me, they were a quirky bunch of misunderstood characters in the animal kingdom.

The gator tucked its little feet against its body and propelled itself forward with its muscular tail.

I readied the net. When the gator opened its mouth to chomp the marshmallow, I swiftly dipped the net into the water and scooped the reptile up, making sure to maneuver the skimmer so the animal twisted and tangled in the mesh. It squirmed and thrashed violently, spraying droplets of water everywhere.

Using a hand-over-fist motion on the pole, I drew the net closer to me, then slowly crouched. The gator was so small that I wasn't too concerned about getting hurt. I flipped the net on the ground, open side down. I kept one knee on the net's handle while my hands went to my duct tape dispenser. I tore off a foot-long piece of silver tape and stuck one end to my left bicep.

Through the net, I clamped one hand firmly around the back of the gator's neck to immobilize it. Its little tail whipped against my forearm but caused no pain—I'd sustained much worse from far more menacing creatures.

Carefully, I lifted the aluminum rim of the pool skimmer and grabbed the reptile with my other hand, dragging it from under the net. I kept it pinned to the ground while I reached for the tape, then wrangled it around its snout.

"Gotcha," I said.

I picked up the gator, resting its slim body on my forearm. The smooth belly felt pleasantly cool against my sunbaked bare skin.

My upturned hand clamped around its stubby front arms and throat. "There we go. We'll get you to somewhere more fun than a pool."

"That was the most awesomest thing I've ever seen," cried the kid.

"Uh, you gonna let him loose in the swamp back there, or what? What if it returns? Then what? Can I shoot it?" The dad gestured to the wild thicket behind the house. "I'll get my Glock and—"

"No, please don't shoot it. It's against the law unless you're in imminent danger. I'll take him far away and he'll never come back. Lemme secure him in my truck then I'll return for my stuff, OK?"

The dad nodded weakly.

It didn't take me long to nestle the alligator in the cage in the back of my beat-up, cherry-red Ford F-150, which used to be Dad's and happened to be almost the same color as my Gator Queen shirt. I paused to clean my hands with some lavender-scented hand wipes while taking in the neighborhood.

This was one of many new subdivisions in Wahoo, making the town look more like a suburban outpost of a big city than a small central Florida village. The homes here in Osprey Landing—that was the name of this development—were crammed together, generic stucco buildings with uniform electric-green lawns the size of mattresses. When I was growing up, this had been an orange grove, and my twin sister and I used to steal the sweet fruit and eat it at the edge of the swamp. Our hands and faces would be sticky with juice and we'd ride our bikes home.

Now there wasn't an orange tree in sight, much less kids on bicycles.

With a sigh, I returned to the backyard for the last of my gear.

The boy was sitting with his feet in the pool, hunched over his phone. I scooped up my trusty duffel bag and sauntered over to Bruce, his brow furrowed with a mix of confusion and mild disbelief. He stood there, scratching his hairy shoulder as he surveyed the pool, likely questioning the sanity of his decision to settle in a place where prehistoric creatures appeared to have an open invitation to party in his backyard.

My sister's voice popped into my head. Since I'd returned home, Vera had insisted that we hand out our business cards. Marketing, she implored.

"Here's my card, in case you need anything else. I trap gators, snakes, iguanas, and turtles. Raccoons and possums aren't my jam. I'm better with reptiles. Oh, and my sister is opening a specialty bookstore downtown. All romance novels. Maybe you and your wife want to stop by. She opens two weeks from today. I'm helping out. The address is on the other side of the card."

My sister had affixed cute stickers with the store's name and address to the back of my gator cards. She claimed that the combo was so quirky it would almost certainly draw business to the bookstore. I wasn't so sure. It seemed a little weird, but this was Wahoo, a place so eccentric that this tactic just might work.

Bruce took the shiny red card and turned it over. "Wow. A girl who traps gators. Gator Queen," he read slowly, totally ignoring my pitch for the store. "Weird, I thought I called a business called Gator King. A neighbor suggested you. You were actually the second place I called. I, uh, left a message for the first place, but they never called back."

"The Gator King was Logan Andrews, my dad. He was the county's contracted nuisance alligator trapper. He passed a few months ago and I took over his business and rebranded. I'd always go on calls with him when I was a kid, so he called me the Gator Queen." Even mentioning Dad made my chest feel heavy. "This is actually my first job since taking over the business."

He nodded slowly. "I see. Well, great job. How much do I owe you?"

"Fifty dollars."

"Fifty bucks? That seems cheap."

"It's what private trappers are allowed to charge in Florida."

"That's a shame, considering you put your life on the line. You have a dangerous job, especially for a girl."

I took a fortifying inhale. I'd expected some casual sexism, but maybe not in my first hour on the job. He extracted his wallet and counted five tens before handing them to me with a grin.

"Thanks again, Maggie. It was pretty crazy, finding a gator in the pool. That brute looked like it could eat my dog."

"Nah, he's actually a young'un. You should see some of the gators in the swamps. Fifteen-footers. That's why I recommend the pool enclosure."

"What do you do with the gators, anyway? Turn them into boots and belts? I heard that people here in Florida eat gator meat. I can't even—" He pantomimed a gag.

"I'm the only trapper in the region who doesn't kill the gators. Most trappers bring the big ones to a processor for meat and hide. The ones under four feet, I'll take to a nearby swamp and release them. I can't set the bigger ones loose because they'll fight each other, so I bring those to my uncle, who runs the reptile sanctuary here in town. It's called Tropical Acres, you might want to check it out, he does private tours. It's a pretty interesting place and your son might enjoy it."

"That's nice you don't kill 'em, I guess. Lemme walk you out. And tell me more about what's in that swamp back there behind the house."

I waved goodbye to the kid, who ignored me for his phone. "Well, there's a bunch of turtles, some bass fish, and the gators in the canal. They roam around for food. So be careful. And please don't feed them. That's how they become nuisances. I only used the marshmallows today so we could take care of this quickly."

We were at the back gate and he swung it open. "I'll be honest, I was shocked when you drove up. You're what, all of five feet, a hundred pounds soaking wet. I didn't think a girl like you would show up to trap a gator."

I raised myself up to my full height and attempted a cool stare. My sister called this my "intimidating garden gnome" look, which made no sense, but that was Vera.

His eyes fixed on my crotch, then back up to my chest. I shot him a glare. Pig.

Hoo boy. Even in Boston, when I worked at the zoo, men had always commented how I was too small, or too young, to be handling reptiles. Dad used to laugh at comments like that and would proudly say he raised tough-ass girls.

"My family's been trapping gators for four generations in these parts. I caught my first baby gator when I was six. It was about the size of this one."

With a tight smile, I said goodbye and climbed into my truck. It was time to bring the reptile to Gator Heaven.

No, really. That was what my family had dubbed the swamp on the edge of town—Gator Heaven. It was owned by the Covington family, who also farmed citrus. This particular piece of land was too wet to plant orange trees, and the family had kept it wild and undeveloped for decades. Because my grandfather had grown up with one of the Covington boys, he'd gotten permission to release the wildlife that we trapped into the wetland on the property. We'd been going there for decades with our little gators.

It took me two attempts to exit the subdivision because every street looked identical. I pulled over to study the map on my phone so I could decipher the twisting roads to nowhere. It struck me that the development was probably named after the very thing it displaced—ospreys—and I breathed a sigh of relief when I finally pulled out onto a more familiar street.

I headed west out of town, passing one of the two remaining orange groves in Wahoo. Workers with heavy burlap sacks slung around their bodies picked the last of the season's ripe fruit off the trees, reminding me that I should probably stop at my favorite produce stand at some point to grab a bag. I'd been here for more than a month and hadn't had a single glass of freshly squeezed juice.

My mouth watered when I thought about the sugary liquid sunshine mixed with a shot of vodka. Mmm. Screwdrivers.

At the stop sign next to a gas station, I banged a left, then slowed about a mile down the road. I hadn't been to this swamp in years and frowned when approaching what I thought was the dirt road leading to the wetland. A heavy chain attached to two wooden posts stretched across the road.

There was also a sign with a photo of a house similar to the one I'd just left. I slowed the truck to a stop and gaped in horror.

COMING SOON: Sunny Meadows
Homes starting at $500K!

"What the hell? Come on!" My voice bounced around the cab of the truck and I slammed my palm on the steering wheel.

Chapter Two

When had the Covingtons sold the property? And who in their right mind would pay a half million bucks for a home in a swamp, where mosquitoes were thicker than humidity in August?

Also, wasn't it illegal to build on a swamp? Possibly, but it was Florida, where developers didn't care about stuff like that.

"Shit," I muttered, while calling Vera.

She picked up on the first ring and her squeaky voice hit my ear. "Well, that's pretty quick for a giant gator. Did you have to wrassle him?"

Even though she wasn't technically involved in my business, she'd trapped more than a few reptiles in her time.

"It was a two-footer. A baby. Grabbed him with a pool net and some marshmallows. Listen. I'm at Gator Heaven and there's a chain across the road and a sign saying that the property's becoming a housing development. What's going on? What should I do with the alligator?"

She emitted a screech that made me hold the phone away from my ear. "Shut the front door! The Covingtons finally sold the parcel? I heard the deal was in the works but didn't know it actually went through. The city council hasn't approved the development, so maybe there's still hope. You know I've been fighting that for months."

Vera protested almost all new developments in town, hoping to keep the undeveloped parts of Wahoo pristine. Well, as pristine as a small town with a pill problem and a heavy dose of Florida shadiness could be. Yet amid the chaos of eccentric locals, drug dealers, and the occasional illegal business enterprise, Vera stood firm in her mission, tirelessly fighting to preserve the town's questionable charm. Bless her stubborn soul.

She was a member of Friends of the Everglades, or FOE. Now that I thought about it, there were a lot of cute acronyms in the Sunshine State.

"OK, we can talk about your activism later." I drummed my fingers on the steering wheel.

"Meet me for lunch downtown and I'll try to find out more on the land deal."

"I can't bring the gator to lunch and don't want to leave him in my truck." Sometimes my twin sister could be a little airheaded. She was a human exclamation point, whereas I was more of a comma in the grand scheme of things.

Necessary for structure, but not at all flashy.

"Right. Bring the gator to Uncle Bert. I'll call and let him know you're on the way."

"Thanks. I'll see you in a little while. Text me the name of the restaurant."

We hung up and I peeled out, annoyed. It took me another ten minutes to reach Bert's place on the edge of town. It was a kitschy roadside tourist attraction that had been in my family for decades. He and his wife, Lolo, lived a few doors down from me and Vera, but the sanctuary was Bert's true home.

When I parked in front of the tired-looking, homemade wooden sign that read SEE LIVE GATORS HERE AT TROPICAL ACRES, my phone pinged with a text from my sister.

> *I just ran into Bert downtown. He said to use the key under the Skunk Ape statue to get into the kennel area. Use the green door to the left, then the keys for the kennels are on a hook.*

She also included the name of the restaurant, a place I'd heard about but had never been. Unlike Uncle Bert, who was firmly still living in Old Florida, downtown was dotted with several new hip cafés and bars, the kind that served oat milk lattes and kombucha cocktails. So much had changed here in Wahoo since I moved away eight years ago, but Vera—who had moved back years before I did—had kept me mostly up to date.

k, I texted back.

First, I located the Skunk Ape statue, which was at the far end of the parking lot. It was about three feet high and made of a lightweight plastic. It resembled a yeti crossed with Chewbacca. Now that I was staring at it for the first time in years, I realized it might actually be Chewbacca, and not a Skunk Ape, which was Florida's version of Bigfoot. I lifted it up and scooted out a dirt-covered key with the toe of my sneaker.

I blew the sandy dirt off the key, then went to unlock the green door. Because the place hadn't changed in decades, a sense of childhood familiarity washed over me as I passed through a canopy of bamboo, which led to the outdoor kennels.

Made up of fiberglass-walled cubes and sturdy steel gates, this was the intake area for the new reptiles. I peered into each cage, curious to see the latest critters, but today the six bays were empty. I found the kennel keys on a hook and unlocked the first bay. There was a stack of large empty plastic tubs and a nearby spigot, and I filled two of them and placed them inside the kennel.

I returned to my truck, grabbed the gator, carefully removed the duct tape, and released it into the cubby, making sure the latch was secure so it wouldn't escape. The reptile could chill in this shady spot until my uncle returned, and then he could decide where to let the creature loose. The sanctuary had a pond and a small swampy area, plus a huge man-made pond for the well-behaved smaller reptiles.

It was also possible that Bert knew of some other swamp to release the gator into. He was an expert trapper and fisherman, and had identified all sorts of secret wild spots. He'd promised to help me with the gator business, since I'd need assistance with any calls involving gators over about eight feet. Even though I was fast and careful with the reptiles, it paid to have someone help with the bigger critters.

Still, most people didn't call about those. It was the young juveniles that gave folks problems.

As long as the reptiles were safe, weren't harassing anyone, and were not turned into belts, I didn't give a crap where they lived. Dad hadn't killed gators unless it was absolutely necessary, and I wasn't about to either.

After locking up, I made sure the key went back under the Skunk Ape statue.

Back in my truck, I sniffed my hands and reached for the wipes again. Gators smell like damp earth and rotten fish, with a hint of algae. It's the only downside to trapping them. Well, that and the potential for danger, but I'd long since accepted that.

I'd prefer to take my chances with a gator than most humans, to be honest.

I roared out of the parking lot and drove to town, still salty about the probable development of the swamp. Why did everything beautiful in Florida have to be paved over?

Downtown was packed, with too few parking spaces for too many locals and tourists, all of whom drifted in and out of the little shops on Main Street. It was January in Florida, which meant the weather was peak perfection for both locals and tourists: sunny, dry, and relatively cool.

Me? I was still used to the cold weather of Boston, so by the time I got out of the truck, I was sweating my tits off.

Vera had asked me to meet her at a place called Cheesy Does It, a new and popular café in town. She knew of my love for toasted cheese sandwiches since we'd always made them as kids, so it was natural that she'd picked this place. The parking gods smiled on me, and a spot opened up right in front of the restaurant.

It was next door to one of the many reasons I'd come home: Vera was now the proud owner of Straight From the Heart, a store devoted to romance novels. She'd dreamed of opening a bookstore since we were teens, and we'd brainstormed the romance idea in college because we adored the genre.

During the pandemic, we'd both decided to follow our hearts and pursue our bliss. Or maybe this was a quarter-life crisis, a concept I'd long classified as clickbait. Either way, the two of us were going a little sideways in the career department this year.

She'd quit her job at the town library to open the bookstore, and opening day was in two short weeks. Meanwhile, I'd walked away from my job as a reptile feeder at the Boston Zoo and moved home, all to help Vera and keep Dad's legacy alive.

My decision to come back to Wahoo had come at the end of a long and shitty year. When Dad was diagnosed with cancer, he'd asked me for two favors: take care of Vera and take over his gator trapping business. A global pandemic and his death were the universe's way of telling me that I needed to make a life change and come home to be with my twin sister.

Vera and I figured that we'd help each other's businesses with our collective money, time, and brainpower. She could help me trap gators and I could work at the store. We could both manage the short-term rentals of the three cabins on her property. Win-win.

And so I was back, in a place where I wasn't sure I still belonged. Most of the six weeks I'd been home had been spent taking care of paperwork for our respective businesses and trying to feel normal again. That, and the holidays.

I wound my way inside Cheesy Does It, passing through a throng of people waiting for tables. Vera, who knew everyone in town, had gotten a prime seat by the window. She waved me over, and I plunked down across from her, my stomach growling at the delicious smell of grilled buttered bread and ooey-gooey cheese in the air.

"I'm shocked you're already here," I said.

"I'm trying to get better about being on time." She was infamous in our family for being late for everything. She'd even been late to our father's funeral.

She smiled, and it was like a blast of sunshine poured into the room. With her bright blue eyes, her milky skin, and the smattering of freckles on her nose, my sister had that special kind of inner beauty glow. Make no mistake, though: she could wrestle a ten-foot gator into submission if necessary. And she was only growing fiercer since starting that Krav Maga class. I eyed her defined arm muscles.

"Have you eaten here since you got home?" she asked.

I shook my head. I'd been too busy sorting through Dad's estate and wrapping up the details of my former life. And getting reacquainted with my new one. For some reason, I'd been hesitant about slipping back into the Wahoo social scene since I'd arrived home. I'd even waited until after the holidays to officially begin trapping critters and, until today, had sent all gator calls to a man in the next town over.

I just didn't feel like people-ing. Maybe it was because I'd dealt with so many in my job at the zoo, but all I wanted was to hang out at home with my kitten and read.

"I ordered you the toasted gouda cheese and tomato soup. And your sweet tea should be coming soon too."

That was the benefit of being a twin, even a non-identical one. Vera always knew what I wanted in cases like this, and I intuitively sensed her preferences too. It used to annoy us as teens, but now it provided a comforting familiarity in a world turned upside down.

"Thanks."

"So, how'd it go? How did it feel to trap again?"

"It was pretty easy. I'd hoped for something far more exciting." I removed my sunglasses and rubbed my eyes. "What's the deal with the Covington property?"

"Oh, I got the dirt. Old man Covington's going into a nursing home. His kids decided to sell. They're all out of state, you know."

"Ah. So they got greedy and gave in to a developer. Douche canoes."

"You've really become quite foul-mouthed." Vera glared at me. For some reason, she'd never embraced the family tradition of colorful swearing. "It was some out-of-town guy from up north."

"Do you think the city council will approve the development? That sign on the property seems pretty final."

She raised her voice to be heard over the din of conversation. "A new council was just sworn in at the beginning of the year. There's a new member who might shake things up a lot. The vote on rezoning the property is coming up soon."

"The new council member, do you know how they'll vote on the rezoning?" I couldn't believe that I, a twenty-five-year-old woman who had more college debt than years left in life, was talking about adult things like zoning. Between this and dealing with Dad's estate, I barely recognized myself.

Vera shrugged. "During the campaign, he refused to say what he thought about that particular parcel of land."

"Which probably means he's in favor of development."

"Maybe not." She had a defensive tone in her voice. "We'll see."

"Who's the new council member? Anyone we know?"

"Tyler Carr." She stared at her napkin as if she'd never seen one before.

"Tyler Carr, as in homecoming king and Wahoo High football quarterback? The guy who called us nerds and geeks and whores and sluts for several long and terrible years?"

"He's not so bad now," she mumbled.

I snorted out a *hmph* sound. "By 'not so bad,' do you mean he's not cooking meth like half of our graduating class? Or do you mean he's found some white-collar job that allows him to perform some lucrative grift so he can drive around in a stupidly expensive luxury vehicle?"

"Shhhh." Vera leaned in. "He's sitting at that table nearest to the kitchen. Don't be too obvious but look a little to the left. He's a legitimate businessman, Maggie. Not everyone in Florida is corrupt, or criminal, or shady."

"Yeah, right," I muttered.

With a sly little grin, I shifted my eyes and scanned the crowd. Tyler was far across the crowded room. He was a generically handsome guy with close-cropped brown hair and a midnight-blue suit. The glint of an expensive-looking wristwatch caught my attention. He was dining with a man I didn't recognize. "Oh yeah, there he is. He looks as smarmy as I remember. Eight years hasn't changed his ass face."

Vera's expression pinched. "You should give him another chance. He's a decent guy."

I shifted back into my seat and stared at my sister warily. She'd recently gone blonder and done some special Brazilian keratin treatment to straighten her hair. This set us apart as twins even more. My hair was natural, curly, and the color of toasted chestnuts.

At least, that's what my hairdresser up north had said.

Vera had always been the prettier, daintier twin. Although she'd probably deny that since she'd gotten vitiligo, a condition that turned patches of her skin white, back when we were in high school. That had made her insecure about her looks ever since.

I sensed that she didn't want to talk about Tyler. Hell. I hoped she wasn't secretly dating him. Since I'd arrived home, she'd been uncharacteristically cagey about her private life. She'd also been taking a ton of exercise classes. Vera had the worst taste in men, and at the ripe old age of twenty-five was desperate for the happy-ever-after she read about in books.

Me? I was taking a break from men. At least for the next year or two. Not because I'd been burned or scorned or anything dramatic. It was time to focus on me. I'd had enough shitty relationships, enough dates with dudes who wanted to screw and scram.

I changed the subject. "We're going to have to find a new place to release the small gators."

The server appeared with our food, and Vera took a stack of business cards out of her purse and handed one to her.

"In case you need a wildlife trapper, or"—she flipped the card over—"a new book!"

The server, a teenager who was probably not even old enough to vote, pocketed the card. "Wow, that's some combo."

"You're relentless," I muttered to Vera as the server walked away.

"It's brilliant, isn't it? That's the fifth card I've given away today. I'm sprinkling them around town like pixie dust." She smiled triumphantly.

Between bites, we debated other necessities for the store and talked about which nearby pond or swamp would be best for the catch-and-release critters. Admittedly, our dual passions—gators and romance novels—didn't really go together like peanut butter and chocolate.

But for Vera and me, it was all part of our upbringing. Dad had trapped reptiles, Mom had read romance. To us, it made sense. Since they were both gone, it was our way of honoring them.

"There's a park on the east side of town, but it's owned by the county so we'd have to get permission to release the gators," Vera said, adding that a friend of hers owned a small cattle ranch that had a river on the property, but she wasn't sure if he'd want gators near his cows.

The river in back of Vera's property—well, our property—was also a possibility, but neither of us wanted a gaggle of gators congregating in the yard. We loved them, but not that much.

"I'll ask around. Don't worry." She took a bite of her spicy chicken bacon ranch melted sandwich.

"How's things going with the store? Did you get the final occupancy permits?"

"I went to City Hall this morning. There are a couple of minor obstacles."

I wiped my mouth with a napkin. "Like what?"

"We need special permits if we're going to serve food. I didn't realize that. What the fluff is that about?" She opened her mouth as if to say more, then closed it. Although she hadn't planned to serve food right away, it seemed like a snag not to have the necessary permits in hand before opening.

"What's going on? Tell me," I probed. "Do you need me to step in and handle that? You've got a full plate with the redecorating. Also, you look a little tired. I think you need to slow down a bit. Maybe take a day off."

"You didn't come home to run the bookstore. And you didn't come home to take care of me," she said in a defensive tone. "Stop trying to fix everything. Nothing's broken. You're doing it again, I can tell."

"Doing what?" I'd never told Vera that Dad had asked me to look after her. He'd thought she was a bit of a fragile snowflake, like Mom had been. Dad and I were of sturdier stock. Or so I believed.

"Worrying. Dictating. Controlling."

"Jesus, Vera, you make me sound like a terrible human. I came home to help you. I came home so we could be a team." As I studied her in the bright sunshine filtering through the window, I spotted a new patch of white vitiligo under her left eye. It was obvious that she'd tried to cover it with heavy makeup. Why she went to those lengths, I wasn't sure—she was fanatical about not getting any sun, so her normal skin wasn't that dark to begin with.

I wondered if she was purposefully not telling me certain things about the business or her personal life. Or if she was worried about the spread of her white patches. She'd mentioned that it had overtaken her shoulders and most of her back.

Her gaze darted over my head.

"Oh fluff," she said. *Fluff* was her go-to alternative swear word.

"What?"

"Gene's here."

"Shit," I whispered, contorting my face into a grimace. It was always bad news when the Andrews sisters were under the same roof as Gator Gene.

Chapter Three

"**D**on't make eye contact," Vera hissed. "He smells fear. Like a shark, but not as smart."

"Pfft. Like I'm afraid of that prick." Maybe Gene wouldn't notice us and would move along, since the restaurant was so crowded.

Vera stared at her half-eaten sandwich, her lips pursed in downward disgust.

Gene was the other alligator trapper in Wahoo, one with a long-standing grudge against my family. The biggest skirmish had happened right when we were graduating from high school, when Dad trapped an elusive nine-hundred-pound gator on the Wahoo Country Club golf course. Gene had wanted the capture in the worst way, thinking it would bring him notoriety and more business.

Instead, my dad nabbed the beast and found himself on the front page of the *Orlando Sentinel*. Because he'd turned the gator over to my uncle's sanctuary instead of selling the creature for its lucrative skin, Dad had received a humane society award. That burned Gene's biscuit.

That was his true fault: greed. Somehow, he thought that trapping gators would make him rich or famous. Which was absurd. As Dad used to say, humane trapping was a public service and a way to honor wildlife, not a route to fame or money.

Gene was the reason I'd referred all trapping queries that came my way to the guy in Sunny Shores these past six weeks while I was getting my act together. Sending any business to Gene was out of the question.

The sound of heavy footsteps reached my ears, followed by the smell of fish wafting into my nostrils.

"Good afternoon, girls."

It had been ages since I last heard Gene's voice, but as soon as he spoke, it came rushing back to me like an unpleasant blast from the past. Phlegmy, just as I remembered it.

"Oh. Gene. Thought I heard the clown car pull up. What do you want?" My sister clutched her tea glass, probably readying to douse him. Yikes on bikes. She disliked him more than anyone in town. I'd learned patience since I last saw Gene. I wasn't sure if Vera had.

This situation needed a peacemaker, fast.

Gene grabbed an empty chair from a nearby table, not even asking the diners if he could take it, which made them stare in disbelief. He set it against our small square table and straddled the seat backwards.

His tan fishing vest was open, revealing a black T-shirt with white lettering that said *I'm not a gynecologist but I'll take a look.*

I visibly grimaced at both the grammar and the sentiment.

Ever since I could remember, he had been skeevy, sexist, and surly. Usually all three at once. Dad used to say that "the cheese had slid off Gene's cracker," and it was hard to disagree with that assessment. I simply thought he was a pimple on the ass of progress.

"Gene," I said, my tone dripping with sarcasm. "How long has it been since we've seen each other?"

"Not long enough," Vera muttered.

"Truth," I murmured back.

"Cut the BS, Margaret. I know you're home for good. Couldn't hack it in Boston, could you? That fancy biology degree you got didn't amount to a hill of beans, did it?"

That set my teeth on edge. No one called me Margaret except for Mom and Dad, and they were gone. And exactly what had Gene heard around town about me? Asshat.

"What do you want?" The frostiness in my sister's tone lowered the temperature in this place by ten degrees.

"You know why I'm here. You stole that gator from me." He stabbed a porky finger in my direction.

I batted my eyelashes innocently and stared at his brown hair, which was styled in something resembling a pompadour. Gene was about ten years older than us, which meant he was around thirty-five. A memory of him offering to buy us beer and "party" when Vera and I were sophomores in high school surfaced, and I fought back nausea.

"What gator?"

"The one at Osprey Landing."

The tops of my sister's cheeks had flared pink, and her fingers around the sweet tea glass were white.

I held up my hand. "The homeowner said he left a message for another trapper but didn't hear back, then called me. He was in a panic. If he called you first, well, you snooze, you lose."

"I thought when your father passed—may his soul rest in heaven—that I'd be done with your family." He sucked on his teeth. Or what was left of them.

"This gator wasn't up your alley, anyway." I stirred my tomato soup. "It was only a two-footer. Under state regulations, you would've had to let it go. Not like you pay attention to the law, though."

He glared at me with eyes the color of dirty denim.

Gene wouldn't have released the baby gator into the wild. Everyone in town knew he ignored the state's rules about relocating small alligators, opting to sell them to clandestine hide processors. Or so the rumor went. All we knew was that he was extremely competitive for the reptiles, whose skins were worth more than the fifty-dollar trapping stipend.

Since baby gators had those distinctive stripes, they were prized by the illegal processors, who made them into belts and small purses.

"There are enough gators to go around. Don't be ridiculous," my sister piped up.

"Don't you two have a dirty bookstore to open?"

My sister's hand slid to her butter knife. I reached to cover her fingers with my palm.

"Gene, if you don't mind, we're enjoying lunch. Or were," I said. "And Vera's bookstore's specialty is romance novels, not pornography. Maybe if men read more romance, they'd understand women better."

"I don't need any help in that department."

My sister snorted. "That's not what your wife says."

"Vera." I shot her a warning look.

He stood and glared down at us. "You girls better watch yourselves and not steal any more jobs from me. It's not like you need the money, with what your father left you. I'm doing a reality TV show about my trapping business, and I won't have you interfering. And that's why I really came over to talk to you."

"Who would want to watch your ugly face on TV?" Vera retorted.

He smirked, which made me want to throat-punch him. "Plenty of people. And I'm hearing that the producers of the show have asked you two to participate. Probably because they want some eye candy on the show."

I pressed my back into the chair and looked at my sister with wide eyes. Show? What show? This was the first I'd heard of it.

Vera swallowed hard and evaded my gaze. She turned to Gene and calmly said, "Maggie doesn't know if she'll be participating. The producers only contacted me yesterday, and we haven't had a chance to talk about it. It's not our top priority. We're busy women."

Yesterday? I wanted to scream. Why hadn't she said something about it then? Trapping was my business! And she had the nerve to call me a control freak. Sheesh.

My suspicions that Vera was keeping secrets from me were well founded, apparently.

I kept my mouth shut and glared at Gene.

"I don't care what they asked you girls. I'm warning you. Stay away from my gators and my TV show. This is my town now, and I'm the star of the show."

"Is that a threat?" I asked. Anything that Gene wanted us to do, I was against, so perhaps I'd think about going on the TV program in a bikini with sparklers shooting off my tits. All to spite that shitgibbon sitting next to me.

"Yes, it most certainly is," Gene barked. The café turned quiet, and I sensed several pairs of eyes on our table. I rubbed the back of my neck and noticed that Tyler Carr was taking a particular interest in us.

"Well, I guess we'll give up because a man asked us to," Vera scoffed, then followed up with a whispered, "slimeball."

I widened my eyes, imploring my sister not to escalate the situation. I snickered nervously. I couldn't help it—I sometimes laughed when I was stressed, a defense mechanism whenever I felt particularly uncomfortable. This trait hadn't done me any favors, like how I'd chuckled heartily when I gave my notice at my job in Boston. Or when I'd broken up with my on-again, off-again boyfriend.

"Trapping ain't a woman's business," he yelled.

OK, now he'd gone too far, and I hooted aloud, throwing back my head for effect. My sister and I had been working with gators since we were kids, and learned from not only our dad, but our grandparents as well. Hell, our granny had been all of five feet tall and she could wrestle an alligator in no time. I smacked my hand against the table.

"Gene, this conversation's over. If you don't leave, we're going to have to get the cops involved. I won't hesitate to get a restraining order against you. Now let us eat in peace."

"Who's threatening who now?" He shot me a menacing look for three long seconds, then he stood, turned on his heel, and stalked out of the restaurant, elbowing a woman out of the way.

Vera and I exhaled in tandem. She pushed her plate away. "So much for my appetite. Jeez, I despise that man."

I studied her without blinking. "When were you going to tell me about the TV show? Why did you get the call, and not me?"

She waved me away. "The producer stopped by the store yesterday. He was filming downtown and had heard about Dad, and our family. Someone told him about the bookstore. I knew you wouldn't be interested, so I didn't bother telling you."

"How do you know I wouldn't be interested?"

"Because you hate reality TV."

"That's because you watch the gross shows like *Zit Zappers*. I don't hate all reality TV. You know I like that one show about the naked people in the jungle."

And that was only because that one dude's butt was nice to look at. At night, I sometimes fantasized about the two of us taking a steamy trip to Pleasureville under the moonlight on a deserted beach.

"What was the proposal?"

"They wanted you, or us, to be in a few episodes. You

know, go out on some gator calls, basically be the rival trappers to Gene's operation. They thought it was sexy for two young women to be involved in gator hunting. Especially since we also own the bookstore."

"Oh. No, no, no. No way. Gene's right about one thing: they want us as eye candy. Next thing you know, they'll ask us to hunt gators in bikinis."

She leaned in, a familiar pleading look on her face. "But it would be such great promo for the bookstore. And we'd get paid for it."

"I don't care. I'm not participating in a reality TV circus freak show. It's going to be classist and show off the worst Florida Man and southern stereotypes imaginable, especially if Gene's involved. We don't want to contribute to that narrative. No way, Vera."

Her nostrils flared. "I knew you'd say something like that."

"Because you know I'm right."

"You might be." A little smile tugged at the corners of her mouth. "They did mention us doing promo pics in the swamp in Lara Croft–like camo gear."

"Gross. They want to use sex to sell the show, because Gene's ugly face sure won't. That will almost certainly cause the ratings to tank." I tore a piece of crust off my toasted cheese, chewed, and swallowed. "But he doesn't need to know we're not doing the show. Let him squirm a little. Screw him."

I dipped my spoon into the soup and stirred. A quick taste revealed a delicious, tangy tomato explosion in my mouth, and I scooped up a larger spoonful. There was no way Gene should ruin such a tasty lunch. I ate in silence while Vera picked at her napkin.

"Anyway, forget about Gene," I said. "He's not worth it."

"He's literally the worst. In the last couple of years he's been swaggering around town like he owns it. He's gotten in with some of the local officials, and I've heard that he wants to use that TV show to run for political office. Can you imagine?"

"You lie down with dogs and you're going to get fleas." That was another one of Dad's sayings, and Vera grinned.

"In speaking of Dad . . ."—she twisted her paper napkin into an accordion shape—"could you check on the probate paperwork again today? I'm hoping the case will be closed soon. It will make me feel better to have that money officially in our bank account."

I nodded. Even though Dad had a will, his entire estate had gone to probate court for reasons I still couldn't grasp. It was all I could do to understand the basics of the situation, and I was thankful for our attorney, who had been a friend of Dad's. Vera and I were the only beneficiaries, but we needed to do things properly. Dad had left us a decent-sized nest egg, but we couldn't touch it just yet. The long process had been incredibly confusing and frustrating.

We thought we had properly filed all the paperwork six weeks ago, but then Dad's ex-girlfriend filed a claim against the estate. As it turned out, she'd wanted five old record albums of Dad's, which we gave to her. But her claim had seemingly sent the estate paperwork into some realm of court purgatory, and we were struggling to get it out. With the help of our lawyer, of course, who was also busy defending a myriad of insurance fraud perpetrators.

"You sure everything's OK?" I asked softly.

"Totally fine." Vera glanced at her watch. "Oh, crud, I've got a call today with a book distributor, and I need to get to the post office. Plus some other stuff. You headed home?"

She obviously didn't want to linger. "Yeah, I have a bunch to do. And it's hotter than Satan's house cat out there."

"Your blood sure has gotten thick. You used to be able to stay outside all day in the Florida sun. And it's only January."

"I don't remember it being this hot this early in the year."

She looked at me for a beat. "It's always this temperature in January. It's you that's changed."

Maybe I had. The thought left me slightly depressed, for some reason. "I'll see you back home."

My sister dropped the napkin on her half-eaten plate of food. "Oh, I almost forgot. There's a new tenant coming to one of the guest cabins today."

Dad and Vera had bought the large property where she—and now I—lived. There were three cabins on the property, and we'd decided to rent them to tourists for extra cash. It was the third prong in our fledgling and shaky business empire.

I gaped at my sister. "Here for the weekend? Is the cabin ready?"

She leaned in, her eyes glittering. "No. He rented it for six entire months. And yes, it is."

"Six months?" Maybe we should have discussed long-term rentals. I wasn't sure how I felt about that. It would be like having a roommate almost. What if he was a perv?

"Get this. He's a professor from Miami, on sabbatical. He's writing a book. I think you two will get along."

"Why, because he's an old book nerd and weird?"

"No, because he's young and interesting. And hot. OK, maybe not exactly our age, but not *that* much older. I had a long conversation with him over a Zoom call when he booked the place. Did I mention that he's cute?"

"Don't try to play matchmaker." I held up my hand. "Being single doesn't mean I'm automatically attracted to author dudes. Getting involved with one was enough for a lifetime."

"I'm merely giving you the facts." She blinked innocently.

"Don't want a man. Don't need one. Just because your biological clock is ticking, doesn't mean I'm hearing the same sound."

She pawed around in her giant canvas purse. Several receipts fell out and she bent to scoop them up. When she righted herself, she clutched a fistful of paper and waved it in my direction. "Only giving you the backstory, Maggie. Don't flip out. He's a really interesting guy. Apparently, he's writing a book about serial killers. I mean, he's also handsome if you're into that sort of thing."

I raised an eyebrow. "What sort of thing? Serial killers?"

"Single men who like books." She unfurled a wicked smile and waggled her fingers in a wave. "See you tonight."

"Maybe he's a better prospect for you. Later." I slurped up more of my tomato soup, wondering if I should get a quart to go.

Vera's taste in men was questionable at best. She'd always been attracted to the muscular jocks and the frat bros, while I preferred the nerdier guys with glasses and lean bodies. I snuck a glance at her and watched as she approached Tyler Carr's table across the room.

She flashed him a brilliant smile, then tucked her hair behind her ears. It was a sure sign that she was nervous. He wiped his mouth, then rose, a smarmy grin plastered on his face. He'd been an awful bully in high school and I'd never forgiven him for it.

Maybe that was unfair of me. Surely we'd all changed since high school.

He and Vera hugged, and then he reached out and tugged a lock of her hair. She let out a giggle that sounded like a porpoise mating call, one that I could hear over the voices of the other customers. I knew when my sister was flirting, and this was a prime example. I noted that Tyler didn't appear to introduce her to his dining companion, which rankled me.

I also wondered why he hadn't been a gentleman and stepped in when Gene was acting like a jerk at our table.

She handed Tyler a business card. Ugh. I wasn't looking forward to him slithering around the store.

I returned to my soup. Vera was an adult, and despite my best efforts over the years, I couldn't change who she was attracted to. Dating was a touchy subject, because she'd always been insecure about her looks and skin. She never felt good enough, or pretty enough— almost the opposite of me. I didn't care what people thought.

I finished my lunch in peace while reading a few pages of a new mystery novel on my phone. When I was finished with the chapter and my food, I paid the bill.

Probably I should've gone up to Tyler's table to say hello on my way out in an effort to make nice with Wahoo's newest city council member, but I decided against it. I'd had enough human contact for one day.

Instead, I walked past the bookstore on the way to my truck. Brown paper covered the windows. Vera really needed to get the new sign up, and soon. Sometimes she hyper-focused on certain things, while ignoring others. She saw the trees, while I saw the forest.

At home, I quickly showered then tackled the tough stuff first from my newly set-up desk in the guest room of Vera's house. My office setup was one of the few things I'd brought from Boston. I'd chosen blond and white wood for the desk and bookcase, along with a gold overstuffed chair and two giant potted rubber plants. A macramé wall hanging and a pretty print of butterflies from the Boston Zoo added a nice touch. I called it boho chic, and it felt relaxed yet clean and organized.

Vera preferred stacks of books and froofy, messy farmhouse decor.

First, I checked the probate records for Dad's estate, which made my chest feel heavy with sadness. It seemed unfair that my colorful father's life was reduced to dry, dull paperwork. Then I turned my attention to another unpleasant task, my 401k forms from the Boston Zoo. I'd worked there four years—well, five, if you counted my college internship—and had a meager chunk of savings to show for it.

My plan was to withdraw some of it to help Vera's bookstore in the short term, because she needed cash, fast. Neither of us had anticipated that Dad's estate would take this long. He'd died in April, and now here it was, nine months later.

After two hours on the computer combined with all that bright sunshine earlier in the day, my eyelids felt heavy. I desperately needed a siesta. I padded around the house, going from room to room, looking for our kitten, Catsy.

I found her in the back room, soaking up the rays streaming through the floor-to-ceiling windows. The little white kitty was on her back, her belly exposed. We'd adopted Catsy the week I returned, when her mother—a beat-up, mean feral named Snowball—had broken into the house and raised her two kittens in the room where Dad had died.

Aunt Lolo had adopted the other kitten and Snowball. Vera and I had claimed our kitten and named her after Dad's favorite singer, Patsy Cline.

"Silly girl." I clicked on the overhead fan then knelt to scratch Catsy's belly.

This was my favorite room in the house. It was essentially a porch-slash-solarium, and in the winter Vera took the glass out and added screens. The room also had a door leading to the peaceful backyard, which was filled with stately live oak trees dripping with Spanish moss. A shell rock path curved through the trees and forked. To the right were the rental cabins, and to the left was the Snake River. The path and its shells were so white they almost glowed in the afternoon sun.

From the comfy daybed aimed right underneath the air-conditioning vent, you could almost see the canoe launch at the far end of the property. That was one of many things that made this property special; you could paddle right from the backyard and end up a quarter mile downstream at Crystal Spring, a stunning swimming hole where the glass-clear water was seventy-two degrees year-round.

"If I was more ambitious, I'd go out for a paddle," I said to Catsy, flopping down on the daybed. "But I'm not, so I'm here with your fluffy butt."

She flipped over and let out a *brrap* sound. I shut my eyes and within a few seconds I felt her hop up on the daybed and snuggle into my side. My fingers went into her soft fur, which was scorching from the sun. Catsy was unable to watch anyone sleeping without napping herself—she was like an Olympic champion of snoozing.

When she wasn't zooming around the house like a maniac.

The sound of her purr and the singing birds outdoors

lulled me into a peaceful sleep. I could've probably stayed there until dark, but I woke to bright sunshine and the crunch of approaching footsteps.

Chapter Four

Trying to move as few muscles as possible, I opened one eye and glanced at the cat next to me. She was zonked out, belly up, wholly unconcerned about the possibility of imminent danger.

Where was my phone? Oh, right. On the table next to the daybed.

A sharp rap on the metal part of the screen door made my eyes peel wide open and a surge of fear shoot through me. There had been zero unexpected visitors to my apartment back in the city. Just the way I liked it.

Catsy righted herself and yowled, digging her claws into my thigh. As I swore aloud, she darted into the living room, a blur of white fur.

"Hello?" the male baritone called through the screen door. "Anyone home?"

I sat up and twisted my body in the direction of the door. A shirtless, black-haired man, with equally dark stubble on his face, was on the other side. He looked slightly wild, standing there in jeans and sneakers, scratching his bare olive-skinned chest. A very muscular bare chest. I spotted a couple of tattoos, one on his left bicep and another over his heart.

He looked like a romance novel cover come to life. One

about a motorcycle gang leader, possibly. Or a mafioso. He was hot as hell. But that didn't mean I trusted him one bit. In fact, it made me trust him less.

"Hi. Can I help you?" I climbed to my feet, scooping up my cell along the way. I'd call the cops if this guy was dangerous, although police in town were sparse, generally useless, and easily ten minutes away. I didn't get a threatening vibe from him, but still.

One could never be too careful. In my mind, I played out how I'd kick him in the nuts then make a run for Dad's shotgun, which was mounted on the wall in the living room.

I stood about a foot from the door, peering at his startlingly handsome face. My eyes flitted down at the handle to make sure it was locked. Like that would make a difference if he wanted to get in. My fingers gripped the cell.

He must've noticed my discomfort because he stepped back a foot or two. I spotted he was holding one of our Gator Queen–bookstore business cards in his hand.

"Sorry to bother you, I thought Vera would be home. No worries. I can call her on the number on the card." He ran a hand through his mop of unruly black hair. "I'm checking in and had a question."

In my fuzzy brain, I recalled how Vera had said the new guest was coming today. This must be him. "Oh, hey. I'm her sister, Maggie. I live here too. Well, recently moved back."

"Maggie! Vera told me all about you. You lived in

Boston and worked with reptiles, if I remember correctly."

"Yeah." The guy was at least a foot taller than me, and seemed a little older, probably in his mid-to-late thirties. He was definitely easy on the eyes, in a bad boy kind of way. Although he wasn't a boy. He was all man, with those muscles. The tattoo on his chest was a lightning bolt, and the other, on his bicep, a detailed and lifelike shark.

"And you are?"

He smiled ferally, showing off dazzling white teeth. "I'm the new renter. The name's Jack Bianchi. Got here an hour ago."

With a name like that, he sounded like an extra in *The Sopranos*. "The university professor? Writing about serial killers?" I squinted. It had been a while since I'd graduated with a degree in animal biology, and I'd had plenty of contact with professors in Boston. I didn't recall any teacher looking this hot. Huh. Maybe things were different in Miami.

He chuckled and looked down at his chest, running a hand over his muscles. He looked like one of those Italian underwear models you see in a men's magazine. "Sorry. I don't seem too professional today. It's hotter than hell out here in this swamp. Worked up quite a sweat moving my things in."

This was the guy staying for six months? I licked my lips as my eye caught a trickle of perspiration trailing down his rock-hard pectoral muscle. "Is everything OK? Is the keyless lock not working?"

"It's perfect. I got into town a little early and did some shopping because check-in wasn't until 4 p.m. When I arrived, everything about the place looked great."

"Well, that's good to hear." Then why was he standing here? Probably to show off his physique.

"It's exactly what I need for my sabbatical. I came over because there's a problem with the bathroom sink."

"Oh dear." After a glance around to see if Catsy was near—and seeing that she wasn't—I edged closer to the still-locked door. I considered opening it, but decided against that. "We need to get that fixed."

"I think it's a washer, something super simple. I could easily run to the hardware store and grab the parts. But I wanted to check with Vera first."

I rubbed my eye. What time was it? Time in Florida seemed to bend and stretch because the days were so filled with sunshine. I'd fallen asleep around three, and it could be three thirty or six, by the way the sky was still bright.

"If you could do it, that would be amazing. I'll be sure to tell Vera. Bring us the receipt and we'll reimburse you."

"Sure thing. And hey, maybe we can all hang out sometime. I make a mean lasagna and a killer tiramisu."

My mouth watered at his words. One thing I missed about Boston was all the delicious Italian restaurants. Wahoo had a lot to offer: my sister, crystal-clear springs, a cool tubing river, exotic wildlife, a great grilled cheese joint.

It did not have lasagna or tiramisu. Or maybe now it

did. My stare was fixed on Jack, whose smirk brimmed with an unsettling confidence. His eyes were an abyss of black, reminiscent of the night sky. It begged the question: why wasn't my sister hot for him? He had all the makings of a perfect match for her.

"That would be—"

The opening saxophone notes of the song "See You Later, Alligator" interrupted my words. It was a gator call. I pointed at my cell. "I need to grab that."

"Of course. Thanks again. I'll go to the hardware store today. After a while, crocodile." He sauntered off and I watched him make his way down the white path. He could sure fill out the backside of those jeans.

Weird. OK. Shaking my head, I jabbed at the green button on my phone.

It was a blocked number and I braced myself for a telemarketing pitch about auto warranties.

"Gator Queen, this is Maggie. How can I help you?"

"We've got a nuisance alligator out here." The male voice sounded faraway and tinny, like the person was on speakerphone in a windstorm.

"OK, sir, I can try to help. Can you speak into the phone a little more? I'm having a hard time hearing you."

"Sure." The muffled sound of thumps and crackles hit my ear. "Is this better? I'm driving."

"Kind of. Anyway. Tell me about the situation and where you are."

"It's at the Palm Industrial Park. You know where that is? Off of State Highway 19?"

"Yes, I know it."

"The gator's out back, in the river. You need to come get it."

"Sir, I don't trap gators unless they're a problem. If it's swimming in the water, it's not a threat. The river is gator habitat. That's where it's supposed to be."

"Oh, this one's a threat all right. It came into the parking lot and tried to attack one of my guys. Almost chomped his leg off."

I frowned and went into the kitchen, where Vera kept a notebook and pen on the counter. Contrary to popular belief, gator attacks were pretty rare, even in weird Florida. "Was he hurt?"

"No. He managed to get away, but now the gator's back. Listen, can you come take a look? Maybe find him and lug him off? I'll pay big money."

"I'll assess the situation. That's the best I can do. Can you repeat the address?"

"Palm Industrial Park. In the river behind the warehouse, almost right across from the back door. There's a table outside. I was just looking at the critter before I left. He's on the riverbank."

"And what's your name?"

"Bob."

"Bob what?"

"Just Bob. But I won't be there. One of my guys will be waiting for you. He'll have the cash."

I cleared my throat. Something about this call was off, but I couldn't put my finger on exactly what. "What time will you be there? And what's your employee's name?"

"It's nearly 5 p.m. and I have to get to a dinner with

the wife. Go there and see what you think. I'll call you back in a little while."

He hung up before I could say anything else. A quick check of the time revealed that it was indeed almost five. I'd slept that long?

We still had another half hour or so of daylight so I had time to drive to the industrial park to check out the gator.

I tapped out a quick text to my sister. *Where are you? Everything OK? I got a call about a gator and I'm headed to check it out. Palm Industrial Park, if you want to meet me.*

I waited for her response, but none came.

"What's up with her?" I muttered. Usually Vera was a quick texter, an oversharer, even in her messages. When I lived in Boston, I'd tell her not to text me multiple paragraphs because I couldn't take the time at work to read everything while flinging fish into the mouths of crocodiles.

Catsy's meow interrupted my thoughts. She was like a tiny trumpet, announcing her displeasure with a surprisingly powerful sound despite her teeny frame. I looked up from my phone. She was sitting near her half-full food dish and looked at me with giant round eyes.

"You have kibble. Come on, stinker."

She wailed again as if I were intentionally starving her. "OK, OK. I get it. You can see the bottom and that's unacceptable."

Normally I wouldn't give her more, since she was already a bit chubby. But who knew how long I'd be gone, or when Vera would be home. Catsy was a growing kitten and she needed sustenance.

I grabbed the bag out of the pantry and poured the stinky food into her bowl so she'd quiet down. My hair was a mess after my nap and I scraped it into a ponytail, slipped on my boots, and grabbed my gator go bag.

Vera and I had identical kits; they were filled with our tools of the trade. Dad had assembled the bags and had given one to Vera years ago, when she moved back to town after graduating college. Hers was hot pink. I had Dad's old bag, a worn black canvas duffel.

The items inside included the marshmallows, a change of clothes, duct tape, rope, zip ties, hand wipes, bear spray, and a .22 caliber pistol with some extra ammo. Fortunately, I'd never had to shoot a gator before, but it paid to be prepared. Dad had taught us well.

I headed to the truck and fired it up.

Vera's house was on the north edge of town. The sprawling old Florida home sat far back from the road, and most of her neighbors had similarly secluded properties. The sun dipped low in the sky as I drove to the industrial park, which was all the way on the south side of town.

It was better to take the back roads in an attempt to avoid downtown, because I knew that tourists and traffic would jam Main Street at dinnertime. Plus, I loved the rural landscape at this hour when the shadows were longer and the light was a filtered, hazy Creamsicle-orange peeking through the Spanish moss.

Wahoo had murky origins. It began its existence as a small Native American outpost near a swamp, with syphilis-ridden Europeans showing up to pillage the place in the mid-1500s. It got its name after the verdant green winged elm trees—also known as wahoo trees—that dotted the landscape. It had a bloody and pivotal history in the Second Seminole War during the nineteenth century.

Later, it became a stop for weary northerners on their way to the Gulf Coast beaches or even Miami. Quirky roadside attractions popped up in the fifties and sixties, and the town's population grew and ebbed over the decades. I'd always thought it was in a perfect location: fifteen miles from sugar sand beaches, four hours from Miami, and smack dab on the banks of a cool freshwater river.

It boasted lots of positives, if one could overlook the many minuses of Florida.

I passed the back entrance to the Crystal Springs State Park, a grapefruit grove, and a strawberry farm. Since I'd only been back home for a short time, I hadn't gotten a chance to drive down this way. The fact that none of these places had been developed yet made my heart soar, and I selected my favorite playlist and cranked up the volume.

Joining in with a Taylor Swift song, I zipped along, the wind in my hair from the open window. This was why I'd returned home. I'd fulfilled my dream of city life, but this was where I belonged. Fresh air, humidity, sunshine. It was my past and my future, the best of both of my worlds.

I'd help animals, carry on Dad's legacy, and Vera's bookstore would rock the romance world like no other indie bookstore ever had. It would draw tourists from across the nation, I was sure of it.

Upon approaching the industrial park turnoff, I slowed the truck. Unlike industrial parks in bigger cities with modern concrete structures, this was a lone, long brick building. It had to be a hundred years old, and I vaguely recalled my grandfather talking about how it had been a cigar factory in his youth. Over the decades, the property had been bought and sold, then renovated and abandoned several times.

Last I knew—well, last Dad had told me during one of our marathon phone gossip sessions a few years ago—it had been purchased by an entrepreneur who wanted to turn it into some sort of community arts center. But seeing that it was five miles from the bustling downtown, and on a quiet two-lane road that wasn't visually appealing save for some scrubby-looking palm trees and fat cattle, the plan for an arts renaissance here in Wahoo had stalled.

I slowed the truck to a crawl as I scanned the parking lot. This place was in even worse shape than when I'd seen it last, which was probably when I was in high school. That was back during one of its abandoned phases, and groups of kids would come here to drink and smoke cigarettes. Vera had talked me into coming a couple of times because she was trying to impress a boy. I spent most of the parties at the river's edge, skipping stones alone in the dark. I was a weird kid.

A few of the building's windows were broken, and the once majestic red brick was crumbling in places. Too bad that the arts idea never took off, because this building really was an impressive structure.

I steered the truck around the side, passing two faded green dumpsters. There was another strip of asphalt behind the building, but it was in even worse shape than the parking lot. I steered around two potholes and kept an eye on the building. Bob had said he'd seen the gator from the main back door.

Four concrete steps leading to gray metal double doors lay smack in the middle of the building. A weathered wooden picnic table sat nearby, probably used when workers took smoke breaks. That must be what Bob was talking about.

Apparently, the factory had been located this close to the river so the workers could unload raw cigar materials from Cuba and load finished cigars back on boats for points north. I spotted an old concrete ramp and a rusted railing down to the water. It was hard to believe that the river had been busy enough—or high enough—to facilitate commercial traffic. These days, all the development between here and north Florida had caused the water level to drop.

The river was now more lazy than fuctional.

I steered the truck in a C shape, to scan the riverbank through my windshield, and parked next to the only car in the lot, the noses of both our vehicles facing the river. Maybe it was Bob's employee. What kind of business had set up shop in this spooky old building?

It was a new truck, and I peered in. The windows were tinted so I couldn't see if anyone was inside.

I climbed out and went around the front of the other truck. Oddly, no one was inside but the headlights were on. So was the engine. I walked to the driver's side and tapped on it.

No answer.

Weird.

My gaze went to the side of the truck. A magnetic sign was stuck on the extended cab door, and the words sent a chill up my spine despite the thick, warm humidity.

Gator Gene: I trap 'em, you snack 'em

I scrunched up my nose. What the hell? That made no sense! Even his slogan was ridiculous. Snack what? Such a dick. Why was *he* here, anyway?

I hustled back to my own truck and locked the door once I was safely inside. If Gene was already trying to catch the gator, there was no reason I should hang around. The last thing I wanted was another confrontation with him, especially if we were the only two here.

I leaned forward. In the fading daylight, I thought I spotted what looked like a good-sized gator sitting on the bank, near the left side of the ramp. It was difficult to tell exactly, because the area was overgrown with scrub brush and covered in what appeared to be several plastic bags filled with trash. The late-day shadows could also be playing tricks with my vision, but it sure looked like a dark gray reptile.

But if the gator was there, where was Gene? His truck was running, but he was nowhere in sight.

My hand went to the roomy glove compartment, where I stashed my favorite pink industrial-strength flashlight. I set it in my lap.

The sun had faded to a deep orange-red glow. Gators were most active at dusk and dawn. Gene was probably in the brush somewhere with a weapon, waiting to ambush and kill the creature. I'd heard he sometimes preferred shooting them with a semi-automatic. No way did I want to get caught in that crossfire.

I eased the truck forward, intending to get a peek and drive away.

I slowly accelerated and stopped just before the ramp, giving myself enough clearance to peel away if Gene appeared. After pressing on the brake, I put the vehicle in park.

To get a better look, I rolled down my window and grabbed the flashlight, clicking it to life with my thumb. When I aimed the beam of light out the open window, I expected to stare into the glowing red eyes of an angry gator.

Instead, the ray of illumination revealed something far worse.

A bloody and lifeless Gator Gene.

Chapter Five

An hour and a half later, I was still trembling as I sat in my truck in the parking lot, watching crime scene techs comb the riverbank. The horrific sight of Gene's body face down in a puddle of blood and muck was burned into my brain.

So was the image of a bullet hole in the back of his skull.

It was fully dark now, and the bright police spotlights that had been erected atop makeshift poles threw off an eerie glow that made the gently swirling river take on a menacing, inky hue. Gene's body was covered in a blue tarp, and every time one of the officers pulled it aside, I had to look away. I'd seen enough already.

I clutched my phone in my right hand, checking it every thirty seconds. The only person I wanted to talk with wasn't answering my messages and calls.

Hey, where are you? I texted my sister. *Something terrible is happening here at the industrial park. Call me ASAP.*

I included a gif of a cat on its hind legs, pressing its front paws together in a pleading gesture, figuring she might be more likely to respond if I included a cute animal image.

Thirty minutes dragged by, and still she didn't respond.

I fiddled with the air conditioner, turning it to full blast. It wasn't like Vera to not return my texts. Where was she? Keeping the details of what I'd seen bottled up inside was making me queasy.

A tap-tap-tap on the driver's side window startled me, and I yelped.

I rolled the window down. A man in a light blue button-down and a dark gray tie loomed large on the other side. He held up a badge, its gold metal glinting in the wan light. A cop. Just what I'd been waiting for.

"Ms. Margaret Andrews?"

"That's me. But you can call me Maggie."

"I'd like to ask you a few questions. Would you mind stepping out of the vehicle?"

"Of course. The responding officer told me to hang out because a detective would eventually want to talk with me. Since I found the body and all. I didn't think it would take this long," I babbled while fumbling to turn off the truck's engine.

My legs felt rubbery as I climbed out.

"Detective Alex Holt," the officer said, extending his hand. "I'm with the Wahoo Police Department."

We shook. He was extremely tall, with broad shoulders, muscular forearms, a mop of curly, dirty-blond hair, and a close-cropped beard of the same hue. I didn't think cops could grow beards, but maybe the rules were relaxed for detectives here in Wahoo.

"Why don't we step over here, out of the fray?" He pointed to the worn wooden picnic table near the back door of the warehouse.

We walked in silence and sat opposite each other at the table, which was pockmarked with cigarette burns and carved initials. A lamp above the door had come on, casting a sickly yellow light over us.

He set a worn brown leather portfolio holding a yellow legal pad on the table in front of him, then clicked a pen three times. I waved off a circling mosquito.

"Can you spell your name and give me your contact information? Address and cell phone, please."

"Here's my details." I reached into the pocket of my cargo pants and pulled out a Gator Queen business card. This probably wasn't the networking Vera had in mind when she told me to hand them out.

I pushed the card toward him and spelled my name.

"You're a local?" He tilted his head.

"Born and raised in Wahoo. Left for college in Boston and stayed for a while. Just returned in November."

"What did you do up there?"

"I worked at a zoo. My specialty was reptiles."

"Reptiles?"

"Yeah, I was the assistant to the assistant director of the Slimy Scaly Spectacular."

He blinked, and I quickly followed up with, "It was a permanent exhibit at the Boston Zoo. Iguanas, crocodiles, pythons. You get the picture."

"And now?"

"I'm a gator trapper. And I'm helping my sister with her new romance bookstore in town. It's opening soon." I flipped the card over and tapped on it twice.

He shook his head. "Romance bookstore?"

"It's all romance novels. Most popular genre of fiction. Readers will come from all over. We hope," I offered warmly, but I was met with silence.

I ran my tongue over my top teeth, wondering if he wanted me to talk more. I decided to keep quiet for once.

"So you and your sister are bookstore owners and in your spare time, you're . . ."—he picked up our glossy red business card and turned it over—"Gator Queens?"

He said it like he wasn't quite sure if I was playing a prank.

"The bookstore's really her business, and the trapping operation is mine, but we're planning on helping each other. It's a family business, the trapping at least. Our dad was known as the Gator King. He was kind of a local celebrity. I wanted to keep his business alive. We grew up catching gators with him. I'm sure you've heard of him, Logan Andrews."

"I haven't."

So, he was new in town. I expected him to elaborate, to tell me how long he'd been on the force. But he didn't.

"Why'd you come back to Wahoo, Maggie? Quite a change from Boston."

"Yeah, it is. I wanted to be near my sister. We're twins, and both our parents are gone. Dad passed not long ago. There's nothing like Florida, you know? I wanted something familiar. The pandemic made my sister and me realize that we were too far apart."

I didn't say that I'd taken the biggest risk of my life, walking away from a good job in a smart city to come home to semi-rural, weird Wahoo. I'd taken a chance on starting a new business at the tail end of a global pandemic in a shit economy. Some days, I barely understood the decision myself.

And now that I'd stumbled upon the dead body of my biggest nemesis, I was really rethinking things.

The detective stared at me, and I noticed even in the dim yellow light that his eyes were a piercing, electric blue. Even though I was completely innocent of any crime, I still felt like he was pinning me down and trying to entice me to confess something. Sweat bloomed on the back of my neck.

"Tell me why you were here at this abandoned warehouse, close to dark, by yourself."

I straightened my spine. His question was on the razor's edge of being sexist. "You mean, what's a little girl like me doing in a wild place like this?"

The muscles in his jaw bunched. "Something like that."

"At around five I received a call about a gator. The caller said he worked here"—I gestured to the brick building—"and reported a monster gator that had chased one of his employees."

"No one works here," he said in a flat tone. "This place has been empty for years."

I lifted both hands. "Really? I don't know. I'm only telling you what the caller said. I agreed to come down and take a look."

"Did you get a name? A number?"

"Bob. Didn't give a last name, said he was leaving to

take his wife to dinner. And no, the number was private on my phone."

Holt lifted an eyebrow. "You came out here when a guy named Bob, no last name, no number, called you?"

"Yeah. That's what I do. I respond to gator calls. And iguanas and other problem reptiles."

"Why didn't your sister come with you?"

His tone made me bristle. I drew from a well of patience, the kind that I'd needed as an assistant zoo-keeper when people asked if they could climb into the crocodile exhibit and take a selfie.

"Because, like I said, this is my business. I came to check out the gator and would've called her if the situation warranted backup. Believe it or not, most gator calls don't end in a trap. Many people call when they see a gator in the water. That's where they're supposed to be, so I end up doing nothing. A lot of my job is simply reassuring folks that wild animals are safe if they're left alone."

He nodded slowly. "Tell me what you saw when you arrived. Be as detailed as possible."

I explained how I'd driven up and parked next to Gene's truck.

"The engine was on, which was a bit strange. I thought he'd kept it running for some reason, and figured he was somewhere trying to trap the gator."

"You didn't call anyone when you saw the empty, yet running, truck?"

I frowned. "No. Why would I?"

More scribbles on the yellow legal pad. I was

beginning to doubt my judgment. Should I have called the authorities?

"I spotted what looked like an alligator, so I drove closer with my flashlight. When I saw it was Gene, and that he was hurt, I got out of the truck to see if I could help. That's when I saw the gunshot hole in the back of his head, and realized he was dead. I didn't touch him because I was too shaken up after seeing all that blood." I shivered.

"Your call to 911 specifically said that you knew it was Gene Robinson. How did you know that?"

"I recognized his face. And from the sign on the side of the truck."

"Are you acquainted with the deceased?"

"Unfortunately, yes," I muttered.

His eyes widened, and I followed up quickly with an explanation.

"You see, Detective Holt—"

"Alex. Call me Alex."

I nodded once. "Alex. Got it. I've known Gator Gene for years."

"Gator Gene? Is that his nickname?"

"Are you not from around here?"

"Came here from Tallahassee last month."

"A-ha. You don't know the dynamics of this area."

"I'm learning on the job."

"Gator Gene is—was—the other trapper in town. He was difficult, if you know what I mean."

"I don't. Please explain."

I took a deep breath. "He wanted to be the only

trapper in Wahoo. He had an intense rivalry with my father. My family's been trapping gators in this area for generations. Years ago, when I was in high school, Gene thought he could muscle his way in on the business. There were usually enough gators to go around for both my dad and him, but . . ."

I flashed back to the scene Gene had caused in the café earlier in the day.

"But what?" prodded Alex.

"But Gene always saw my family as competition. After my father passed, Gene figured he'd be the only game in town, gator-wise. But I decided to continue the business. Today, in fact, Gene confronted my sister and I while we were eating lunch."

"Confronted?"

"Gene had a nasty attitude. It was on full display today. He came to our table while we were eating and gave us an earful. He was a total jerk, in fact."

"Where were you?"

"Cheesy Does It, that café downtown. Great grilled sandwiches, by the way. Gene accused me of stealing a gator call earlier in the day."

"Did you steal the job?"

Stupidly, I giggled from sheer nervousness. "Of course not. A client called, and I went. I caught the reptile. It was in his pool, a baby gator. Then I left."

"Did Gene say anything else?"

"He was obnoxious, like he always was. Caused a bit of a scene. Said he was filming a reality TV show about his trapping business and warned me not to interfere.

The TV producers wanted me and Vera to go on the show as foils for Gene. That's what my sister told me, anyway. It doesn't matter because I'm not going on any show, and I had nothing to do with his death."

He scribbled in his notebook and lifted his head. "Vera's your sister? Older or younger?"

"We're twins."

"Identical?"

I shook my head. "We look nothing alike."

"You have a number for her?"

I rattled off her digits.

Alex cleared his throat. "Maggie, can you tell me what you were doing between the hours of noon and approximately 6 p.m.?"

"I had lunch with my sister, like I told you. Around one thirty, I went home. Well, to my sister's home. I'm staying with her now, basically we're living together until I decide if I want to buy a place or what."

He clicked his pen twice and the sound seemed to take on a life of its own. "You were home. Alone?"

"Yep, with my cat. I did some paperwork for the bookstore, had some things to take care of with my father's probate case. Oh, and I took a nap."

"A nap?"

I nodded, wondering if I was speaking a language other than English and that's why he kept repeating my words.

"Was your sister there with you?"

I shook my head and my stomach sank. I'd been by myself, for hours. Possibly right at the time Gene was killed. Eep. Did I need an alibi? A lawyer? No, that was stupid to even consider.

"Am I being questioned for murder?" I let out a laugh, which caused Alex to look even more confused. "I'm totally innocent."

Which is exactly what a guilty person would say. I needed to stop laughing and shut up.

"We'll probably want a more formal statement from you. Is there anyone who can vouch for your where-abouts today?"

"Well, my sister, and the server at the café. And . . ." I racked my brain. "Oh! My sister's tenant. I spoke with him around four-thirty-ish, right before I received the gator call."

"Hm. Tenant? Have a name?"

"Jack Bianchi."

Alex's eyes narrowed faintly, as if he didn't believe me.

"He's a professor from the University of Miami. He's on sabbatical and here writing a book."

"OK. Thank you." There was an awkward pause while he slid my business card into his chest pocket.

"Am I free to go?"

He nodded curtly. "I'd advise you not to leave town for the next few days. I'll be in touch."

"Thanks. I hope you get to the bottom of this. Even though I didn't like Gene, no one deserves to die out here, like this. I'm happy to help with anything." I flashed him a tight smile.

We both rose from the picnic table and walked toward my truck.

"If you happen to know of anyone who had it in for Gene, let me know, OK?" His voice was a touch less flinty, and my shoulders relaxed away from my ears.

"Vera's the best source for that because she knows everyone in town. She's probably at home. Or you can find her at the shop tomorrow." I gave him the address, which was silly because it was on our business card.

"Good deal," he said, then pulled out a business card of his own. "Here's my number, in case you think of any-thing else."

I thanked him and climbed into my truck, reaching for my cell. Vera still hadn't called. Now I was truly con-cerned. It took all of my remaining patience not to gun the engine out of the parking lot and peel away in frus-tration, but I managed.

#

I raced home, and exhaled when I saw lights in the windows of my sister's sprawling home. After running up the front steps, I shook as I unlocked the door.

"Vera, where are you?" I cried, feeling feverish and sweaty.

She was sitting on the overstuffed tan sofa, glass of wine in hand. In the matching recliner chair was Jack, who was sitting with his feet up. Catsy was stretched on Jack's chest and was purring so loud that I could hear her from ten feet away.

I paused and stared at him. He beamed at me. This was no time to flirt.

"Catsy, get down." I waved my arm and of course she ignored me because someone was giving her attention. "Is she bothering you?"

Jack shook his head, looking shockingly cozy with my kitty. "We're bonding. Is that her name? Catsy?"

"Short for Catsy Cline," I replied, probably a bit too curt.

"Thank goodness you're home." Vera drained her glass and reached for the open bottle on the coffee table. "You're not going to believe what happened to me."

"You're not going to believe what happened to *me*," I countered. "Why didn't you answer my calls?"

"Here, we have a glass for you." She grabbed an empty tumbler and poured. "What happened to you?"

"No, you first. I need a drink or three." I sank down next to her and took a gulp.

"OK. Well, after you and I had lunch, I went to the post office. It took so long, gah." I noticed that her face was free of makeup, which made her vitiligo more visible. Not by a lot, and not enough to mar her beauty—in my opinion, at least. "Then I went to the park for a walk. You know, the one with the boardwalks over the swamp. Needed to clear my head after that situation with Gene at lunch, since he really frosted my butt. I left everything but my key in the car. Didn't even take my cell."

I gaped at her. "You didn't take your cell? Why? That's dangerous."

She threw her hand in the air. "I dunno. Sometimes I like to be unplugged. I hate being tethered all the time to a phone."

Maybe it was years of living in the city, but that didn't sit well with me. I needed to have a talk with her about safety. "Go on," I prodded.

"I had a great walk, felt much more balanced and sane after a half hour in nature, and came back to find my car had been broken into. The driver's window was smashed to pieces."

"Oh no." I let out a groan. "So your phone was stolen?"

"Everything. The phone, my purse, my IDs, and my credit cards."

"Gosh. I'm sorry. So that's why I wasn't able to reach you."

She nodded. "And get this. They also took my go bag. My duffel. With all the gator stuff. And my gun, and the extra ammo."

My eyes widened in horror. "Vera, what the hell? You left your gun in the car?"

"I know, I'm not supposed to. It was in the trunk and I thought it was hidden well. This is a small town, Maggie. Sometimes I keep it in there so I don't have to haul it into the store and out again, and then back here at home."

I rubbed my temple. "Dad taught us to never leave a gun unattended."

"I know," she whined.

Her revelation about the gun was shocking and irresponsible. Vera was disorganized but usually not careless. That, combined with her evasiveness at lunch, made me worry even more. What was going on with her?

"This could get complicated real quick if the gun is used in the commission of a crime," Jack piped up. He pressed his hand to Catsy's back. His palm almost covered her entire body. "I'm merely giving you my opinion as a criminology professor."

Until now, he'd been silent, so quiet that I almost forgot he was there. I looked up to see him stroking my kitten's back. Tonight he was wearing jeans and a black T-shirt with what looked like a band name on the front.

I looked to Jack, then to Vera, a sense of growing resentment welling in my chest. What was he doing here, anyway? Had she invited him over in a ham-handed attempt at matchmaking? I wanted to talk to my sister alone. Especially now.

But maybe he could be of use to us, given that he knew the law.

"Did you report this to the cops?" I demanded.

She nodded. "When I got home, I called and gave a report over the phone. The dispatcher's an acquaintance and she said the officers were out at some crime scene but wouldn't tell me what was going on. I'm expecting a call any minute now to follow up, but you know the local police. There are only like three of them and it might take a few days to return a call if it doesn't involve drugs, drinking, or something violent."

"But they definitely took a report? This is serious."

"They did. I feel awful. Hopefully they'll find it." She took a long gulp of her wine. "How about you? Tell me about your night."

I laughed nervously and set the wine on the coffee table, then pulled the scrunchie out of my hair, shaking it loose. "You're not going to believe this, but I went to an alligator call at the industrial park and found Gator Gene lying dead in the water. Dead as a doornail. Tits up. Probably murdered. So yeah. It was quite a night."

Bile rose in my throat at the memory of Gene's body and I swallowed, trying to push the image deep inside.

Vera gasped and pressed a hand to her chest. Jack righted the recliner so abruptly that Catsy jumped down with a disgruntled meow and ran out of the room.

"What?" Vera cried.

"Who's Gator Gene?" Jack asked.

While Vera sat with her mouth open, I shifted to look into Jack's brown eyes. For some reason, his *GQ* cover looks annoyed me tonight. I didn't need a thirst trap distracting my sister, not with everything going on.

"Gene Robinson is the other gator trapper in Wahoo. He is, or was, an unpleasant dick. Just today he threatened Vera and me while we were eating lunch."

Jack's eyebrows lifted. "Wild."

"Gene's hated our family for years. He has, or had, the intellectual capacity of a Roomba without a charging station."

Vera exhaled. "Gene didn't like the idea of two women being better trappers than him."

"Dad actually gave Gene a lot of trapping tips twenty years ago, and Gene started his own business and felt that our dad was his rival," I explained. "Gene was also lecherous and nasty. Total perv. We've had run-ins with him, but nothing recent."

"Run-ins?" Jack looked at me, and Vera, probably wondering why he'd ever left Miami. "You two seem harmless."

Vera gestured with her thumb at me, her little-girl voice filled with a mixture of pride and embarrassment. "She slashed Gene's tire when we were sixteen."

I smirked. "It was because he brushed against Vera at the roller-skating rink and acted all pervy by grabbing her butt. I wasn't going to let that asshat do that to my sister. No one messes with my twin, especially not a withered fruit roll-up like Gene."

I braced myself for a round of mansplaining from Jack. Probably he'd spout some BS about the law or the statute of limitations.

"Fair enough," he said, to my surprise. "Sounds like he got what he deserved."

My stomach rumbled, and I realized I hadn't eaten anything since the grilled cheese and tomato soup at lunch. "Probably I shouldn't have resorted to vigilante vandalism, but I was a teen and my brain wasn't fully developed. Anyway. Today Gene told us not to steal his gator calls. He also informed us that he was the star of a reality TV show about his trapping business, and warned us not to interfere with that either."

"I guess someone else interfered," snorted Jack.

"I wonder who." Vera grabbed a pillow embroidered with a palm tree and held it against her stomach. "I wonder what happened."

I quickly recounted how Bob had called, and how I'd parked next to Gene's truck, then spotted his body near the riverbank, on the edge of the concrete boat ramp. "I thought Gene might still be alive, so that's why I got out of the truck to get a closer look. But when I saw the bullet hole in his head, I realized he was gone and I called 911."

Vera reached for my hand, and I twined my fingers into hers. "I'm sorry you had to see that," she whispered.

"Oh, and get this. The detective might want to speak with you."

Vera yanked her hand from mine. "Why?"

"Because I told him about our run-in with Gene at lunch."

Her face fell. "Did you also tell him you slashed Gene's tire?"

"No, I very much did not tell him about that."

"Good. I know how you're incapable of lying."

"Why would I lie? I have nothing to lie about. It didn't even cross my mind to discuss that. It happened years ago, and until now the only ones who knew I'd slashed Gene's tire were you, me, and Dad. And now Jack."

We both looked to him, and he pantomimed zipping his mouth closed. "I'm a bit concerned about your stolen gun," he said.

"Do you think I'll be charged or cited?" Vera squeaked.

Jack shook his head. "They'll probably give you a warning and tell you to lock up your other firearms."

"I don't have any other firearms."

I chimed in. "Well, apart from Dad's shotgun . . ." I pointed to where it hung on the wall. "But it's hella old and I doubt it even works. We only carry because of the gators. It's our last line of defense if things get really bad on a call. Even though Vera's only helping me out, she has a gun just in case."

Jack's face lit up with excitement. "Have you ever had to fire at an animal?"

Vera and I shook our heads.

"Our dad taught us the art of nonviolent rescue. We want the gators alive so they can return to where they belong in nature," I said.

"Or to our uncle's sanctuary, the one I was telling you about. That's the best place for a problem gator that can't be relocated," Vera added. "But I don't like the idea of someone out there, having my gun. What if they commit a crime and shoot someone? What if . . . oh, no."

"What?" I asked, wondering why her face was suddenly so pale.

Jack's mouth was set in a hard line as he finished Vera's sentence. "What if your gun was used to kill Gene? The theft and the murder seemed to happen within hours of each other, from what it sounds like. Very unusual events in a small place like this."

"Hadn't thought of that," I whispered.

"Maybe it was suicide?" Vera asked.

Jack leaned forward in the recliner and steepled his fingers. His dark eyes smoldered with determination, and his chiseled jawline hinted at the ruggedness that lay beneath his casual clothes. Great. Exactly what we needed. A hot Sherlock Holmes.

"Maggie, did you see a weapon?" he asked.

"No. I don't think it was suicide." I paused as a fresh chill went down my spine. "Unless he was extremely proficient with a gun, but I don't think Gene was that talented. He was shot in the back of his head."

My gaze met Vera's. Our eyes were the same color—it was one of the few physical characteristics we shared as nonidentical twins—and I knew that the panic in her expression mirrored my own.

Chapter Six

Despite my still-shaky insides, the next morning I went into the bookstore. Vera had errands to run, thankless tasks like the tax collector, the bank, and most importantly, the police station. She wanted to make sure her stolen gun report was indeed logged in the system, and I figured I'd help her get a head start on taming the chaos that swirled in her mind and probably in the store.

I unlocked the glass door. The smell of fresh paper and ink, along with a hint of lavender, greeted me. She said she'd gotten several book shipments in, and a few boxes of nonbook items, like notebooks, planners, and cards.

I flicked on the lights and passed all the boxes that she hadn't yet unpacked on my way to the back room, where I stowed my go bag.

My sister had found this space on Main Street a year ago, when it was a tired, bland office-supply store. She'd called me, breathless, and said it was the place of her childhood dreams.

At first, I'd resisted the idea of coming home. The job at the zoo was secure and paid well. I had plenty of friends and Boston was an interesting city. But one monster snowstorm, one week of dealing with poorly behaved rugrats throwing French fries into the iguana exhibit, and one lackluster date with my then-boyfriend later, I'd made up my mind to return to Florida. That was all before Dad died.

I loved Boston, don't get me wrong.

But it never quite felt like home the way Wahoo did. The older I got, the more I yearned for my little town located smack in the middle of Florida's swampland. Plus, the pandemic. Not being able to travel freely to see Vera and Dad was physically painful; before, I'd tried to visit them every few months. I didn't want to be in that situation ever again.

Unfortunately, it took a while to set the wheels in motion to leave, and Dad had died during that time. The guilt I felt over that was still palpable. If only I hadn't dithered and screwed around in Boston. It had only strengthened my resolve to follow my bliss. Life was short.

But now that I was home, I felt a bit unmoored. Wahoo without Dad seemed like a different place, and I wondered if I'd made the right decision. Seeing first-hand all the work it took to open a store, and ramp up the trapping operation, made me wonder if Vera and I really were cut out as small business owners.

Everything felt out of order, especially the store. We were only days away from our soft opening and this fact stressed me out immensely.

Boxes littered the large space, and the shelves lining the walls were empty. Two wooden tables were hap-hazardly jammed in the back near a wall, as was a floral-print loveseat. I wasn't sure what Vera had planned for that, but she had an eye for quirky beauty and decoration, so I hadn't asked.

Truthfully, I didn't have a clue how the store should look. Vera, on the other hand, had done watercolor mockups of the interior. She'd already set a vase of fresh pink and white roses on the new wooden counter, near the electronic cash register. I paused to smell the flowers, then noticed a card stuck on a plastic stick.

I plucked it out and opened it.

I don't want to set the world on fire, I want to start a flame in your heart. -Ty

I rolled my eyes so hard that I thought I might go blind. What a cheese-fest. Gah. I made a retching noise out loud. So she was dating Tyler Carr, who communicated in clichés. I nestled the card back into the arrangement.

No wonder she'd been so evasive. She knew I wouldn't approve, given how mean he'd been to us in high school. But it was my sister's life and choice, not mine. I'd have to deal with whoever she chose.

I took out the to-do list she'd stuffed into my hand when I left the house. Vera was forever making lists in an effort to be more organized. I'd bought her countless planners and notebooks over the years, but as far as I could tell, she was still using plain yellow Post-it notes because, as she maintained, the planners were "too darned pretty" to write in.

Still, she'd made some progress on her organizational skills, since she'd left me a list of things to do.

Essential oil diffuser on the counter: press the button that says MIST.

I located the contraption and turned it on, sending a stream of lavender vapor and scent through the air.

Check the mail.

Put the sign on the sidewalk.

There was no mail yet, but the sign rested by the front door. I wrangled the two-foot-high wooden frame out the door and set it outside, trying to place it where people would see it and where it wouldn't impede foot traffic.

MARK YOUR CALENDARS, it read in loopy cursive, **Straight From the Heart, a romance-only bookstore, is coming to this space soon!**

Soon. Thirteen days by my count. Vera seemed to be cutting it pretty close with every task, a fact that made my palms sweat.

As I tried to rub a dark scuff mark off the top of the white wood, I heard someone calling my name and looked up.

"It is a blessing to see your face out here, Ms. Maggie Andrews." The male voice made me smile.

"Rodney!" I cried, walking over to the tall older man, who folded me into a hug.

Rodney Heath was the president of the chamber of commerce, which had its offices downtown. He'd been a close friend of Dad's since high school.

"You're looking good," I said, studying his dark-skinned face and brown eyes. "How's Ginny and the kids?"

He laughed. "She's out of town for a few days, visiting the grandkids in Fort Lauderdale."

"How many do you have now?"

"Three."

"Wow!" This, of course, was a reminder for me that Dad never had the chance to be a grandfather. He'd never pushed us, of course, but since his death it had been in the back of my mind that he'd never meet our children. If we had any, that is. I wasn't sure if I wanted them. Vera, on the other hand, did. My thoughts went to smarmy Tyler and I shoved them into the recesses of my brain. That was the last thing I wanted, to spend holidays and family milestones with him and his crotch goblins.

"We're working to get everything set for the store's grand opening," I said, changing the subject while rubbing my hands together.

"I'm glad you're home and helping Vera out. I think she could use your levelheadedness."

A slight frown crossed my face. What did he mean by that? "It feels good to be home."

"I'm sure it does. I haven't seen you since your dad's funeral."

We looked at each other glumly. "You miss him, don't you?"

He nodded his head. "Something fierce." He paused. "Hey, did you hear what happened last night?"

Prickles of awareness flowed through my body. "Not sure," I hedged.

"Gator Gene was found dead." His voice dropped. "Word around town is that he was murdered."

I cleared my throat. "Actually, I was the one who found him."

"No! Oh, sweetheart." He reached to squeeze my upper arm.

I nodded. "I was out on a gator call."

"Oh, hon, I'm sorry. That's terrible. I heard that a woman found him, but didn't know it was you."

"If it was murder, I wonder who killed him?"

Rodney shrugged. "Could be anybody. It's not as though he was well liked around town. Well, he was well liked, but by a certain type of person."

I nodded. I wasn't sure what he meant by that, but I could guess. Sketchy biker gangs, off the grid white supremacists, meth dealers . . . they were Gene's brand of buddies.

"Although . . ." Rodney tapped his chin with a long finger and I perked up. "I'm hearing that his wife stands to get a substantial life insurance payout."

I squinted. "I thought he was divorced? I remember last year my dad said something about it. You know how Dad would call me every week to update me on the gossip in town."

Chuckling, Rodney shook his head. "That's right. Your father told me he did that. But Gene and Barbie, they were going to split but never did. She filed but then rescinded the paperwork."

"Weird. Maybe she stuck around hoping he'd get that reality TV show and some instant fame and money. Where'd you hear about the life insurance thing?"

"You know. Gossip at the Crow's Nest." He let out a rich chuckle.

That was the local coffee shop. Every cell in my body

cried out for a cup of their strong brew. I hadn't had time to make my morning coffee because I'd stayed in bed a little later than anticipated. Sleep had eluded me for most of the night because I couldn't stop thinking about finding Gene's body, and I loathed being late or behind schedule.

"Maggie, what are your plans, anyway? Are you staying in town for long?"

"I'm home for good. Taking over Dad's business, going to help with the store."

"That's what your dad always wanted."

I swallowed a lump in my throat and nodded. "Listen, I need to get back inside, I'm supposed to answer a call from a book distributor this morning for Vera. Let's catch up later, OK?"

He squeezed my shoulder. "Will do, Maggie. Welcome home."

I sauntered back in, feeling a weird mix of emotions. On one hand, it felt good to be back where people knew me and cared about my well-being. But Gene's death had cast a pall over my homecoming. Something about it didn't sit right with me, and as I made notes for my upcoming call, I couldn't shake the image of his ugly dead body from my mind.

I'd read a lot of suspense novels, some pretty gritty. I had a strong stomach for fictional crime, but now that I'd seen the real deal, I was shaken to my core. One thing was sure: I wouldn't be reading any mysteries anytime soon. Probably I'd stick to something more uplifting, like rom-coms.

Also, the situation with my sister's stolen gun made me uneasy.

I tried to forget about everything and concentrate on the book order. I was looking at some of the bestselling historical romances when the bells attached to the front door jingled. I automatically called out, "We're not open yet, I'm so sorry!"

I peeked around the computer, expecting to see someone I knew, or a curious tourist.

Instead, it was Detective Alex Holt in a dark blue police uniform, looking far more official than he had the previous night. His beard was gone this morning, making him look younger and more square-jawed. He removed his hat and looked around with a slightly dazed expression.

"Why, hello, detective." I put on my cheeriest voice.

His blue-eyed gaze landed on me and I set my pen on the counter. He seemed far larger in broad daylight, and something about his wide shoulders, along with the crisp uniform, made him stand out in the messy store.

"Ms. Maggie Andrews, good morning." Why did his tone have to be so stern? I wasn't a general fan of cops and he wasn't helping matters.

"Can I help you? Did you decide to come in to ask for a romance novel recommendation?" I waved my hand at the boxes. "Unfortunately, we don't have any books on display yet. I'd advise you to return in a couple of weeks when we're officially open."

That earned me an upward twitch of his mouth, which I took as a victory. "I'll admit that I've never read a romance. Walking in here is like coming to a foreign country."

"Allow me to be your ambassador." Today I'd worn my cutest dress, a fit-and-flare red number printed with pink conversation hearts that said HUGS, SWEET, and XOXO, along with a pair of white sandals. I curtseyed. "More men should study romance novels. It would help them understand women. What is your choice of reading material?"

"I like military history, cyber-thrillers, that sort of thing." A slight frown pulled on his brow. "You seem a lot shorter today."

"Maybe it's because I'm not in my T-shirt, cargo pants, and boots. I clean up good when I'm not hunting gators."

"Gotcha. I'm glad you're here, because I wanted to ask you something. And I'm here to talk with your sister. Is she in?"

My muscles stiffened. "She's running some errands. Should be here soon, if you'd like to grab a coffee down the street and come back."

He studied my face for a beat, which made me uncomfortable. "I think I'll wait, if you don't mind."

"Of course. Uh, there's a seat over there."

I pointed to the floral loveseat in the corner. He wove his way around some boxes on those long, muscular legs and plopped down. It was kind of comical, this giant lawman on a frilly-looking piece of furniture, and I snickered.

Of course, there was nothing funny about this situation. I picked up a box cutter and wondered whether I should call a lawyer.

"So, any news in Gene's case?" I asked nonchalantly.

"We're following up on several leads." He fidgeted with his hat. "Have you heard anything around town?"

"Well . . ." I ran the cutter across the top of a box and it made a satisfying ripping sound against the tape. "I did hear that Gene's wife stands to inherit a large life insurance payout."

"I see." He seemed unimpressed. This guy was good-looking, but we had the chemistry of orange juice and mint toothpaste.

"How did Gene die, anyway? I mean, it looked to me like he was shot."

"That's correct." Geez, this one was a real talker.

"Probably not suicide, since the bullet wound was in the back of his head. I did notice that." I tried to sound casual while fishing for information. "Hard to commit suicide by shooting yourself from behind."

"Smart observation," he replied dryly.

"Gene was obviously a very troubled man, and who knows what kind of messy stuff he was involved in. Or what kind of debts he owed."

"Do you have any knowledge of his debts? Or messy business dealings?"

I shook my head. "There's a lot of gossip around town. But Gene never struck me as someone who was fiscally responsible. His get-rich plan seemed to hinge on trapping gators and a reality TV show. Hard to say, though, because I always got the sense that he stretched the truth a bit."

There was a long pause and I pulled out a few paranormal romances, inspected them, then settled them back into the box.

"It's definitely a homicide."

I froze, the box cutter in midair. It took every ounce of willpower I had not to giggle. "Oh, dear."

"I can tell you another piece of information." Alex's tone was a touch too ominous for my liking.

I set the cutter on an unopened box and walked over to him, folding my arms across my chest. "What's that?"

"Your business card was found near the deceased."

"My business card?"

"Well, your Gator Queen card. The bookstore card."

"That's odd." Had a card somehow slipped out of my pocket when I approached the body? "Maybe someone gave it to Gene. I know my sister has been handing them out like candy to promote the bookstore and my trapping business."

Alex tilted his head. "It wasn't on his person. It was underneath his body. Which is one reason I came here. I'd like to take your gun and do some ballistics tests."

"What? My gun? It's been in my possession at all times. I haven't lost it."

I pulled at my earlobe, feeling a bone-crushing sense of heaviness descend upon me, as if I'd suddenly donned a suit of chain metal. As I absorbed this suspicious development about our business card at a murder scene, the bells on the front door jangled.

The sound made me flinch.

"Excuse me." I scampered off, gliding to the front of the store with my skirt swooshing around my legs.

It was my sister. She was wearing the cutest macramé wedge sandals, form-fitting white capri pants, and a gauzy long-sleeved pink blouse, probably because she wanted to hide her speckled arms. Oversized black sunglasses completed the outfit. She looked like she was on her way to a garden party in Palm Beach.

"Thank goodness you're here. Vera—"

She cut me off. "I've had the worst morning, I swear. Maggie, the police—"

"Shh," I hissed.

"What? Listen, I'm still super annoyed by that officer. You know, Jason? He was two years behind us in high school? The one who was in the band and played trombone and who once put glue in my flute? I went over to the police station and he said—"

I reached out to grip her bicep. "Vera, hush," I warned, staring at her in an attempt to shut her up.

"You're hurting me," she protested, giving me flashbacks to when we'd squabbled as kids.

"Don't be a drama queen. I'm barely squeezing your arm. There's a—"

"What?" she interrupted and wriggled out of my grip, her voice rising. "You're not going to believe this. My gun was definitely used to kill Gene. That's what Jason said at the cop shop. Rumors are spreading around town. Do you know what this is going to do to me? To the store? To us?"

My heart slammed against my ribs. Rumors could sink the bookstore even before we opened the door to customers. I could only imagine the national headlines about a romance bookstore owner, her gator-hunting sister, and the murder of a rival alligator trapper.

It had Florida Woman vibes all over it, and people around the country would laugh their butts off. We'd be a staple for late-night talk show hosts and online tabloids. Probably we'd even trend on social media.

And no one would come to the bookstore unless it was to take ironic selfies with the horny, gator-trapping, bookstore-owning murder twins. Just perfect.

I could almost feel our savings, our inheritance, and our dignity fly away with the wind. Things had taken a colossally craptastic turn in the past twenty-four hours, through no fault of our own. Well, maybe it was my sister's fault, a bit; she'd been careless with her gun.

"Vera, it's OK. We'll work it all out." I tried to use my most soothing voice, if only to calm myself down.

Heavy footsteps echoed on the tile floor behind us, and Vera's gaze skittered over my shoulder. Her eyes widened.

"Who's that?"

I waved my hand manically in the air. "Uh, this is the detective I talked with last night. He's investigating Gene's murder."

My sister swallowed hard as she sized up Alex's large frame. "Oh. Hello. I'm Vera. A few minutes ago, I was talking with some of your colleagues down at the station."

"I'm Alex Holt. Wahoo's newest detective. Well, only detective." He politely extended his hand and they shook. It was actually kind of surprising how tender his tone had become. "Do you have a place where we can talk in private?"

I reached for my sister's arm and leaned into her ear. "Do you want me to call Mr. Carpenter?"

Chris Carpenter was the lawyer handling my father's probate case. I didn't know if he did criminal law, but since he was the only attorney I could think of, I figured his counsel would be better than nothing. If he wasn't playing golf or with a client.

Vera shook her head. "No, why? I'm innocent. I didn't shoot Gene."

Well, neither did I, but that didn't seem to be stopping Detective Alex Holt from suspecting us.

###

Vera and Alex had been in the back office for an hour and I was starting to sweat. What could they be talking about?

With shaking hands, I answered the call from the book distributor in New York. Thankfully, it was a quicker conversation than anticipated, with me confirming that we'd received a book order. The guy on the other end actually wanted to chat with Vera, but I managed to deflect and extricate myself from the conversation politely.

"Well, that could've been an email," I muttered when I hung up.

My cell immediately rang with the alligator tune. Oh, crap. This wasn't a good time for a reptile call.

"Gator Queen," I said in my most chipper tone.

"Vera?"

"No, this is Maggie." Even though we didn't look alike, everyone always got us confused on the phone.

"Oh, hey, Maggie, I heard you were back in town. This is Amos at the country club."

Amos was the manager there. Like nearly everyone in town, he'd been a friend of Dad's. They'd gotten to know each other quite well during the saga of a giant gator Dad had trapped some years back.

"Hey there, what's going on? You have some reptile trouble out there?"

He sighed. "As a matter of fact, you're not going to believe this. There's a huge gator out here again."

"Yikes. Has it threatened anyone?" It couldn't be the same gator that Dad had trapped, since that particular reptile was at Uncle Bert's.

"Nope. It's been a good citizen and stayed mostly on the banks of the pond. But it's frightening the guests and the staff. It showed up this week and likes to stroll down the fairway, then sun itself by the pond in the late morning and early afternoon."

Not surprising. Gators are cold-blooded, and they love basking in the Florida sunshine. "You know I can't trap it unless it's a nuisance."

"I know, I know. I wanted you to come out and take a look. I'd like your expert opinion on what we should do. Or can do, legally. Please?"

My gaze went to the office door, which was still closed. I didn't feel right about leaving before speaking with Vera. What if Alex dragged her away to jail? "I'll be there as soon as I can. I'm at the bookstore, helping out. My sister's, ah, in a meeting, and I need to wait until she's finished."

A vision of Vera being led out of the store in handcuffs made me say a silent prayer to the universe.

"Excellent. Right now the gator's sunning itself and doesn't look like it's going anywhere. I'll tell folks that the seventh hole is off limits."

"OK. I'll be over as soon as I can."

We hung up, and I gnawed on my bottom lip. Why were Vera and Alex taking so long?

I tried to quiet my mind by dusting the empty shelves, then checked my watch. It was already eleven thirty. The gator probably wouldn't even be around by the time I got there, because once they got too warm they tended to retreat to the water.

The office door swung open and a placid-faced Vera walked out, followed by Alex. He wore a soft smile.

"The call with the book distributor went well," I trilled in a fake and cheery voice. "And I got a gator request. Apparently, there's a large fella over at the country club. I'm going to check it out. I'll change and grab my duffel."

Alex's eyes widened for a second, then his mouth turned into a frown.

"Maggie, I know that you carry a weapon. I'm going to have to confiscate your gun for tests. Do you own more than one handgun?"

"No." I folded my arms. "Do you want the gun now?"

He nodded.

"Fine." I went into the back and carefully took the case out of my duffel. The .22 caliber pistol I carried had been

Dad's. Some gator trappers used rifles, but Dad had preferred this, so I did as well.

I walked out and handed the case to Alex. He set it on the counter and undid the latches, as if he didn't believe it was inside. When he saw that the weapon was where it should be, he nodded and snapped the case shut.

"Thank you. I should have this back to you in a week."

"A week? I might have to trap gators!"

He shook his head. "I'm sorry, Maggie. You be careful out there with that critter."

"Yes sir," I said with a nervous chuckle. Inside I was cursing him. I'd never fired a gun while trapping, but it was good to have in case things went terribly wrong.

"Vera, ma'am, I'll be in touch." He tipped his hat at her and walked out.

So polite, in a southern-boy kinda way.

My sister exhaled and sagged against the counter.

"What happened?" I hissed. "What did he say?"

"Well, they're finishing up the ballistics tests, but it's definite that my gun was used to kill Gene. They want to do more tests and everything could take a while."

"Oh no. Oh shitballs." My hand went to my chest and clutched my fake pearl necklace. So why did he want my weapon? Gah.

"Yeah. And I don't exactly have an alibi for those hours, since I was walking in the park."

I felt my pulse roar in my ears. "Didn't you say you were only there for a half hour? Aren't there surveillance cameras at the park entrance or something? Surely someone saw you go in there. Vera, this is terrible."

"He's going to check on the cameras. It doesn't help that literally everyone in town knows how much I—we—hated Gene."

"I think you should call the lawyer."

Vera shrugged. "Nah. I'm innocent. It will all work itself out, eventually."

"How can you say that? Innocent people are arrested, tried, and convicted all the time. Wrongfully convicted people spend decades in prison, all because of shoddy police work and overzealous prosecutors. I can't spend decades trying to get you off death row." I couldn't believe my sister was taking this so nonchalantly.

She waved me away. "Listen, you'd better get to that gator. I can handle things from here. It's not as though my arrest is imminent. Alex was actually pretty kind about everything and said he was looking into several leads. He admitted that a lot of people probably wanted Gene dead and that I'm not the only suspect."

I allowed my head to flop back and made a strangled noise. "Vera, we need to be proactive."

"Take care of the gator. You can't neglect your business. And after all"—she finally cracked a genuine grin—"you are the only trapper in town now."

With a sigh, I went into the back room. Alex's spicy, masculine aftershave scent hung in the air as I changed out of my cute dress and into cargo pants, boots, and a long-sleeved white T-shirt with the Gator Queen logo on the front. Vera had ordered several shirts, hats, and even stickers printed with my logo, which she'd designed herself.

While lacing up the boots, my mind went to Alex. Thank goodness he'd been gentle while questioning Vera. I hated to think of her being mistreated in any way. This whole situation with her gun and Gene's murder was deeply disturbing to me, and I didn't share her optimism that everything would automatically work out.

Perhaps I needed to have a conversation with Alex in private so I could glean more information. That way, I could push my sister into hiring a lawyer if needed.

I made up my mind to call him after assessing the gator situation, then said a quick goodbye to Vera. She'd put some tunes on the wireless speaker and was humming along to a Lana Del Rey song, probably dreaming of Tyler sweeping her off her feet. She seemed to be in denial about the gravity of her situation.

"Call me if anything comes up, OK? You promise?" I demanded, as I paused with my hand on the doorknob. "And go get yourself a new cell."

"Stop worrying," she called out.

It didn't take me long to reach the country club, which was about a mile from Main Street.

I asked at the golf clubhouse for Amos, and he bustled out. As I remembered, he still had the intense, burnt-orange skin of a man who'd been in the Florida sun for decades, and snow-white hair. We gave each other a quick hug.

"Sorry it took me so long to get here," I said.

"It's OK. The gator hasn't moved. Some of our guests think it's a statue, it's been so still. I've had to tell them to steer clear. C'mon. He's still on the bank of the pond near the seventh hole."

We climbed into a golf cart and whizzed down an asphalt path.

"How 'bout that situation with Gene Robinson? You hear about that? It's all anyone in town's talking about," Amos said, probably in an attempt to make small talk.

"Yeah, pretty wild," I replied, not wanting to get into how I'd found the body or how my sister's pistol was the murder weapon. "Have you heard any gossip?"

Amos slowed the cart to a stop. "I have. But, hey, look. There he is. Isn't he a monster? I swear to God he gets bigger by the day. I wonder what he's eating out there."

He pointed toward the bank of the pond. My gaze followed his finger and I gasped aloud.

It was the biggest damn gator I'd ever seen.

Chapter Seven

I sat in the golf cart, frozen in shock, for a solid minute. My hand went to my sunglasses and I slid them to the top of my head so I could get a clearer look at the beast. Yep. It was enormous.

"Dang," I whispered. I was in awe of its size.

Amos shook his head. "One of our guests from Michigan thought it was a dinosaur. The staff have named it Chubbs."

"Chubbs certainly looks like a dinosaur. I'd say it's about fifteen feet, maybe more. Bigger than the one my dad caught here a few years ago." I leaned forward, studying the behemoth gator. Its dingy grayish-black body contrasted with the vibrant green grass. It looked like it was sleeping, but it was difficult to tell.

Swallowing hard, I tried to imagine trapping it, and went through the mechanics in my mind. I'd have to get a forklift and a bigger truck to haul it away. This was no baby gator in a pool.

On the plus side, my uncle would be thrilled to accept such an enormous alligator into his sanctuary. It would be a tourist draw, that's for sure.

Amos gripped the cart's little steering wheel. "What do you think we can do? It comes out every morning and suns itself on the bank. Scares the heck out of the guests. Around noon it saunters back into the water. How'd it get so big, anyway?"

"Here's an interesting fact. Gators never stop growing. So, the bigger they are, the older they are. This one's probably up there in years. Has Chubbs threatened anyone? God, I hope no one's been an idiot and fed it."

Amos shook his head. "Nope. The one time a golf cart drove near, it scurried away. The people in that cart somehow didn't see it until they were about three feet away. They came back to the clubhouse looking like they'd just had a brush with death."

I giggled. "Gators really aren't normally aggressive. You know that. And it's usually the female gators protecting their nests that get violent."

"Yeah, but this one, it's bad for business."

It took a second to dig my phone out of my purse. I snapped a few photos of Chubbs.

"Amos, with a gator this size, I'm reluctant to do anything if it hasn't caused a problem. We're going to have to call the state on this to get permission to take it. You're not a homeowner, and this is a city-owned public golf course. The only reason my dad was able to trap that other gator was because it tried to attack someone."

He let out a sigh. "I know. But I was hoping you could tell me if you think it might go away. Is it mating season or something? Can we do anything to discourage it from hanging around?"

"Mating season's a few months away. There's not a

lot to do to deter it from sunning itself on your golf course. It thinks this is its habitat. And honestly, it kind of is. They were here first." As if on cue, the alligator pushed itself up and walked slowly toward the pond. It moved deliberately, as if it were an old man with creaky joints.

Amos and I watched as it gracefully slipped into the water and disappeared.

"When the temperature rises in the summer, their metabolism increases, and that's when they go looking for love," I said. "Worst-case scenario, it spends the winter with you, then finds a different home and a girlfriend."

Amos grinned. "Well, people sure do love to stare at him. I'll make sure to keep folks away."

"I'll contact a local officer today and get guidance on this situation. How about that? Since I just got home, I want to find out if any state rules or regulations have changed. We also might have to call the Fish and Wildlife department." I lowered the sunglasses back onto my face. "Also, make sure your staff and the guests know not to feed Chubbs. No bread, no chicken wings, no jalapeño poppers, nothing. That's the biggest reason gators become nuisances, because people feed them and they come to expect snacks."

"Got it. Thanks, Maggie." Amos pressed a button on the golf cart dash and the electric engine hummed to life. He did a U-turn and we headed back to the clubhouse.

"So, back to Gene," I said casually. "What have you heard?"

"Oh, right. Get this. Apparently, his wife is getting a huge life insurance payout."

"I heard that too. Can't believe Gene could even get life insurance, in his line of work." Goodness knows I'd struck out on that front. I'd spent three hours on the phone with one insurance company last week.

"Right? And I'm also hearing that she's been trying to buy out that cupcake shop she's working at. You know the one, it's called Big Sugar?"

"Yeah, I drove by it, but haven't been in."

"She apparently wants to own the place. Oh, and I've heard she's been hanging around with a much younger man lately."

My eyebrows shot up to my hairline. "What's her name again?"

"Barbara, but she goes by Barbie. Barbie Robinson."

"Interesting retro nickname. Timely, though," I murmured, wondering if Alex Holt knew about Barbie-the-cupcake-baker-with-the-younger-side-piece.

"Oh, and here's another detail. One of our caddies is friends with some computer hacker guy. He's an animal rights activist. Apparently, he had a few run-ins with Gene too."

A memory of a decades-old rumor about Gene tormenting racoons popped into my head. "Not surprising. Gene wasn't exactly kind to animals. Did you get a name?"

"I didn't, but the caddy comes in at two. I'll ask and text you."

Who knew that the golf course was a hotbed of gossip?

I was still holding my phone, and itched to pump Alex

Holt for information. When I finally said goodbye to Amos and got to my car, I found his card and my thumbs flew across the screen.

"Wahoo Police. Holt." Goodness, his voice was gruff and masculine.

"Hi," I giggled, sounding a bit like my sister. When I was nervous, I tended to mimic her high-pitched tone. "I'm finished with the gator call, and I was wondering if you have a few moments this afternoon to chat."

"About the gator, or Gene's murder?"

I hummed, hoping to sound coy. "Why not both?"

# # #

As it turned out, Holt's office was a small mobile home nestled in the back of the Wahoo Police Department, right next to a trailered powerboat parked in the weeds and a weathered, rusting crime scene van. This didn't inspire confidence that the department was making a dent in the crime rate.

I rapped on the flimsy door.

"It's open," a male voice called out.

Inside, I found Alex sitting at a tired desk, in an equally exhausted-looking chair. A small window-unit air conditioner wheezed in the direction of a row of gray metal file cabinets. Apparently, the town hadn't put a lot of effort into the decor for its newest detective.

Alex stood, seemingly taking up the entirety of the small space. His desk was neat, possibly more organized than my own.

"Thanks for stopping by. This is only temporary until my office inside the police department is ready. It's under renovation now. All this stuff is leftovers from fifty years ago." He pointed to a cracked leather chair facing his desk. "I've put in a request for some new furniture."

I sat, trying to avoid the crack that looked like it could rip open my pants from its sharp edge. I folded my hands in my lap. He eased his big frame back into his chair.

"So," he said. "Whatcha got for me?"

I figured it was better to begin with the easy subject. "Well, the gator on the golf course is huge. Massive. At least fifteen feet. The staff there call him Chubbs."

He chuckled. "Has it become a problem?"

"So far, no. It enjoys sunning itself near the seventh hole."

"I'm not a fan of removing gators unless they're a nuisance."

That made me smile. "I'm not either! And between us, I'm not sure if I have the chops to catch this gator."

"Have the chops. Good one."

We grinned at each other, and it was as if the little air conditioner unit had switched off, making beads of perspiration form on the back of my neck. I folded my arms over my chest. "I told Amos at the country club not to allow anyone to feed it, and that we'd watch the situation."

"Good plan."

We both nodded and stared at each other. I suspected Alex Holt was only perhaps a few years older than me, but way more serious. In the harsh fluorescent light of the trailer, I noticed small lines near his eyes, and deeper laugh lines. And possibly a dimple. That was surprising.

"So," I said.

He leaned back in his chair and studied me, clasping his hands behind his head. "Gator Gene."

"Yes, Gator Gene." I let out a sigh. "Listen. I'm going to be honest here. I'm worried about my sister."

He pursed his lips. His earlier, easygoing attitude evaporated in an instant. "It's a valid worry. Ballistics came back today and the bullet in Gene's head matched the ones used in your sister's gun."

I opened and closed my mouth several times, trying to take in more air. So it was true. "Oh hell," I whispered.

He held up his hand. "Listen, that's not to say I think she did it. But I'd be remiss if I didn't investigate every-one who had motive to kill Gene."

"Of course."

"I'm a straight shooter, so let me put it to you this way. I haven't ruled you out either."

I pressed my hand to my chest. "You think I might've killed Gene?"

He leaned forward. "I don't, but like I said, I'm thor-ough. You and your sister were among the last people to have contact with him. And you had a verbal altercation. Also, you found the body."

"You think bookstore owners are capable of murder?" I yelped. "Look at us. Together, Vera and I probably weigh less than Gene did."

He tilted his head. "I know that you and Vera are capable of taking down some pretty big alligators. I did my research. I saw the old newspaper photos of the two of you as teens. You are two tough ladies."

"Women," I corrected. "We did not kill Gene Robinson."

"As far as I'm concerned, the case is wide open. I'm looking at all suspects. It could be someone close to Gene. Or it could be someone who just arrived in town. I'm doing ballistics tests on your weapon today."

"Why my weapon? If Vera's has already been tested, why do you need mine?"

"That's police business." He sat there staring at me, implying that, despite his denial, my sister and I were in fact his prime suspects. He was playing some kind of cop mind game with us.

Any earlier, pleasant thoughts I'd had about Detective Alex Holt dried up.

"Well. I've got to be going." I climbed to my feet. "It's not in my best interest to sit here and talk to you."

"Didn't you have something you wanted to tell me about Gene?"

I narrowed my eyes. "Since I'm apparently a suspect, I'm going to ponder whether I need to hire a lawyer. Unlike my sister, I'm not cool with inadvertently incriminating myself. I don't like taking risks."

The corners of his mouth quirked up. "You're a gator trapper who doesn't like taking risks?"

"Gators are more predictable than humans," I snapped. Somehow his smirk annoyed me. Entitled prick. "Have a good day, detective."

Chapter Eight

That night, I took out all of my frustrations on a bowl of Caesar salad dressing. First I whisked the egg yolks to a yellow goo, then added two different oils—that was the secret to great Caesar dressing, olive and grapeseed oil—and finally, crushed four garlic cloves and mashed them to a pulp with a small tin of anchovies. Once everything was well combined, I added a hefty sprinkle of salt and Parmesan, then tossed it all into a bowl with freshly washed romaine.

I'd learned this recipe from a chef I once dated. Too bad he would piss with the door open—even while I was eating breakfast. That infatuation had dried up quickly.

My cell phone pinged with a text, and at first I didn't recognize the number.

"Oh, it's Amos," I muttered aloud.

Hey, FYI. The name of the computer hacker/animal rights guy is Diego Viernes. He lives above Cheesy Does It in the second-floor apartment. You might want to keep your eyes open because he really dislikes gator trappers.

Thanks a bunch, I texted back.

Vera walked into the kitchen. "You think this will be enough food for three people?"

She eyed the ginormous bowl of lettuce while reaching for a baguette.

I stowed my phone in my back pocket.

"Jack said he's making a tray of lasagna." I wiped down the counter with short, furious movements. "A tray implies that he's making a lot of food."

"You don't have to be snippy. It's obvious you don't want Jack here, but I thought it would be neighborly to all have dinner together."

She walked out before I could respond.

I didn't disagree, but I was still annoyed. Just when I'd hoped to have a night with my sister alone to talk about everything—and ask why she was being so evasive—she'd gone and invited Jack over.

It wasn't that I disliked him. He seemed like a decent enough person. But after my day of inadvertently gathering clues, I wanted to share them with Vera and not deal with being a hostess and making small talk with a stranger.

It also meant that I had to keep my bra on for a few more hours. Fricking torture devices, if you ask me.

I heard my sister's chipper voice in the hall. Jack was here, and by the sounds of it, she was gushing over his food.

"Let's put it in the dining room. Oh my gosh, it looks amazing!" she squealed.

I grabbed a corkscrew, a bottle of pinot noir, and three glasses, set them on a tray, and headed out.

"Hello, hello," I called out, pasting on a smile. It was difficult for me to lie about my emotions, but it wasn't fair to take my annoyance out on Jack. After all, he was new in town, staying here for six months, and alone.

I remembered that feeling well from when I moved to Boston.

The smell of garlic, tomato, and cheese hit me when I reached the dining room. True to his word, he'd brought a tray of lasagna, one that was big enough to feed a small army. I had to admit that it smelled divine, and my annoyed mood softened.

"Wow, I can't wait to taste that," I said, setting down the tray with the wine and feeling like a 1950s housewife.

Jack beamed. Tonight, he wore a form-fitting black T-shirt and jeans, along with dark sneakers. I had to hand it to him, he really had that whole "tall, dark, and handsome" vibe down. I'd bet a hundred bucks that his students crushed on him hard.

Behind his back, Vera winked at me, as if to say, *go for it*. I shot her a simpering grimace. If she was so interested, I didn't understand why *she* didn't go for him.

I took a moment to appreciate that in one day I'd been in the presence of two gorgeous men. OK, one had been frustrating and also held my sister's freedom in his hands—and he possibly thought I was a killer. Still.

Being around good-looking guys had been common in Boston, between the professors and scholars. But they were usually arrogant or taken. Decent, handsome men were a rarity in these parts, and I hadn't figured out if Jack or Alex fit into the "decent" category.

And probably never would.

"I think the lasagna came out well. Allow me to do the

honors." He reached for the corkscrew and the wine, and easily opened it with a whisper of a cork pop.

"I'll grab the appetizers and let you two chat," Vera said, scurrying off.

"How was your day? Get a lot of writing done?" I asked as he poured the wine. "It sounds like you're working on a fascinating book."

"Yeah, a thousand words. That's a good day for me." He handed me a glass and I thanked him. "How about you? You make any headway on the murder?"

I looked at him, puzzled. "What do you mean by that?"

"You seem like the curious type. I figured you'd probably snoop around to see what you could find. You know, to clear your sister's name."

The only thing I could clear at the moment was my throat. How had he pegged me for someone who would snoop around? I laughed. "Oh, right. You're a serial killer profiler. You read people."

He raised his glass. "Exactly."

"What's your assessment of me?"

He inhaled and tilted his head, a small grin on his lips. "I think you're curious but not judgmental."

This dude was trying to get in my pants with an answer like that. "Yeah."

He seemed to grasp that I was onto his tactics and his expression sobered. "Anyway, how did it go? The sleuthing, I mean."

"I found out a few interesting tidbits."

Vera was back in the dining room, carrying a plate of pigs in a blanket. I'd hoped she'd serve something a little more sophisticated and with less sodium, but she loved them and had insisted. Now I'd have to listen to her talk about being bloated tomorrow.

"Tidbits about what?" she asked.

"Gene's murder." Jack reached for a pig in a blanket like he was a man clinging to a life preserver. Either he was starving or my sister knew her audience.

As he and Vera munched, I told them what I'd discovered at the country club, while interspersing my story with details about Chubbs the alligator.

"Wait, his name is really Chubbs?" Jack wiped his mouth with a napkin.

"It's common for people to name neighborhood alligators," Vera said.

I added, "I'm not a fan of it because that anthropomorphizes them. It's a step toward feeding the gators, which is bad, bad, bad."

Jack nodded. "Definitely. What happened next?"

"I visited Detective Alex Holt. He's working out of an old trailer in back of the police station."

Vera glanced at me, her mouth turned down. "I hope you were there to talk about the gator, not about me."

"It was a bit of both."

"Maggie, stay out of this. I'm warning you." Her normally bubbly tone was sharp. Harsh, even.

"We'll discuss this later." My annoyance was back. What was Vera hiding, and why?

Jack clapped his hands together. "Why don't we eat?"

#

We didn't discuss Gene for the next two hours. Instead, Jack talked about his book, and Vera and I filled him in on the town, the nearby blue spring, and all things alligator. My sister and I laughed and joked over dessert as we swapped stories and entertained Jack with Wahoo lore and tales of our wacky family.

"So Uncle Bert and Aunt Lolo, they're the ones who live nearby?" Jack asked. It seemed like he was trying to get a handle on the local eccentrics.

I nodded. "Uncle Bert looks like an aging member of an eighties band, with long hair and a gray beard. And Lolo . . ."

Vera chimed in. "You'll see Aunt Lolo on her hot-pink adult tricycle. She has a portable radio on the handlebars and blasts classic rock. There's a basket in front. She takes her chihuahua in the basket and rides around town. Oh, and she wears a neck fan, because of menopause."

We fell silent for a second, absorbing that image.

It was almost like old times with us, and I was beginning to think I'd read too much into Vera's strange behavior. Maybe it was me who had changed. After all, I was the one who'd been gone for seven years, if you counted my time at college.

Jack reached for his second cupcake. "Mind if I have another?"

"Not at all," Vera said. "I got the cupcakes at this bakery downtown. Big Sugar. You should try it, and yes, have all you want. Take some home."

I stared at Vera. "Isn't that where Gene's wife works?

Amos at the country club told me her name is Barbie and that she's trying to buy that place."

She threw her hands in the air. "Why does every conversation lead back to Gene?"

"I dunno. Maybe because I found him dead and you're a prime suspect in his murder?" And I was, too. Possibly.

"Why can't you just let it go? Everything's going to be fine."

"You don't know that. We can't be in denial about this, Vera."

"You can't control everything," she spat.

I reared back, shocked at the harshness in her tone. This was totally unlike my sister.

She stared at her cupcake wrapper. "Listen, I'm going to go upstairs and take a bath and try to relax. It's been a difficult day. Sorry that I'm not in a better frame of mind, Jack," she sighed.

"Totally understandable," he said, seemingly nonplussed by her change of mood. Since his arrival, he sure did roll with the quirky that we'd put on display.

"I don't know if you've noticed, but I have a skin disease," she said, pointing to her face, then her forearm. White spots were interspersed with light tan skin and freckles. "I have an autoimmune condition called vitiligo. It's not contagious and it's not painful. Well, physically. Emotionally it takes its toll, especially when I'm under stress. I'm getting new patches on my feet."

We all looked down at her feet, which were in red flip-flops.

"You're so pale you can't even notice," Jack said.

"Exactly. You should be less self-conscious, Vera. You're gorgeous." I'd told her this a thousand times over the years, but obviously my words hadn't gotten through.

She rose from the table. "*I* notice," she said softly.

"Vera, I'm sorry," I pleaded. "Please stay. I'll make coffee."

She squeezed my shoulder. "It's not you. I can feel a migraine coming on from the chocolate. I'm just under a lot of stress. I'm the one who should be sorry. I love you, Mags."

Jack and I were silent as she walked out. I reached for another delicious cupcake.

"Something's up with her, and I can't quite figure out what it is. It's not just the vitiligo, I don't think. Although I know it bothers her a lot. Always has."

"Hmm. Tell me more."

I got the sense that he really wanted to lend an ear, and that he wasn't prying just to be nosy or to try to get laid.

"Usually my sister and I are on the same wavelength. We're twins. We can't read each other's minds, but we're attuned to each other's moods. But since I've gotten home, she's been secretive. Evasive. It's so weird. And now with this Gene situation, I don't know what to think." I picked a chocolate curl off the top of my cupcake. "I don't believe she killed Gene."

"Of course she didn't. I don't think your sister has a mean bone in her body."

"I wish I could prove that to Alex Holt. Maybe if she

wasn't a suspect in a murder investigation, she'd calm down and tell me what's really going on."

Jack licked his lips, and I swear there was a glint in his near-black eyes. "Well, we could do one thing."

"What's that?"

"We could do a little investigating ourselves."

"Hunh?"

"You've already talked with the guy at the country club. That's a start."

I sipped my wine and pondered this for a moment. "You know . . ." I tapped my finger on the table. "Amos from the country club told me that an animal rights activist had gotten in some sort of fight with Gene. He texted me the guy's name a couple of hours ago and told me where he lives."

"We could start there tomorrow."

"We?"

Jack grinned. "Me and you. I have a criminology background. And you're curious. It's a match made in heaven."

I got the sense that this was an entertaining challenge for Jack, or a diversion. Like a particularly interesting television show. Which was a little strange, but since it was Florida, I was used to odd characters with unusual hobbies.

Or maybe he really did have pants feelings for me. Well, the feeling was mutual, since he was a smoke show. But I wasn't going to act on the many depraved thoughts I'd entertained over dinner.

I knew he had the potential to be helpful with something other than sex.

For me, this was about clearing my sister's name, and making sure our new businesses weren't failures even before they started.

Chapter Nine

The next morning, I made a pot of French press coffee for me and Vera.

She was supposed to be the adult today. Because she knew everyone in town and I'd been gone for years, we'd decided she'd be the one to attend a special weekend edition of the monthly chamber of commerce breakfast at nine. And here it was, a quarter to. Being the punctual one, the mere thought of her leaving so late made my palms all itchy. I poured her favorite Snickers creamer and two sugars into a travel mug in an attempt to subtly push her out the door.

Catsy was up and eager, weaving her little body around my legs, hoping for another dollop of kitty pâté. I'd recently taken to buying a branded "breakfast" cat food, which always made me crack up. As if cats knew it was breakfast time. Although it seemed that Catsy did, since she was meowing for more. Second breakfast had become a thing.

Vera bounced into the kitchen, wearing a yellow sundress, white sandals, and a smile. She looked a thousand times better than last night, and I was glad she'd gotten a good night's sleep.

"Did you feed her?" She pointed at Catsy.

"Of course I did. You look super cute today." I inspected her book-themed enamel earrings.

"Thanks! Why are you up so early?" she asked. Apparently, she wasn't angry at me anymore, or if she was, she was hiding it well.

I yawned and stretched. "Want to get a jump on the day."

"What have you got planned?"

"I want to hit Target for some new sheets. You need anything? I also might look at some apartments." It was all a lie.

She frowned. "You don't have to move out, you know. I like having you here. I was just stressed last night. I'm sorry. Do you not feel welcome?"

I went to hug her. Part of me felt bad about keeping my sleuthing to myself. It was second nature to share everything with my twin. But since she'd been so touchy the previous night, I thought it best to dig around without her knowledge.

"I should probably just see what's out there, in terms of places to live. This is your place. I don't want to over-stay my welcome."

"You're always welcome here. This is your home. You helped Dad and me with the down payment. You know that. Another option is that you stay here until Jack moves out in six months, then you take over the cabin since it's the biggest. That is, if you want your privacy."

"That's an idea. We'll see. Oh, Jack and I might go kay-aking later. Too bad you have to work. You sure you don't want me to come into the store and unpack?"

Please say no. Please say no. Please. I needed to snoop without her.

"No, you've had a weird week. Plus, you know I'm better with decorating."

"This is true." My sister was many things. Flighty, ditzy, a little high-strung. But she was also the most creative person I'd ever met.

"When you go out with Jack today, wear some nice shorts. Not the old ratty olive-colored ones. And a cute T-shirt. Look feminine. Show off your . . ." She waved her hands in front of her boobs. It was now ten minutes to nine. "I'm running a bit late. I'll see you later. Maybe movie night tonight?"

"Absolutely."

I waited until she'd pulled out of the driveway to text Jack.

Vera's gone to work. Come over for coffee and we'll go over the plan.

Five minutes later, there was a rapping sound at the back door. Jack stood there in black sneakers, khaki cargo pants, and a tight-fitting, long-sleeved black Henley that showcased his arm muscles in a visually appealing way. I scowled in his direction while wondering what those muscles would feel like naked.

"Very special-ops," I said, pointing to his outfit. In my mind I imagined him on the cover of a romantic suspense novel. My favorite kind.

"You going like that?" He motioned with his nose at

me. I was wearing pink pajama bottoms and a white T-shirt that said BOSTON in purple letters on the front.

"No. Vera would've known something was up if I was fully dressed at this hour on a Saturday. I'll go change. There's coffee and leftover cupcakes in the kitchen."

While Jack took a left into the kitchen, I made my way to my room and threw on a casual black tank-top dress and a pair of black Converse sneakers. I grabbed my go bag and walked out. We were most definitely not going kayaking, and I felt terrible for telling my sister that lie.

I found Jack in the living room, sipping coffee. Catsy was on his lap, purring away.

"She really likes you." I pointed at my white, almost three-month-old kitten and thought back to how Catsy had hidden under the bed when the electrician came a few weeks ago. "Normally she's shy with men."

"She knows I'm harmless." Catsy head-butted Jack's hand, and he addressed my cat. "Yes, you do, you big floof."

"Here's what I'm thinking," I said, hands on hips. "First we'll stop at Diego Viernes' apartment. It's downtown. If we happen to run into Vera—and there's a chance we will, since the bookstore is near Cheesy Does It—we'll just say that you're tagging along on my apartment search. She already thinks we're on the verge of hooking up anyway."

He raised an eyebrow.

"Also. I need you to be the good cop to my bad cop, if we talk with Diego or anyone else."

"Why am I the good cop?"

I considered this for a second. "Because people would expect you to be the bad cop. It'll throw people off."

He nodded thoughtfully and sipped his coffee. "Seems reasonable."

"After we're finished with Diego, we'll assess and see who else we can talk with."

He carefully set Catsy on the floor then stood up. I reached for the mug. "Let's do this," he said.

After giving the kitten a scratch on the head and putting the empty mug in the kitchen, Jack and I were off.

#

The smell of grilled cheese enveloped us as we walked up a long flight of steep stairs.

"How does he live here with it smelling like that?" Jack asked.

"Right? I'd eat grilled cheese three times a day. After a while, I'm sure it would kill me from all the fat. But what a way to go."

At the top of the steps was a corridor, and we made our way down, pausing at the first door.

Cheesy Does It Office, the sign read.

We kept walking. There was only one other door, at the end of the hall.

"Interesting old building," remarked Jack.

"This was one of the two cigar factories in town. My grandfather used to tell us stories about it. It's always been businesses and an apartment since I remember, though. The other old cigar factory is where I found Gene."

The second door was gray and dingy, which didn't set it apart from the similarly colored walls.

Jack rapped on the door with his knuckles.

We heard footsteps, then a voice. "What do you want?"

"Diego? Is that you?"

Pause. "Who wants to know?"

"We're here to talk about Gator Gene. But we're not cops." I kept my voice neutral and friendly.

The door cracked open a couple of inches, revealing dark Ray-Ban sunglasses over a golden-brown face.

"What about him? Who are you?"

"I'm Maggie and this is Jack. We're trying to find out more info. If we can talk, I'll explain."

Slowly, he opened the door. Diego was a young guy, probably around twenty-one. Cute in a puppy-dog kind of way. He wore baggy jeans and a T-shirt with an anime character on the front. His hair was loose and curly, and in a different life he would have been a heartthrob in a boy band.

"Monkey D," I said, pointing to his shirt.

"You know manga?" He grinned.

"My sister used to be a librarian and she did an entire month highlighting manga."

"Cool. Uh, have a seat." He swept books and papers off a tired-looking brown upholstered couch. The cushions on the end sagged as if they'd seen years of wear. In the corner was an extensive computer setup, with three large screens and two keyboards.

Jack and I sat as Diego quickly snapped shut a laptop, which was on the coffee table. Diego plopped down in a randomly placed computer chair and swiveled to face us.

"What do you want to know about Gator Gene? You sure you aren't cops?"

"Do we look like cops?" Jack asked.

Diego scratched his smooth chin. "Not really. Both of you look too . . ."

"Too what?" I asked, curious.

"I dunno. Soft. You also don't look like assholes."

"OK, listen, bro," Jack said. "You know Gene's dead, right?"

Diego snorted. "I heard. Good riddance."

I fought the urge to raise my eyebrows. "Here's the deal. The actual cops think my twin sister might've killed Gene for reasons I don't want to get into. But—"

"Twins? Do you look alike?" Diego interrupted.

"No," Jack and I answered in tandem.

"Oh, OK."

"Anyway. My sister didn't kill Gene. But we're trying to poke around to, you know . . ." My voice trailed off. This whole idea suddenly seemed absurd. We were essentially doing our own investigation.

"See if someone else killed Gene?" Diego asked.

"Yes," Jack said. "Exactly."

Diego nodded thoughtfully, as if it was the most normal thing in the world to have two strangers—who weren't law enforcement officers—investigating a crime in his living room.

"I didn't kill him," Diego said.

"We never thought you did," Jack said gently.

"But we did hear you had a run-in or two with him," I added in a firm tone.

"Of course I did. I'm the local representative for FETA."

"FETA?"

"Floridians for the Ethical Treatment of Animals."

Jack tilted his head. "You pronounce it fee-tah? Not feta, like the cheese?"

"Of course we wouldn't pronounce it feta like the cheese," Diego said in a snotty tone. "We're vegan."

Jack clicked his tongue. "Of course."

This conversation was going off the rails and I had to steer it back on course. "Anyway. Can you tell us about your dealings with Gene?"

He blew out a breath. "The cops have already been here. I've told them all I know."

"That's OK," Jack said. "We're just snooping around. C'mon, man. Satisfy our curiosity."

"All right, fine. Gene was awful. Really horrible to alligators and other creatures." He balled his hands into fists. "FETA targeted him as one of the top animal abusers in the state, along with two elephant circuses and a roadside monkey zoo in Pasco County. FETA sent me here to take Gene down and I started to run surveillance on him."

I wondered if Diego had taken Gene down after all. Maybe Jack wasn't convinced that Diego was a killer, but I wasn't so sure. "Surveillance?"

"Yeah, I pretended I was doing a student documentary and asked to tag along with him. He was a publicity hog so he said yes. Of course, he was stupid enough not to do any sort of a background check on me. I got a ton of footage of him torturing animals. Want to see? I have it on my computer."

"No." I could handle a lot, including watching one of my former fellow zookeepers get bit by a rattlesnake. Animal abuse was intolerable, though.

"Not now, maybe later," Jack said.

I held up my hand. "Let's talk first. How many times did you video him?"

"Only twice. Then Gene found out who I was." Diego's cute boy-band face crumpled into a glum expression.

"How did he find out?"

"He was in talks to do some stupid reality TV show. It's just like network TV to exploit animals for entertainment. The producers wanted to know if he'd had any fights with animal rights activists, and he said no, but mentioned me later in an offhand comment. The producers looked me up and did some digging. They outed me."

"Sucks," Jack said.

"What happened when Gene found out who you were?" I asked.

"He came here to my apartment and threatened me. Said I wasn't going to screw up his TV deal and his shot at being a millionaire. He didn't grasp that the show was going to make him look bad, like a redneck in the swamp."

"Gene was short on the nuance gene," I muttered.

"I still have a bruise to show for it. This is after three weeks, so you can imagine what it looked like when it was still fresh." He lowered his shades and pointed to his left eye, which did seem a sickly shade of yellow.

"Ouch, that's rough, dude." Jack was doing a great job at being chummy with this guy.

Diego sighed. "He actually destroyed one of my cameras and most of the footage I'd gotten. I'd transferred several minutes onto my computer though."

I leaned forward. "Did you report that assault and property destruction to the police?"

Diego shook his head. "Local cops usually aren't sympathetic to our cause."

"Understandable," Jack chimed in.

"So there's no record of the assault. Hmm. Who do you think killed Gene?" I asked.

He shrugged. "Could be anybody. Anybody but me. Everyone hated the guy."

"Where were you the day he died?"

"Here, mostly. I went downstairs to eat at around two."

He'd been at the restaurant about an hour after Vera and me. "Downstairs? You're a vegan. They serve grilled cheese."

"Their tomato soup is vegan, and they have a vegan grilled cheese on the menu."

As I pondered the sad reality of vegan cheese, Jack slipped into the conversation.

"Dude, we're really just trying to clear her sister's name. Give us some clues to look into. Did Gene mention anything while you two were out? Where did you go? Do us a solid."

"We were on a gator call. Went out in his boat once. Gene mostly talked about selling gators for their hides. And women. He was a total pig when it came to women."

I visibly winced, thinking of the time he'd grabbed Vera's ass at the roller rink when we were in high school. He'd done it in front of a whole crowd of kids, and I'd been pissed. Something like that could've tanked Vera's reputation and mental health, so I'd taken revenge.

"Maybe his wife could've killed him?" I mused aloud.

"Possibly. She's kind of a piece of work herself. Looks like she should be in LA or Miami, not Wahoo Bumpkinville, Florida."

"Hey," I said sharply. "Wahoo's a nice place."

"It's not bad. Better now that Gene's gone."

The hair on the back of my arms prickled. This guy really hated Gene. Couldn't blame him, really, but it was stark hearing that sentiment aloud.

"Did you meet his wife?" Jack asked.

"Nope. Saw her from afar. She looks like a Barbie, let's put it that way."

I scowled. "What's that supposed to mean?"

"She's blonde and curvy. That's all."

Jack and I nodded, although I wasn't ready to condemn her just because she looked a certain way. "Any other women who would've wanted him dead?"

Diego snorted. "Any women who ever met him, probably. Ah, wait. You should check out the Shady Lady bar. He said he had the hots for a bartender there. He hung out there on Fridays and Saturdays. He encouraged me to join him one night, but I didn't."

"Why not?"

"Had a date that night."

This was a possible avenue to explore. The Shady Lady was downtown, famous for its dollar-fifty "shot and a wash"—a shot of generic liquor and a glass of terrible beer. "Thanks. We'll check that out."

I was out of questions and feeling ridiculous. What else could we do? Diego had given us little to go on, and how could we verify his alibi, other than possibly asking the owner of Cheesy Does It if anyone on staff remembered him as a customer that day?

"Well, I guess we'll be going." Jack rose and looked at me. I climbed to my feet. Maybe he had some ideas on how to proceed.

"What did you say your name was again?" Diego walked to the door.

"Jack. I'm a criminology professor at University of Miami. I'm a friend of Maggie and Vera's and writing a book on serial killers."

I anticipated Diego to comment on the serial killer book, but instead he looked at me with a flinty expression.

"Maggie? Vera? The Andrews sisters? Gator Queens?"

"That's us."

"I've heard about you two. Your family's kind of famous around here."

"Don't get any ideas. We don't mistreat alligators. We try to relocate them back to the wild as much as possible."

He nodded slowly. "And your uncle's gator sanctuary? What's up with that?"

"We do take some gators there, the big ones. But he treats them well. I promise you. He'd never sell or hurt a gator."

"That's what I've heard around town and in animal rights circles. But you need to know that I'm monitoring you. Gator Queens is on FETA's watch list." He opened the door. "I know you're not as stupid as Gene, and you won't let me tag along on a gator call. But I have other methods of surveillance. Consider yourself warned."

His words stopped me in my tracks. It was the second time I'd been threatened this week. This kid irked me, even though I knew his heart was probably in the right place.

"I have nothing to hide, and neither does my sister. If you want to come along on a call, just ask. You're welcome anytime."

I turned and stomped down the hall, Jack racing to catch up with me.

Chapter Ten

Many hours later, I was slipping on a red embroidered blouse with flowy sleeves when Vera opened the door to my room. With her hand on the knob, she paused to study my outfit.

"Hot. I approve." She had far better fashion sense than me.

I reached for a tube of lip gloss, the only one I owned. "How was everything today? I created a spreadsheet system for our inventory. We just need a few more titles and we're fully stocked."

"Where are you going? I thought we were having movie night."

I groaned. "Oh, Vera. I'm sorry. I have a . . ." My voice trailed off. I hated lying to her. "Date. I have a date."

Her face fell and my stomach sank in tandem. I was a terrible sister.

She plunked down on my bed and Catsy rolled over to swat her hip with her paw. "With Jack?"

"Mmm-hmm." I swiped on the red lip gloss and felt like Ronald McDonald.

"Wow. That was fast. But I knew you two would get along. Did you go kayaking today with him?"

I shook my head. "We had coffee together and then

went into town for a little while. Stopped at Target. Poked around a few places on Main Street. Then he had writing to do, and I wanted to work on the inventory."

None of that was a lie.

"And then he asked you out?"

"Yeah, it's real casual. Just some appetizers and drinks at the Shady Lady."

She screwed up her face. "That's not a great first-date location."

I shrugged and slipped my ID, a couple twenties, and a credit card in my jeans pocket. "Like I said, it's pretty informal. But listen, I'm sorry. I totally spaced our movie night. Can we do it tomorrow?"

Guilt washed over me. Not only did I hate lying to Vera, but it made me feel awful to break our movie-watching plans. We'd talked about watching a documentary on cults, which was one of our favorite genres.

This effort was all for her, though. Eventually, I'd tell her everything, once her name was cleared.

She waved her hand in the air and smiled. "No worries. You go have fun. I'm just glad you're not sitting around and wishing you were still with whatshisname in Boston."

"Lawrence? Who hated my love of genre fiction?"

She rolled her eyes. "Literary Fiction Larry. God, his writing was insufferable. Dry. And he couldn't write a sex scene to save his life."

I was going to retort with a snarky comment, but I refrained. "How do I look?"

"Gorgeous. Way better now that you have some Florida color in your cheeks. You no longer look Goth like you did when you came home six weeks ago." She climbed to her feet. "But don't get into any fistfights at the Shady Lady. Who knows, you might have to fight off other women with a stick, once they get a look at Jack and his biceps."

We both giggled. "Come on. He's not that good-looking."

She snorted. "Yeah, he is."

"Then why didn't you snag him?" I asked.

She pursed her lips into a pout. "Maybe I've got something else in the works."

I thought back to the cheesy note in the flowers from Tyler. "OK, Miss Secretive. You tell me about your love life when you're ready."

We walked out, and I noticed she ignored my statement.

"Call me if you drink too much," she said, leaning to kiss my cheek. "I'll come get you."

"Thanks," I said. "I'm really sorry about ditching you tonight."

She yawned. "Don't apologize. I'm going to bed early."

I walked out the back door and to Jack's cabin. I knocked twice and he opened the door. He was in a similar outfit as earlier, except he'd changed into a different black T-shirt. This one had a band name on the front. His hair was slightly damp and a fresh, soapy smell surrounded him.

"I'll drive," he said.

We climbed in his car, a Prius. I gave him instructions on how to get to the Shady Lady.

"It's at the end of Main Street. Across from the Catholic church." I pointed. "It's the oldest bar in Wahoo, by the way."

"A slice of history."

"It's what passes for history here," I said. "Well, that and the original Kentucky Fried Chicken building. It was the first KFC in Florida."

We found a parking space in back and walked slowly to the front door.

"What's the plan?" he said.

I shrugged. "I figured we'd have a beer and try to talk up anyone who looks like a regular. And the bartender, especially if it's a woman."

"We doing the good cop, bad cop thing again?"

I laughed. "I dunno. Not sure it really worked well with Diego."

Jack opened the glass door of the bar for me. We strolled in, the dark lighting and the smell of beer invading our senses. The place was nothing to write home about. It was filled with tired plywood tables, old wooden chairs, three pinball machines, and an old Galaga video game.

An eighties heavy metal band played softly on overhead speakers. The Shady Lady wasn't where one went for atmosphere. It was a place for tired, fed-up people to do some hard drinking at the end of a long workday.

Possibly because it was only eight at night, the place was no more than half full. Or maybe the hard drinkers had come and gone. It was difficult to tell.

"Looks like there's a band tonight," Jack said, stuffing his hands into his pockets.

I eyed the four musicians on the stage, who were setting up amps and guitars. I didn't recognize any of them. Come to think of it, I didn't recognize anyone in here at all. Over the years, when I'd come home from Boston and stopped here with Vera, I'd know at least a few people from high school.

Now, I guessed, they were all home with their families. I, on the other hand, was out on the town with a total stranger, investigating a homicide. Maybe I wasn't doing this adulting thing right.

We sauntered over to the bar. An older woman was the only other person sitting on the stools, and she was focused on her phone, a thin cigarette in hand. There appeared to be a creature on her shoulder, and I did a double take.

"Jack." I turned so my back was to the woman. "Come closer."

He did, and the scent of his soap—Irish Spring, I detected—was a pleasurable tickle in my nose. "What's up?"

I leaned to whisper in his ear. "Does the person at the end of the bar have a monkey on her shoulder?"

"Literally or metaphorically?"

"Literally."

There was a pause, and he swallowed. "Yes. In fact, she does."

We sat in two of six empty seats, with the monkey lady at the end corner. I tried not to stare, but couldn't help sneaking glances. The monkey appeared to be wearing a little red vest and was attached to a leash. If I wasn't mistaken, it was a capuchin. Between sips of her beer, the woman would pass the monkey a peanut in a shell. It was impressive how his tiny hands cracked open the nut, just like a human would.

The bartender wandered over. She was a young and beautiful Black woman wearing a tank top with the bar's logo on front. It made her slender, muscular arms look incredible. I wondered if this was who Gene had the hots for.

"Hey there," she said warmly. "I'm Farah. What would you two like this evening?"

Jack and I both ordered a local beer on tap and Farah walked away. We swiveled our chairs a few inches to face each other.

"Do you think that's the woman Diego mentioned? The bartender?" I asked in a low voice, trying to put the monkey at the end of the bar out of my thoughts.

"Could be. I'm going to ask."

"Hang on, give it a few minutes. Let's assess the scene first."

Farah brought the two glasses of beer and Jack paid in cash. As we sipped, I tried to make conversation instead of drinking too much. The beer was a dark brown ale, and it tasted bitter on my tongue.

"I told Vera that we're on a date."

He grinned. "Is that an unpleasant thought?"

Was he flirting with me? I smiled back at him. "I . . . guess not?"

"Good," he said.

An adorably awkward pause hung in the air, and

the strains of Night Ranger's one hit came over the speakers. The band seemed nowhere close to starting. I hummed along with the tune.

"You like eighties hair bands?" Jack asked.

I shrugged. "Not really, but I know all the songs because of my parents. They played all this stuff when Vera and I were kids. My father and his brother looked like Mötley Crüe as teenagers—and loved their music. And in their later years, they kind of looked like the guys from ZZ Top. You know, with the beards?"

Jack nodded slowly, as if he wasn't sure if I was joking.

We drank some more while sneaking glances at both the monkey and a group of tough-looking men in the corner. They were all beefy, scarred, and tattooed, the kind of guys who could either be corrupt jail officers or actual criminals, if my years of casual true-crime research were correct.

"Tell me something interesting about yourself," I said.

Jack took a sip and swallowed. "I've been struck by lightning and bitten by a shark."

I laughed. "No, really? That's like a Florida Man cliché. You get the trifecta if you've been bitten by an alligator."

"It's true."

"I need the details."

"Both were actually pretty mundane. I was on a golf course in Fort Lauderdale with my dad when I was ten. A bolt hit a tree about fifty feet away, and I was knocked off my feet. I have a scar on my shoulder."

"Wow. No aftereffects? What did it feel like?"

"Like I was inside a giant bass speaker. But no, no heart attack, brain fry, nothing. It was weird. Just a minor lightning strike. But I still thought I'd become a superhero."

"Maybe you did, and you just haven't had to use the powers yet." I winked at him. "What about the shark?"

"Oh, that was even less dramatic. I was surfing off New Smyrna Beach. I jumped off my board and onto a blacktip shark. It bit me on the foot. Thought I was going to lose my little toe but didn't. Had to go to the hospital."

"Oh!" I cried. "That's why you have the tattoos."

He grinned and nodded. "How about you? Tell me something interesting about you."

I nodded, impressed. "Well, I once caught a gator and a python in the same day. I was seventeen."

His eyes widened. "Whoa, that is badass," he whispered.

Before I could launch into my story about how Dad and I trapped both reptiles that day, Farah returned.

"What do you think of the local beer? I'm hearing it's up for some national awards," she said.

"Very hoppy," I said. "But I don't know anything about beer."

"It has notes of chocolate and espresso," Jack said. "With a hint of toffee."

Her eyes lit up. She went on to explain how the local brewer used flaked oats in the recipe. Farah sure knew her stuff with beer, and I was impressed. I was also amazed at Jack's palate. To me the beer tasted like thick . . . beer.

"You know, I have a question for you, Farah." I scooted closer, so my midsection pressed into the bar.

"Shoot," she said.

"Do you know a guy named Gene Robinson?"

All of the warmth and friendliness on her pretty face disappeared. "Why do you want to know?"

"We'd heard he was a regular here. We were curious about his murder." Jack smiled cockily.

Probably most women would be charmed by him. Farah was not. "You're obviously not cops. What are you, one of those true-crime podcasters?"

"Well," I blurted.

Jack glanced at me, his eyes flashing in surprise for a millisecond. "Yes, we're starting a podcast and Gene's case is our first episode."

Way to roll with the situation.

Farah didn't seem to buy our explanation. She narrowed her eyes. "What's the name?"

"Our names, or the podcast name?" I asked in order to buy time.

"The podcast name."

"We haven't settled on it yet," Jack said smoothly.

"We'll be on Spotify eventually," I added.

"I'm not going on any podcast." Farah picked up a napkin holder sitting on the bar and set it down with a thunk.

"That's OK. We only wanted to know what you thought of Gene."

She pressed her full lips together. "He was a total loser. I hated him and his racist friends, and every time he walked through that door, my night was a thousand times worse. He never took no for an answer. Hated Black people but always lusted after me. Dick."

I had to admit that if we did have a podcast, I would have wanted that quote. "Did you consider him dangerous? Did he ever try to hurt you?"

She fixed a hard stare on me. "Yes, and yes."

My eyes widened. "Oh, shit. I'm sorry."

"One time he waited for me outside after closing and tried to get me into his car. He was pretty drunk and uncoordinated, so I made a break for it and got away. After that, the owner showed up every night I worked to walk me to my car at closing. I was terrified of him. And his friends? Don't get me started. If you're going to keep talking about him, I'm going to have to ask you to leave."

Jack let out a long whistle. "He sure does sound like a jerk."

"I'd prefer not to hear his name ever again in my bar. Good luck with your podcast, I don't think I can help anymore. Let me know if you need another beer." She walked away to help a couple who had just entered the bar.

Jack and I turned to each other and leaned in close. "Wow," he hissed.

"I feel like she knows more, but she's not willing to talk. If he treated her like that, I can't blame her."

He nodded. "We can't push her. I got the impression she was about five seconds from throwing us out."

"What do we do now? I have so many questions. Who were his friends? When was the last time she saw him? Where was she the night he died?"

Jack sipped from his beer. I did the same, lost in thought.

Just then, I felt a presence appear behind us. I swiveled my barstool and gasped. It was the woman and the monkey in the red vest.

"I couldn't help but overhear your conversation. I love podcasts." Her voice was a smoker's rasp, and I noticed that her nails were painted coral and decorated with little monkey faces. Her hair was an odd shade of orangey-red, and her lips matched her hair. She wore a blue muumuu. She appeared to be around sixty, and I wondered if she was new in town—certainly I would've remembered someone this eccentric around Wahoo.

She had a similar vibe to my Aunt Lolo, who also wore muumuus (except when she was on her adult tricycle).

Jack and I stared, open-mouthed. Now the pair were closer, I noted that the monkey wore a diaper. Mötley Crüe's "Home Sweet Home" wafted over the speakers. Maybe I'd stepped into some alternate reality. Wahoo had always been weird, but I didn't recall it being quite this surreal. I glanced around for TV cameras, wondering if this was a prank.

"Oh, this is Jane." She stroked the animal's foot.

"Hi Jane. You're beautiful," I said. It was the truth. I wasn't a fan of wild animals like monkeys being kept as pets, but even in the smoky bar her fur was glossy, and she looked like a healthy animal. She grinned, showing a mouthful of teeth, and I burst out laughing.

"Listen." The woman leaned in, and a strong scent hit me. It was a mix of hay, whiskey, and rose perfume. "Jane and I have been coming here almost every night for two years. Gene was absolutely up to something shady."

Jane reached out her little hand—paw?—and set it on Jack's shoulder.

"She likes you," the woman chuckled. The monkey started to stroke Jack's dark hair.

"What was Gene up to?" he asked.

"I'm not sure. It has something to do with politics. You might want to ask his wife. She came in here one night last week and ripped him a new one. Was screaming about his TV show and how he'd helped some powerful people and how he was in way over his head. That's what she said. 'You piece of shit, you're in way over your head.'" The woman shook her finger in the air. "It didn't make sense. But I think it's all tied to his death."

"Do you think his wife killed him?" I asked.

The woman shrugged. "Maybe."

"Did you ever talk with Gene?"

She shook her head. "Not really. One time he came over to meet Jane, but she hissed at him. She's a good judge of character."

I glanced at the monkey, who was intently stroking the stubble on Jack's chin. "Yes, she is."

"But Gene never talked with me. I was about forty years too old for him. Thank God."

"Who did he hang out with?" I asked.

"All sorts of unsavory people. Bikers, skinheads. Recently, though, his drinking companions were different. I didn't recognize them. A bald guy. A couple of guys in suits. They were scuzzy in a different way, if you know what I mean. Real oily looking, like used car salesmen or politicians. They'd sit over in that corner and talk." She pointed to an empty table in a low-lit corner near a dartboard.

"I wonder if his wife would chat with us," Jack mused.

"She might. She seemed like she was wilder than him. He talked at the top of his voice about how much they fought. Apparently, she liked three-ways."

I allowed that revolting detail to sink in. The mere idea of Gene having sex with anyone was enough to turn me celibate for life.

"You know anything about a life insurance policy?" My thumb worked at peeling the label off my beer bottle.

She shook her head. "I only know what I'm telling you. He came in on the weekends."

"Well, thanks for the tips. What's your name, anyway?"

She waved her hand in the air. "It's not important. We gotta run. It's Jane's bedtime."

With her muumuu billowing behind her, she and the monkey walked out of the bar.

Jack and I stared at each other. "That was really weird," I murmured.

He nodded. "Quite mysterious. I think we need to pay the grieving widow Mrs. Robinson a visit."

"Agreed."

We finished our beers, waved goodbye to Farah, and headed to the car. Our investigation suddenly felt far more official. And surreal, given that a woman with a monkey on her shoulder had walked up to us in a bar and given us some tips.

"Do you know where Gene's house is?"

I stopped next to Jack's car and shook my head. "I used to, but I'm not sure if he still lives there."

He tossed me the keys. "You drive."

"OK. Why?" I went around to the driver's side.

"I'm going to look up his address and navigate."

"I like your style," I said.

We climbed in and Jack swiped and tapped on his phone. "I'm looking at the county property appraiser's office. Thank God for open public records here in Florida . . . aha. Here it is."

He read off the address.

"I'm not familiar with that. Sounds like one of those new subdivisions."

Jack looked up the address on the GPS and the disembodied mechanical voice described where I needed to go.

He tapped and swiped again at his phone screen and let out a low whistle. "I guess gator trapping is a lucrative gig, huh?"

I put the car in drive. "What? No. Trappers make hardly any money."

"Well, according to the property appraiser, Gene lived in a million-dollar home."

I scrunched up my face. "Really? When I was in high school, he lived in an old trailer on the edge of town."

"Says here he's the owner of a five-bedroom, five-bath home with a pool. He just bought it a month ago."

"Hmm. That's suspicious, right?"

"Could be. You said he was in line for a TV show. Maybe he'd signed a contract and got some sort of advance."

"I guess that's a possibility."

Silence filled the car as Jack became absorbed in his phone. Every couple of miles, the GPS voice gave directions. I turned down a road, and the GPS said the destination was on the right, five hundred feet. We were in a rural part of town, not far from my sister's house. But instead of the homes on large lots being old Florida wood cabins, these were new, sprawling McMansions.

I slowed the car to a crawl. "Should be right up here."

All we could see in the distance was a behemoth of a home, and I slowed. It was one of those new structures that had architectural details from several periods and cultures. Spanish tile on the roof, beige stucco on the outside, plantation columns, and white shutters. There were lion statues flanking the end of the driveway, and a fountain with a dolphin in the middle. It was tacky as all get out.

I cruised toward the Robinson home at five miles an hour. There were no streetlights out here, and it was dark enough to see stars.

"What should we do? Turn in the driveway?"

We craned our necks to the right as we rolled by. The house was dark, with no lights in any of the windows. There also weren't any cars in the driveway, although there was a large, three-bay garage.

"Doesn't look like anyone's there," Jack said.

We were past the house now, and I kept driving. "It's ten at night, so probably best if we don't knock now. Maybe she's sleeping."

"Or maybe she's not home."

"I guess she could be over at his mom's house. I think she's still alive, but I'm not sure." Gene's mom hadn't come up in my dad's updates on town gossip.

"Yeah, we might want to put a pause on this visit for now." Jack sighed. "I hoped there would be a bunch of cars, maybe some sort of gathering for Gene. That way, we could've said we were in the area and were stopping by to give our condolences. Blend in."

"Right. That would've been good." I swung the car around in the middle of the empty road. "Guess I'll just head home, then. We're pretty close, actually."

As I drove, Jack read aloud more details of Gene's house. Things like the square footage, date of the pool deck addition, how much he paid in taxes.

I pulled up to our house and killed the engine, then handed him the keys.

"Interesting information, but nothing that will exonerate my sister, or me, from being a suspect."

"Sadly, no. Not yet. Don't lose hope."

We got out of the car and walked up to the front door. I paused, house keys in my hand. This was the awkward part. Tonight had felt a little like a date. But since we were sleuthing, it wasn't. Although we had flirted a little, and I'd recognized a glimmer of interest in his eyes at various points in the night.

Should we shake hands goodbye? Hug? A kiss on the cheek? Blergh. I was terrible at this. I had to admit that I'd love to find out if he was a good kisser. "Uh, thanks for coming with me tonight. For wanting to help."

"Hey, anytime. Seriously. I'd love to help with this.

I don't want you and your sister wrongly accused. It happens a lot, you know."

I nodded. I'd read stories of people who were falsely accused. People who'd even served time who proclaimed their innocence for decades. The gravity of the situation hit me and I grasped the doorframe.

"It's a little scary, honestly. Makes me dizzy to think about it."

He nodded grimly. "We'll work it out. Or you'll get a good lawyer."

"Or both."

"Don't worry yet. Get some rest. We'll talk tomorrow." He reached out and gently brushed a lock of my hair off my face. It was a sweet gesture, one that sent a little zing of desire through me. Hmm. I hadn't felt that in years. It was probably a good idea to get the hell out of here before I climbed him like a tree.

"Night," I said quickly.

"See you later, alligator." He winked, and I stood frozen, slightly amazed at both his goofiness and his handsome face. It had been a strange evening, from the details we'd learned, to the monkey, to Jack's gentle flirtatiousness. He seemed like a good man. Maybe my sister was right, and I should give him a chance.

Or perhaps I was diverting my attention away from the problem right in front of me: the fact that my sister's gun had been used in the commission of a crime. That was what I needed to focus on. Well, that, and the new store. And my gator business.

I didn't need to crush on a guy who'd blown into

town a couple of days ago and would eventually leave. I needed to solve a murder. But why was Jack so insistent about helping me, anyway?

Alex Holt's words from earlier popped into my mind. It could be someone who just arrived in town, he'd said.

Jack started to walk away, and I called to him. "Um, Jack?"

When he turned and stopped, I ran up to him. We were under a large oak tree. His eyes widened and he grinned lazily, probably because he thought I was going to plant a kiss on those full lips of his. How I wish it were that simple. He casually leaned against the tree, and I wanted to swoon from his cool confidence.

"Hey," he said with a foxy grin.

"How do I know I can trust you?" I blurted, then laughed nervously.

He ran a hand through his dark hair while still smiling. "Trust me how?"

"How do I know *you* didn't kill Gene?"

That got him to frown and snort a laugh. "Why would I want to kill Gene? I never met Gene."

I shrugged. "I don't know you from Adam. You arrived the same day that Gene died. You're the only newcomer in town."

"Other than you."

"I'm not a newcomer. Well, not really. And I didn't kill him."

"Neither did I. But as a criminology professor, I think it's smart that you ask these questions. If you wanted to do your research, you could google me." He reached for his wallet and opened it, a smirk on his face. "And, I have a receipt here for Arby's at twelve thirty on the day I arrived in Wahoo."

He handed it to me and I used my phone's flashlight to illuminate the paper. It was the fast-food restaurant in the strip mall road into town, the one near the interstate. "Loaded Turkey Sandwich with Horsey Sauce. Good choice."

"Here's a receipt for 1 p.m. I stopped into the Foot Locker and bought some of those Adidas slide shoes. Figured I needed something for the water."

I studied that piece of paper.

"And a third. At one forty-five. I bought towels at Target. And—" He looked at two receipts, then showed them to me. "Two thirty, Office Depot, where I bought paper, some pens, and a pack of notebooks. And at three, I bought some groceries."

He handed me another paper. It was a long receipt totaling a hundred and ten dollars of groceries that included pasta, tomato sauce, and onions. I nodded, while noting that he had also purchased cleaning items, shampoo, and toothpaste. Those grooming products alone immediately elevated him above at least half the men in Wahoo. The fact that he used proper grammar *and* had all his teeth meant he was the crème de la crème in this town.

"At around four I arrived here, and a half hour later, showed up on your doorstep."

I handed him the stack of papers and grinned. "You're very thorough."

He shrugged. "Taxes."

"Thanks for proving you're not a killer." Elated, I leaned up to kiss him on the cheek. My heart banged against my chest as I pressed my lips to his stubble. Meanwhile, pleasurable tingles flowed through me when I heard him inhale sharply as I kissed him. I paused with my lips against his face so I could take in his soapy man smell.

Yum.

I pulled away, then walked backwards. "Goodnight, Jack Bianchi, my new partner in crime."

And the new star of all my flirty fantasies, is what I didn't say aloud. I needed to replace that guy with the nice ass from the reality TV show anyway.

Chapter Eleven

When I lived in Boston, my Sunday routine went like this: I'd wake up and walk three blocks to the neighborhood bagel bakery. Rain, shine, or blizzard. There, I'd buy a garlic bagel with lox, cream cheese, onions, tomato, and capers—two, if my boyfriend (now ex) was staying over. I always paid because he never had cash.

Then I'd stroll back home and make a pot of coffee. The rest of the day would be spent lounging and reading, catching up with the latest novel for my book club.

Since I'd only been back in Wahoo about a month and a half, I didn't yet have a Sunday routine. This morning, Catsy snoozed on my bed. She'd woken me at four, clamoring for a bowl of wet kitten food, so I didn't need to attend to her culinary needs just yet.

I pulled on a pair of jeans, a T-shirt, and some flip-flops, and shuffled into the kitchen. Crud. We were out of coffee. And it didn't look like we had much in the way of breakfast either. My sister and I had to get into a routine for grocery shopping. We did have basic pancake supplies, but no syrup.

I dug around the cabinets and found a jar of instant coffee that had probably been knocking around since the Obama administration.

Vera wasn't awake yet. I pondered whether I should pound on Jack's door for some java, but after my cheek kiss, I hesitated. Probably shouldn't feed my attraction or curiosity about him. That didn't stop me from doing a quick Google search on his name while standing in the kitchen and boiling some hot water in a kettle so I could make instant coffee.

Catsy sauntered in. Whenever anyone was in the kitchen, she correctly assumed food was on the horizon.

"Whoa," I whispered when I saw his CV. He'd published several articles about mass murderers and serial killers, and was the founding editor of a peer-reviewed journal called *Homicide Studies*. I noted that he'd been an expert on several networks over the years, and had been quoted extensively in the *New York Times* when a serial killer had been arrested.

I stirred my instant coffee, reading a three-year-old *Miami Herald* profile about Jack. It noted that he enjoyed long bicycle rides, hamburgers, and Cuban jazz. I skimmed the article, wondering how such an interesting human had landed in our backyard. Well, actually, that was a lie. I was thinking far dirtier thoughts.

Like riding him while listening to jazz, then eating burgers afterward.

Bianchi is married to another University of Miami professor, Dr. Lisette Garcia. She teaches Latin American literature.

I spat the instant coffee into the sink, partially because it tasted so horrible but mostly because I was so shocked.

Jack was married?

I slipped the phone in my back pocket. I'd made a point last night to check his ring finger, and it had been bare. Maybe he was divorced?

"Thought he was one of the good ones," I grumbled to Catsy.

She looked up with frosty blue eyes. She didn't give a crap. All she wanted was her Fin-Tastic Fish Bites.

I dumped the instant coffee into the sink. This was yet another reason why I should stay away from men. Like Vera, I never picked the right ones—although my poor choices were nowhere near as bad as hers.

It would be a lie to say I wasn't disappointed. I grabbed my keys and purse, pushing Jack's marital status to the corners of my brain. I needed to get on with life, and that could only happen if I was properly caffeinated.

Today I would surprise Vera with a box of donuts and fancy coffee. There was no way I could drink that instant dreck.

As I pulled out of the driveway and onto the main road, I thought back to the previous night. Something felt unfinished. The sleuthing, not the kiss. I approached the turn to Gene's house.

I didn't need Jack for this.

On a last-second whim, I took a sharp right down Gene's street. It was nine in the morning, and some in town were probably preparing for church. Gene never struck me as the church type, so perhaps his wife, Barbie, wasn't either. Plus, if their family was anything like mine, there would be folks gathered at the house, offering condolences for Gene's passing.

Unlike last night, I didn't cruise slowly by the house—I boldly pulled into the driveway like I belonged here. Today, there was an SUV parked by the garage, and I noted that it was a new-looking blue BMW. Shockingly, that was the only car. Maybe his truck had been impounded by the cops for evidence? That must be it.

But why wasn't anyone else here?

Didn't Gene have a large extended family? That's what I recalled from my days in high school; I'd even been in class with a few of his nieces or cousins.

Perhaps they were all at Gene's mother's house. It seemed odd that his widow would be left alone to grieve, though. Poor woman.

I turned off the engine to my truck and climbed out. It was a gorgeous, sun-filled morning, with a brilliant blue Florida sky and a light breeze that rustled the palm trees flanking the walkway to the front door. The humidity was already thick, and I was in full sweat mode by the time I reached the porch. I rang the doorbell and heard the echo of a dog bark.

The door swung open. I expected it to be a woman, but instead it was a young man, probably in his early twenties. He was in a tank top and board shorts, and he looked like a male model with his muscular build and close-cropped hair.

When had the guys in Wahoo gotten so handsome? I didn't recognize this person at all, and he was about my age. I knew Gene had a couple of nephews, but most sported mullets and frequented the crime blotter in the local newspaper. This guy looked like he should be in a toothpaste ad, his smile was so blindingly white.

"Hi there. Gosh, what a gorgeous day, isn't it?" His tone was positively bubbly. Which was odd, since I expected anyone in this house to be somber over Gene's recent death. A tawny brown dog raced into view, and he caught the animal by its collar.

"Uh, hi. I was wondering if Barbie's here. I was in the area and wanted to stop by and give my condolences. I'm an old acquaintance of Gene's. I'm so sorry for your family's, er, your, loss."

"Thank you. Of course, of course. Come in." He stood aside while holding the dog, and I caught such a strong whiff of men's cologne that it nearly made my eyes water. "Barbie's outside. One second, let me put the dog in the other room."

I stood in the foyer, studying a large painting. It was of Gene and a blonde woman. I assumed it was Barbie. In the portrait, he was sitting on what looked like a gilded throne, wearing a khaki shirt and pants. There was an alligator at his feet, with its mouth fused shut with duct tape. The woman stood behind him in a low-cut white dress and big hair. Both had slightly bunched-up looks on their faces, as if the artist had told them to look serious. The result was that they both looked constipated.

It had all the class of a Velvet Elvis and I wondered why anyone would pose for a painting looking like tacky royalty. Was that a tiara? I leaned in for a better look. There was no accounting for taste.

"Hey, follow me. She's in the pool."

I flinched at the guy's voice. "Thanks."

We walked through the large house, which was decorated in what I could only describe as a poor man's version of a rich person's home. Everything was done up in gold and baroque, with lots of scrolls and ornaments and rich colors. I spotted the throne-like chair that I'd seen in the portrait.

The decor didn't mesh with the views of palm trees and tropical foliage out every large window, and the effect was harsh on the eyes. Plus, it smelled overwhelmingly like coconut—not a crisp tropical smell, but something chemical and rancid, like an air freshener gone bad. I coughed.

The guy opened the back door and pointed. "Barbie! There's a visitor." He turned to me. "Just go on out. And help yourself to a Bloody Mary on the table. They're pretty strong, so watch out."

I let myself into a screened-in pool enclosure. The space was far prettier than what I'd seen inside. At one end was a tasteful sitting area with a rattan sofa, matching loveseat, and coffee table. A rattan bar stood nearby. On the other side, there was a glass table and cast-iron chairs with tropical-print pillows. A pitcher of red liquid sat nestled in a bowl of ice, and a half dozen blue glasses sat empty. An appropriate neon sign read *It's Five O'Clock Somewhere*.

My gaze landed on the pool. Barbie was in the middle, perched on a pink donut-shaped float. She wore a white bikini, and her platinum-blonde hair was piled atop her head. Oversized black sunglasses completed the look. She was quite pretty and buxom, giving off a retro Hollywood starlet vibe.

"Well, hi there," she said in a throaty southern accent. She held a blue plastic cup with a straw in one hand, and dragged her other through the water, propelling herself toward me. "You don't look familiar. Do I know you? Or were you one of Gene's customers?" She narrowed her eyes. "You're not that gator groupie from Tallahassee, are you?"

I stood at the edge of the pool and cleared my throat. Were women vying to sleep with wildlife trappers? The concept of a "gator groupie" made me want to puke in my mouth.

"You don't know me. I'm Maggie Andrews. My family and I have known Gene for years, and I wanted to come by and offer my condolences. I'm so sorry for what happened. I don't know if you realize, but I was the one who, ah, found him. It was just terrible, and I hope you've found a measure of peace in his absence. My dad died not long ago, so I know what it's like to lose a loved one. You need to be tender with yourself." I mightily fought back a nervous giggle. Sometimes if I rambled, I wouldn't laugh. Thankfully, this was one of those times.

The rubber float bumped up against the side of the pool, and I expected her to hop out. Or start crying. Instead, she extended her arm with the glass.

"Would you be a sweetheart and pour me a refill? Grab one for yourself, too. You must try these Bloody Marys. Chad's recipe is simply incredible."

"Chad?" I said weakly, trying to recover from the shock of both gator groupies and Barbie not acknowledging my babbling monologue.

"The guy inside. Isn't he a looker?" She waved the cup at me, and I bent down to grab it.

This was way weirder than I'd anticipated. Drinking with her probably would set her at ease, but it was also not even ten in the morning. I poured her drink, then gave myself a splash in a matching plastic cup. Screw it.

In Wahoo, it was always five o'clock.

I handed her the full cup. She was holding on to the edge of the pool, but as soon as she took the cup from me, she allowed herself to float away.

"Cheers." She held up her drink and took a long sip.

I did the same, but coughed when the liquid hit my mouth. It was the spiciest Bloody Mary I'd ever tasted. It felt like I'd opened my mouth to swallow a flamethrower. "Wow, that sure has a kick to it."

She laughed, a raspy, genuine sound. "That's how we celebrate around here."

"Celebrate?" I sputtered, a little of my drink leaking into my sinus cavity.

She tilted her head back, allowing the screen-filtered sun to beat on her face. That's when I noticed she was wearing glossy red lipstick. This certainly didn't seem like a grieving widow to me, but what did I know? I'd laughed from nerves when I helped pick out my father's casket. Grief affected people in different ways.

"My husband's gone, and I couldn't be happier. He was a son of a bitch. I'm sorry if that opinion makes you uncomfortable, but it's time I own my truth."

My eyes widened. I'd be lying if I disagreed, but I also didn't want to speak ill of the dead. "Oh."

She snorted aloud. "Come on. I've heard of your family. I know you found him. Gene always talked about you and your sister and your dad, and how much he hated all of you. Gene was a prick, you know it and I know it. The world's better now that he's gone."

"Well, he did seem rather difficult at times." That was the best I could do without lying. I might have grown up in a trailer, but I was raised to be polite during funerals and weddings.

"Pfft. That's the understatement of the year. I should've never married him. But," she sighed dramatically, "I'd have never gotten this house or this fabulous pool. Or a bunch of other things. The future looks bright! What a gorgeous morning!"

She cackled and a chill ran up my spine. She was positively gleeful. I tried to steer the conversation back to my fact-finding mission.

"I felt terrible that he was murdered."

"These things happen." She shrugged and took a sip of her drink.

Holy shit. I wondered if Alex Holt had interviewed her, and if she'd acted like this with him. "No one deserves to die like that."

"I suppose not."

"I can't imagine what you're going through." I paused. What I really wanted to know was where she was the day of the murder. "It must have been terrible, finding out while you were going about your business."

"I got a call from the cops. They asked me if I was sitting down." For the first time, her voice quivered.

"Aww," I murmured, hoping she'd talk more. "Where were you when they called?"

"I was actually in my car. Coming back from Orlando. I go there twice a week for an advanced baking class. Each class is eight hours, and I'm just glad the cops didn't call while I was there. I would've hated to mess up my project. I was making the best cake. SpongeBob-themed."

"I see." It sure sounded like she had an alibi, but Christ on a bike, this was messed up. "It must have been quite a shock."

"Honestly, not really. Gene upset so many people and had been threatened over the years. There's no telling who did it."

I knelt down. "Really? Who threatened him? Who do you think killed him? Did you share any theories with the police?"

Barbie lifted her sunglasses and perched them on top of her head. "I don't know who killed him, and I don't really care. That's what I told that new detective. Alex Holt. My word, is that man handsome. Have you seen him?"

"I have."

"I think every woman in this town's going to be after him."

Every woman but me. "Uh, but what about Gene?"

"What about him?"

"Who could've killed him?"

"Oh, right. It could be the animal rights people, I suppose. Gene fought with them so many times. He also owed money to a few guys because he liked to gamble. I've also heard around town that it was possibly your sister. Or . . . you."

I swallowed hard. "We didn't kill your husband."

She waved her hand in the air dismissively. "I don't believe you killed him. I don't think women are capable of shooting someone in the head, unless it's self-defense, and trust me, I had to defend myself against Gene a couple of times. Let's just say it's a good thing I didn't have access to a gun. No, women are smarter than homicide, you know? When we want revenge against a man, we play the long game."

Her smile was positively feral. Despite the heat and the spice of the drink, a chill went through me.

"I suppose you're right," I said slowly. I was glad she didn't think Vera or I had anything to do with it. But her cavalier attitude toward her husband's murder was unsettling.

Understandable, but problematic.

"When's the funeral, anyway?"

"Tuesday. He wouldn't have wanted a church service. If we wheeled his casket into a church, it would burn to the ground. So we're doing it at the Mortimer Funeral Home downtown. I'd be honored if you came."

I nodded. "OK."

She floated in silence and I attempted another sip of the liquid inferno Bloody Mary. "Well, I hope you can find a measure of peace. Be kind to yourself, OK? It's hard losing someone."

She swirled her free hand in the water. "Thanks. There was a time that I loved Gene, but those days were long gone when he died. Now I'm just relieved that I don't have to put up with his abusive crap. And I can pursue my passion."

"Which is?" I couldn't help my curiosity about this strange woman.

"Cupcakes. Now I can buy the cupcake bakery downtown. We had the money before, but Gene insisted it was a bad investment. He didn't want his wife to be covered in flour during his stupid reality TV show. I thought it would be cute. But he forbade me and refused to allow me to buy the business." She took several long drags from her Bloody Mary straw. "Now I can live my life the way I want. Men are only good for one thing."

She was slurring her words now, practically shouting. I didn't ask what the one thing was, but I kind of suspected. Thinking of Gene, I felt some bile and Bloody Mary creep up my esophagus.

"Well, good for you. I'll come by for a dozen cupcakes," I said, edging toward the table, where I set down my glass of liquid fire. "Thanks again for the cocktail. You take care, you hear?"

I gave a little wave and scurried back inside. There was no sign of the young guy—who was he to Barbie, anyway?—and I took a right, thinking I was headed toward the front door. The place was sprawling and disorienting.

Instead, I found myself in the kitchen. I paused, trying to get my bearings, because this didn't look like anything I'd passed on the way to the pool. My gaze scanned the room and landed on the granite island counter.

There was a framed portrait of Gene as a young man lying next to a stack of photos. Since a large white poster board and a tube of glue also rested nearby, I assumed this would end up as a collage for the funeral. I quickly looked at the top photo in the stack. It was of Gene and Barbie. From the looks of Gene, it was taken several years and many pounds ago. He was shirtless and tan, she was in a bikini.

Knowing that I probably shouldn't—but unable to help myself—I rifled through the photos. Surprisingly, they weren't raunchy or tacky. There was Gene as a baby, then in grade school missing a front tooth, then a photo of him in a maroon cap and gown, in front of Wahoo High School.

Where had he taken a wrong turn in life?

There were others of him on boats, and posing with gators. I came to the second to last in the stack and paused, bringing the photo closer to my face.

It was of Gene. He was wearing a white T-shirt that said *Do you like pancakes? Well, how 'bout IHOP on that ass?*

I had to hand it to him. Gene had been a master of the tacky T-shirt.

But that's not what had captured my attention. There was a massive gator and two other men. One was Tyler Carr, my sister's boyfriend. Even thinking that made me throw up in my mouth a little. The other guy wore sunglasses and a fishing hat, and between the white-hot Florida sun and the gator's tail that partially obscured his face, it was hard to know what he really looked like. Had I seen that man before? He looked vaguely familiar.

I held the photo between my thumb and forefinger, briefly wondering if I should slip it into my purse. Vera needed to see a photo of her crush next to Gene. But taking the photo was theft, and that wasn't cool or legal.

Glancing about to make sure no one was around, I slipped the phone out of my back pocket and snapped a picture of the photo. Once I'd arranged everything the way I found it, I wandered off, trying to find the front door. Okay, maybe I paused to snoop a little.

I ended up in a long hallway, stopping to inspect a photo on the wall. It was of Barbie, in a bikini, standing next to a strung-up dead alligator suspended from a hook. I winced.

The sound of a male voice coming from a nearby room with a half-open door hit my ears. It could be Chad, but I wasn't sure. I stepped closer, but not enough so that I'd be spotted, and flattened myself against the wall. My heart started to pound, and I held my breath as I listened.

"No, she's not going to tell anyone anything. Don't worry. She doesn't know much at all. Gene kept her in the dark."

A panting noise filled the air. It got closer. Oh, crap. The dog. The sound of nails clicking on tile echoed. I tilted my head, hoping to hear a little more. The dog was next to me now, pushing its snout into my crotch. I tried to wave it away.

"And she doesn't follow politics, read the paper, or watch the news. Her head is filled with sugar and spice and cupcakes. And shoes, of course." Chad chuckled.

"There's no way anyone will figure out it was us. We have an airtight plan. Don't sweat it."

The dog let out a short, sharp bark. I was seconds away from being discovered so I turned and ran down the hall, then made a left. The dog followed, its tail wagging. It thought it was a game.

"Shoo," I hissed.

I wove my way around a gilded leopard-print fainting couch. Where was the front door? Ah, there. By the tacky painting of Gene on the throne. I opened the door just as I heard Chad's voice bounce off the walls of the living room.

"What is it, Brownie? What's wrong, boy?"

The dog wuffed again. I shut the door softly, sprinted to my truck, and peeled out of the driveway, wondering what the newly elected Tyler Carr had in common with the newly dead Gator Gene.

Chapter Twelve

It took me a solid fifteen minutes of driving aimlessly to calm down. Now I wished Jack had been with me, because I desperately wanted to discuss what I'd just seen and heard with someone. I'd tell Jack later, although I also pondered whether I should let my sister in on my snooping secret.

Probably not the best idea.

Although, did I want to tell Jack? Since he was married and all? He was knowledgeable about crime, though. I'd have to think on this.

After stopping at the Crow's Nest and buying two giant coffees and a dozen of Vera's favorite maple bacon donuts, I drove home, vowing to keep my mouth shut around my sister about Barbie and Chad.

Vera was on the sofa watching a rerun of a hot-dog-eating contest when I walked in. I handed her a coffee and she beamed.

"Oh, thank God. I broke into the stash of instant. But it was so gross." She made a squealing noise when she spotted the donut box. "You didn't have to do this."

"We deserve it after last week."

She opened the box and grabbed a donut, and I did the same. I sat in the recliner and we munched silently.

The donut was surprisingly light, considering it was a hunk of fried dough covered in maple glaze and chunks of bacon. I reached for a second.

Vera broke the silence. "I'm sorry I've been moody lately."

"You don't have to ever apologize to me. But what's going on? I mean, if you want to share." Years ago, I would have never uttered that kind of caveat. Until now, I'd always assumed Vera wanted to share every detail of her life with me, as I did with her.

She tucked her legs under her and sipped her coffee. "Dad dying and us turning twenty-five have really done a number on me. I feel my mortality. It's a quarter-life crisis."

I still wasn't convinced that was a thing, but I nodded anyway. Dad's death from cancer had been something of a shock, since he'd been healthy as a horse prior to his diagnosis. I didn't share her view on getting older, though. As far as I was concerned, life was far better now than in my teens, and it could only improve.

"Why do you think that is?" My goal for this conversation was to be as nonjudgmental as possible, while also drawing information out of Vera.

"Probably because Mom died in her early thirties. Don't you ever wonder about that? By our age, she had two three-year-olds."

I frowned. Our mother had died in a car crash when we were in middle school, and Dad became an instant single parent after that. "I try not to dwell on the past. It's too painful."

"I just wonder what I'm doing with my life. You've already had one successful career. I've had zip."

"Vera, that's not true. You graduated with honors for your undergraduate degree in library science. You had a great job at a nationally recognized library. Now you're chasing your dream. Success with a new business doesn't happen overnight. And I think you have a pretty rosy view of my career in Boston. It wasn't that exciting or successful. I was the assistant to the assistant reptile director. Not exactly the stuff career dreams are made of."

She lifted a shoulder. "And I know you joke about my biological clock, but I really do want to be married and a mom. There's not enough time left. Or men."

"Of course there is. Are. Whatever. I'm sure plenty of men are interested in you. Didn't you say you had a prospect?" I mentally crossed my fingers in hopes she'd spill the tea.

Her lips lifted at the corners. "I don't know if he's marriage material. We'll see."

"You have to start somewhere." I practically chomped on my tongue to prevent myself from asking the guy's name. *Please don't let it be Tyler Carr . . .*

She took a long gulp of her coffee. "He's really ambitious."

"Oh, yeah?"

"You probably won't approve."

I rolled my eyes. Considering I'd seen Tyler's photo in Gene's house just an hour ago, no, I probably wouldn't be keen on their relationship. "Vera, my approval means nothing. If he's good to you and treats you like a queen, then maybe I'll like him. Who is it?"

"Tyler Carr."

Gah. I nodded slowly, hoping my expression didn't betray my true, dismal feelings. That photo of a grinning Tyler and Gene flashed again in my mind, and I wondered if I should show it to her. "I see. Well."

"I was afraid to tell you."

I had to think fast. If I flashed the photo now, she wouldn't share anything further with me. I needed more information about his and Gene's dealings, especially given that conversation I'd overheard. My heart pounded against my ribcage at the thought of Vera dating such a sketchy character.

"Vera, don't be silly. Just because I hated—well, disliked—him in high school doesn't mean anything now. People change. How'd you two get together, anyway?" I thought about how he'd called her a "Dalmatian" in high school because of the white vitiligo spots on her face and neck, and hated him with a renewed ferocity.

"I was at that new wine bar downtown one night with a couple of friends. He was there, and we started to talk. I told him all about our bookstore idea, and . . ." Her voice trailed off.

"And?"

She waved her hand dismissively. "And we got to talking about business and how he was running for office. This was a couple of months ago. One thing led to another, and we went out to dinner. Went all the way to Orlando. He's been really busy with the campaign, but we've managed to hang out a few times. I'm not head over heels but he's fun, and I'm seeing where it's going."

This didn't sound like a solid relationship to me, but I kept quiet. "Does he know how much you've protested new developments around town?"

She nodded. "He's aware. During the campaign he said that was why we couldn't be seen around town together, and we went to Sarasota."

I licked my lips. Something seemed odd about her story, but maybe it was my overprotective attitude when it came to my twin. We'd both gone to colleges in Boston—me at BU, her at Boston College—and I recalled how she'd dated a really sketchy older disc jockey. I'd hated him, and she'd gotten defensive. This situation was reminding me of that debacle; the DJ had ghosted her after three months.

She was so stubborn that if I pushed her now, our conversation would end in a fight. "Hmm."

"See, I can tell you're judging him already," she cried.

"No. I'm not. Honest. Now that he's been elected to office, I assume you two are free to be seen around town, right?"

She sighed. "I thought so, but we haven't gone out in public together since the election. Sometimes he texts and I go to his house at night. After his mom's asleep."

"He's an elected official who's texting you for a booty call while he lives with his mommy? Vera, what the hell?" My lip curled. I could no longer tamp down my dislike of the guy.

She let out a strangled groan. "Here we go."

"He should be proud of you. You are brilliant and beautiful and accomplished. There's no man in this town who's worthy of you. Tyler should want to show you off. He should worship at your feet. He should wake up and thank the universe every day that you exist."

"Well, now with Gene's murder, he sure as heck doesn't want to show me off. He was just elected to office and doesn't want it getting out that he's dating a murder suspect."

I rolled my eyes. "Ass clown. He should be over here helping us clear your name. Our name."

"He wants to stay out of it."

"Yeah, that's marriage material right there, he'll stick by you through thick and thin," I spat. Maybe he wasn't helping Vera out of this situation with the gun because he knew a little too much about Gene. A frisson of fear lodged in my gut.

"All I'm asking is that you don't mess this up for me," she said, her voice quivering.

"I'm happy to keep ignoring him, like I've done since our high school graduation day."

"Well, actually . . ." She stared at me with pleading eyes.

"What?"

"We're supposed to go out tonight and I was wondering if maybe you'd join us. You know, to get to know him. I want you to like him as much as I do. We'll have so much fun, you'll see. Please?"

She was looking at me in the same way as when she was ten. Back then, she'd had an idea to hitchhike to

Orlando so we could buy new Beanie Babies with our birthday money. Her logic seemed so solid, and she'd been so convincing, that I eventually said yes. Our plans were foiled when Dad drove by as we stuck our thumbs out on State Road 19.

"Don't make that face," she whined.

"What face?"

"The one where you look like you're going to pass gas."

"Spending an evening with Tyler Carr isn't high on my list of pleasurable activities. Passing gas is a party, comparatively."

She let out an impatient groan. "You don't even know him. The last time you saw him was when he was seventeen. No one is at their best as a teenager."

"No, the last time I saw him was the other day at Cheesy Does It, and I know that he wasn't gentleman enough to come over and defend you against Gene." Perhaps because he and Gene were buddies, if that photo was any indication. I was seconds away from telling her.

"I don't expect a man to defend me," my sister said, her tone haughty.

"You know what I mean. Plus, I'll feel like a third wheel."

"I spent several nights with you and Literary Fiction Larry. Don't you think I felt left out?"

She had me there. I blew a sigh out of my nose. "OK, fine. I'll meet you guys for a drink. One."

Vera clapped her hands together and squealed. "And

changing the subject, what did you and Jack do last night?"

"We hung out and had a beer together. That's all." My chest squeezed a little, thinking about how thrilling it had been to kiss him on the cheek, only to find out less than twelve hours later that he was married.

"Any chemistry? Chemistry is everything, you know."

I didn't feel like telling her about the tsunami of desire I'd felt when Jack and I locked eyes, or about his marital status, so I shrugged. It also turned my stomach to think that my sister had chemistry with the bully who'd tormented us in high school. "Maybe. Dunno. Not really thinking of him in that way."

"Oh, Maggie, what am I going to do with you? I'd always hoped we'd have kids at the same time, so we could raise babies together."

I smiled, but it was a half-grimace. The idea of Tyler Carr as my brother-in-law was too horrible to consider. And possibly too dangerous.

"Well, I need to go see if Jack's up. I promised him we'd go to Target and Home Depot today." I stretched. This seemed like a good excuse to get out of the house.

She squinted. "I thought you two went to Target the other day."

"Oh, uh." I grabbed the donut box. I'd forgotten I'd already used that excuse. "He wants to build a bookshelf for my room. We're going to pick out wood and stain and stuff."

"And stuff," she said, her face lighting up.

Gah. I hated lying to my sister.

Chapter Thirteen

I was a little out of breath from nerves and rage when Jack opened the door to his cabin. He wore low-slung jeans, rumpled hair, and nothing else. Perhaps he didn't own many shirts.

Admittedly, he looked hot, especially with those abs, but I had more pressing issues on my mind. Like his marital status. And a murder case. Both were intertwined in my mind, because whether he had a wife might influence whether I wanted to continue sleuthing with him.

"Morning, sunshine," he beamed, motioning for me to enter. For a married guy, he sure seemed happy to see me.

I handed him the donuts and walked inside. "I come bearing gifts. Maple bacon."

"You might be the perfect woman." He bit into a donut and groaned. "Holy hell, that's a good donut."

"About that." I put my hands on my hips and scowled.

"I'm definitely a fan of donuts," he replied.

"No. Women. About women."

He swallowed and cocked an eyebrow. "You're going to have to elaborate."

"Are you married?" I blurted, then laughed. Lord, I was so inappropriate.

He looked confused, probably because I was still chuckling.

"Sorry. I laugh when I'm nervous. And, uh, I googled you, like you suggested, and read the *Miami Herald* profile about you and your wife."

"Oh, now I understand." He paused. "No. I'm not married. Our divorce was finalized last summer."

I let out a breath, unsure how to take this news. He was single. Probably looking for a rebound hookup. This opened up several questions and possibilities, ones that I didn't have the bandwidth to deal with at the moment.

"Well, good for you, if that's what you wanted," I said in a hearty tone, adding a little pump of my fist for emphasis.

"We grew apart, and she took a teaching position in Spain and I didn't want to go. No kids, so we parted as friends. It's what we both wanted."

We stood there awkwardly, as Jack finished his first donut, still shirtless. His alluring self seemed to fill the room, and I was here for it. There was definitely an attraction between us. I wasn't *that* dense. And now that he was single, he was definitely fair game.

Wait. I didn't want a relationship. But I wouldn't mind a friends-with-benefits kind of thing.

He licked his thumb and stared at me with those brown eyes, and my mouth watered a little. I wondered if he was going to ask me if I was dating anyone.

He didn't, so I babbled, because I was a certified dork. "Yeah, being single after college is weird. All those dating apps and shit. Weird."

"That it is."

"Full disclosure: I just got out of a relationship," I offered.

"I know, your sister told me all about it. The novelist in Boston. Literary Fiction Larry."

"Great. Way to go, Vera." I rolled my eyes. "His name was Lawrence."

"An excellent name for a lit fic bro." Jack grinned and inhaled the second donut. "Did he write anything I've heard of?"

"Probably not. He wrote a book about the existential crisis of a teaching assistant at an Ivy League school who then bones several blonde co-eds."

"Sounds scintillating. A bit clichéd, though."

I chuckled.

"These are incredible donuts. Where'd you get them?" he said in between bites.

I mentioned the bakery. "So, do you like the digs?" I waved my hand in the air, wanting to change the subject. I almost wanted to ask him to put on a shirt, but Horny Me wouldn't allow that.

His place was a small two-room cabin, with wood logs for walls and high, exposed beams. Vera had decorated it in a tropical cozy style, with soft, airy tones and dark accents. There was a comfy rattan sofa, sheer fabric curtains over the windows, and a few strategically placed zebra-print pillows. On the walls were framed maps of Spanish Florida and a black-and-white print of our dad on an airboat in the Everglades, his long beard flapping in the wind.

An antique mahogany desk was covered with two computer screens, books, and papers, and I turned to Jack. "Is that where you write?"

"That's where the magic happens, such that it is. Love the cabin. It's perfect for what I need."

"Did I interrupt your writing? I'm sorry." I bit my lip.

He shook his head. "You can interrupt me anytime, Maggie, especially if you bring donuts. Do you want some coffee?"

I was already well caffeinated, but what the heck. "Sure. I'm here to discuss some stuff. Not just ask about your marital status. I mean, I was curious about that, but I have other things to tell you." I groaned and shook my head. "Sorry. I'm quite overwhelmed this morning. Some really weird stuff went down. Super strange. It's about Gene."

He quirked a black eyebrow and went to the coffee pot. "Weirder than an anonymous woman with a monkey?"

I plunked onto the sofa with a sigh. "Actually, yes. I think it's significant for our, ah . . . what are we calling this?"

"Our investigation?"

"Yeah. That. I need to debrief."

"Lay it on me. Cream? Sugar?"

"Black."

He handed me a mug, then threw on a wrinkled button-down shirt, much to my dismay.

Still, that made it easier to tell him about my morning. I was relieved that the attraction between us was dissipating, too.

I described how Gene's wife didn't seem upset in the least, recounted the strange conversation I'd overheard, and showed him the photo I'd snapped of the picture of Gene and Tyler and the other guy.

"I don't recognize the third man, who's holding the gator tail. But wait, there's more." I paused to take a breath and a sip of coffee, realizing I'd left the half-finished coffee I bought back inside the house. I was discombobulated from all the caffeine and chaos swirling in my brain.

Jack reached for a yellow legal pad and a pen and started scribbling. "I need to get this down. This is great stuff. Excellent job."

His praise sent a little fizz of happiness through me, and I told him about my sister and Tyler's down-low relationship. "I'm worried about her. Tyler was a nasty teenager and something tells me he hasn't had a change of heart. And the fact that he went on a hunt with Gene is super sketchy, in my opinion."

Jack tapped the pen on his chin, which was covered in dark stubble. "What does Tyler do, other than city council?"

I lifted my hand in the air. "Dunno. I haven't kept up with anyone from high school. Vera and I left the summer we graduated. We both went to school in Boston. She returned home after college and I stayed up there until about six weeks ago. Can you believe she's been hiding her relationship with Tyler for six whole weeks?" More than anything, this made my chest squeeze with sadness.

"I think it's time we do a little internet sleuthing on Mr. Carr, for starters," he said.

He grabbed a laptop and came to sit next to me on the sofa. I scooted over to make room and noticed a scar on his forearm. I reached to touch it. "What skirmish is this from?"

"Motorcycle accident when I was in college."

The man sure was prone to trouble. Part of me liked that, a lot. Okay, all of me liked it.

He opened his laptop and his fingers flew across the keyboard.

"Here's his campaign website. Let's see." Jack read aloud. "Tyler loves hunting, fishing, and boating. He's a lawyer and, ah, check this out. He works for his family's construction company."

I snapped my fingers. "That's right, his dad is a condo developer."

"Condos. Just what Florida needs more of."

I snorted. "Look how slimy he is. Even his smile gives me the creeps. God, my sister has the worst taste in men. One time she dated a guy with a face tattoo. You know what he'd tattooed on his forehead?"

Jack started to laugh. "What?"

I ran my index finger over my forehead. "'It'll all end in tears.' It's a Jack Kerouac quote. And not even the complete one."

"Wow. That's . . . something."

We stared at the screen for a moment. I was acutely aware of the proximity between us as we sat there. The air crackled with a magnetic energy, making my heart flutter like a startled canary.

"Nothing really stands out in his bio," Jack said, shifting

a millimeter in my direction. "Do you know anything about his recent campaign for city council? Who were his campaign donors, his backers?"

I shook my head. "I guess I should get more acquainted with local politics now that I'm living here again. All I know is that it's a nonpartisan race, so the political parties usually aren't involved."

He navigated to the website of the local weekly paper, the *Wahoo Sentinel*. We skimmed a couple of boring articles about the election. It seemed that Tyler Carr was far more pro-development than his opponent, and much more so than my sister had let on.

"That's troubling, considering she's always fought against new construction on open land in town."

Jack clicked to a different page and leaned an inch closer to the screen. "Well, this is fascinating."

"What?"

He pointed at the screen. "Here are the election night returns. Tyler ran against an incumbent, a guy named Dave Smith. Tyler won by a hundred and twelve votes."

"OK. So? I think it's pretty typical for local races to be that close."

"Right. But get this. There was a third candidate in the race. A person named David H. Smith."

I wrinkled my nose. "That's unusual. Two candidates with essentially the same name? Dave Smith was a council member, and David H. Smith was a challenger? I mean, there are about fifteen thousand people in Wahoo, so I guess it's a possibility. It's a common name."

Jack stroked his chin. "This reminds me of an election

fraud scheme some years ago in Miami. It made the news but no one was ever arrested. Basically, the winner paid a fake candidate with a similar name to run a sham campaign, to siphon votes away from the opposition."

"Is that legal?"

He typed into the newspaper's search bar. "Probably not, but if that's what happened here, it looks like Tyler Carr might have gotten away with it. Or he's under investigation and no one knows yet. Somebody's behind this, that's for sure. I don't see any stories about any scandal. Look here, the newspaper tried to reach David H. Smith and it said he didn't respond to their candidate questionnaire."

I sipped my coffee. "I wonder what this has to do with Gene."

"Maybe nothing. But it sure is oddly coincidental, you finding the photo of him and Tyler, the overheard conversation, and now this. Who was the young guy at Barbie and Gene's house this morning?"

I shrugged. "Never saw him before."

"We need to find out who he was. You're sure the guy who was talking when you left was the same guy who answered the door?"

I nodded. "Definitely. And I know one thing."

"What's that?" He shut his laptop. Goodness, his eyes were so deep and chocolate-colored I felt like I could drown in them.

"I definitely don't want my sister dating Tyler. Corrupt elected officials are a dime a dozen in Florida, and I wouldn't be at all shocked if Tyler is ethically challenged.

But I can't say that to my sister, who's probably infatuated with him."

"What do you think she sees in him, anyway?"

This was the million-dollar question. "Vera tends to like anyone who likes her. She doesn't think she can do better because of her skin condition and her poor self-esteem."

"It's not that visible. She's pretty pale."

"Exactly. Vitiligo's much more emotionally difficult for people with black and brown skin. But I think she just gets self-conscious because it spreads without warning, then goes into remission. Her hands are totally white now, and her shoulders, too. She loves being out in the sun but that makes her normal pigment darker. When we were in high school, she would cry and cry that she couldn't get a bronze tan like the other girls. I used to feel guilty . . ."

My voice trailed off as I remembered those days. I hadn't thought of them in years.

"Why did you feel guilty?" he asked.

"Because we were twins, but I didn't share the skin condition. Only twenty-five percent of twins with vitiligo share the condition, we found out. It made me feel terrible because until that point, we had shared everything in life. We both used to love swimming and were on the swim team in high school, but she quit because she didn't want to show her speckled skin in a bathing suit. I quit in solidarity, because I didn't want to be tan while she was pale." I shrugged. "It was fine with me, because I preferred reading and talking about books with her anyway. I kinda always hated after-school practices."

"Have you always defended your sister?"

I nodded, slipping silently into all the times I'd stuck up for Vera in school. Now I felt even worse about being gone for years, leaving her to fend for herself.

"And yet you two trapped gators outdoors in the bright Florida sun with your dad. Interesting."

"When she got her first white spots on her fingers, she didn't want to go out trapping with our dad because she was worried she'd look weird. But I pleaded with her and we covered up with long sleeves, hats, and pants. I think we single-handedly kept the army surplus store in business." I smiled, thinking of how we'd probably looked like mini versions of Steve Irwin but had made so many memories with Dad. "But that's a long way of explaining why she jumped at the chance to date Tyler. Who bullied her mercilessly in high school. Shit. What am I going to do about this?"

He paused to take a sip of coffee. "It might behoove us not to tell Vera about what we've discovered about Tyler yet."

"Why? At the least, he probably orchestrated some election shenanigans. Oh, and great use of the word behoove. I haven't heard it in a sentence in eons."

He flashed me a smile. "Thanks. About your sister, I was thinking that if we could get her on board with our sleuthing, she could be an informant of sorts. I'll bet she knows more about Tyler than she's letting on. Or could find things out for us."

I sank back into the sofa cushion and gnawed on my thumbnail. The idea of using Vera as a honey trap didn't sit well with me. But what if she did have additional info about him, details she hadn't shared? That left me with a bitter taste in my mouth, more so than the black coffee.

"I'll have to think on that for a few hours. Isn't there something we can do, someone we can talk with, in the meantime? What about that candidate, David H. Smith?"

"Or Dave Smith, the former council member. He's the loser, and he probably has heard some gossip. Do you know him?" Jack opened the computer and made a few clicks. He turned the laptop toward me. A photo of a smiling older man with silver hair was on the screen.

I shook my head. "He looks about my dad's age. Probably Dad knew him, since he knew everyone. Does it say how long he's been in town?"

"Says here that he owns a doggie daycare and training center. Oh, here. He moved to Wahoo three years ago, was elected a year later to the council. He just finished his two-year term."

"We could use the podcast excuse to chat with him. I thought that was pretty smart," I grinned.

Jack let out a laugh. "It was. This guy doesn't look like the podcast type, though. Also, we're not asking him about Gene's death. We're trying to find out about the election."

"True." I tried not to check out Jack's muscular forearms as I pondered the situation. "If only we had a dog."

"I know. We could inquire about training."

"For a fake dog?" I chewed on my cheek.

"No, for Catsy."

I squinted. "Catsy's a cat. She can't be trained. She's ungovernable."

"Of course she can't be trained. But we can go there under the pretense of asking him about training cats, and then talk with him about the election."

"I guess that's logical. Do you think he's open today? I told my sister we were going to Home Depot because you're building me a bookcase. Tomorrow, I need to really spend time at the store with Vera."

"It's Sunday, so probably not. But we could give him a call, I suppose. Do dog daycares ever really close?" Jack reached for his phone and dialed.

"Good morning. Dave Smith? Hey. My girlfriend and I wanted to chat with you about training our pet, Catsy." Jack winked at me. My face felt hot.

Girlfriend?

"Yes, Catsy. Mmm-hmm. Yes. OK. Are we available today? Hon, are we available today at noon?" Jack moved the phone away from his mouth.

"Yes, dear," I called out, a touch too loud, while stifling a giggle.

"Perfect. We'll be there at noon." He tapped on his phone and set it on the coffee table, then leaned back into the sofa.

I turned to him, the thrill of it all surging through me. "Impressive. It's like a romance trope."

"What is?"

With my finger, I motioned to him and then to me. "A common theme in romance novels. Popular with readers. We have a fake relationship."

"Or is it fake? Dun-dun." He mimicked the *Law & Order* theme song and raised his brows. "Now, about that bookcase. I'm not much of a woodworker, but I can give it a shot."

I stared at him with a flirty smile. "Why are you doing this, anyway?"

"Doing what?" He widened his eyes, all innocent-looking.

"Helping me."

He shrugged. "Lots of reasons."

"Give me one."

"Procrastinating writing my book." He bit his lip, those smoldering eyes locked onto mine with a magnetic intensity that sent a pleasurable shiver down my spine.

My cheeks flushed, feeling like they were about to burst into flames. Clearing my throat, I mustered all the self-control I had left.

"All right, time to get moving," I managed to say, attempting to sound nonchalant. Deep down, I knew that if I lingered any longer in this small cabin with Jack, I'd pounce on him like a Florida panther on a tree limb, consequences be damned.

Chapter Fourteen

Dave's Doggie Daycare and Training Center was located in Dave's house. From the address, I knew it was in one of the stately old craftsman bungalows that lined the residential streets near downtown. As we drove there, I took Jack down a back road and pointed at a pasture with several large black animals grazing in the sunshine.

"I'm giving you the two-cent tour. There's the beefalo farm."

"Beefalo?"

"A cross between a buffalo and a cow. Beefalo. They're quite tasty. If you want to try some, the specialty market downtown sells the meat. I heard the beefalo owner is expanding to ostrich and emu meat soon."

"You are a wealth of local information, Ms. Andrews."

I pointed out a few more landmarks along the way—a home decorated with hundreds of bowling balls in the yard, a rough and tumble roadside bar where a famous serial killer had her last drink, and the spot of a Skunk Ape sighting.

"There's a lot going on in Wahoo. We might have to check out that bar for research purposes," he murmured. "And when was the Sasquatch sighting?"

"Skunk Ape. Not Sasquatch. It was when I was in fifth grade. I mean, there might have been more in recent years. I'm not sure. I stopped paying attention a while ago."

We eventually made it downtown, and I asked him to turn on one of the residential streets. Being with Jack made me excited about showing him every detail about Wahoo.

"See that gray trailer, with the brown door? The one with the rickety porch?" I pointed.

Jack hummed a yes.

"That's where Vera and I grew up. Man, I had a lot of good times in that place." Between the jasmine vine growing over the arch of the back gate to the two windows on the side—where Vera and I had our bedroom—just seeing the house made my heart swell with memories.

"Don't kill yourself, girls," Dad would yell, as we'd pop wheelies on our bikes in the street. "You're of no use to me dead!"

Of course, he'd been the one who taught us how to do a wheelie on our bikes. We were fully free-range kids. Driving past the house made me miss my father and his eccentric ways desperately, and I could almost see him standing on the porch, watching me and Vera race up and down the street on our bikes.

"I'll bet this was a great place to grow up." Jack's deep voice brought me back to the present.

"It was. There used to be an old pharmacy with an authentic soda fountain counter, and we'd walk over for root beer floats. And we'd ride over to the creek and catch frogs. It was idyllic. Oh, turn left. It's a shortcut to Dave's street."

A few minutes later, we pulled up to the front of the home, which was a large two-story bungalow. I stared at it for a beat. "I think my third-grade teacher used to live here. She was arrested years later for insurance fraud."

"Florida." Jack shook his head.

Like the other houses in the area, it was landscaped with a lush green lawn in the front, a squat palm tree, and a neatly trimmed hedge near the porch. We made our way up the walkway and rang the old-fashioned brass doorbell. A cacophony of barking dogs followed.

"C-A-T," I whispered to Jack, who put his finger to his lips.

An older man wearing a lime-green polo shirt and khaki pants greeted us.

"You the folks who called earlier?" he said with a smile.

"We are. Pleased to meet you." Jack gave the man his name and the two shook hands. "This is my girlfriend, Margaret."

I stared at Jack adoringly. He blew me a kiss, which made me giggle, but also sent a little whoosh of desire through me. This fake relationship thing was going pretty well, in my opinion.

Dave looked at our feet and behind our shoulders, at the Prius next to the curb. "Where's your furry friend?"

"Oh, we wanted to talk first. Like a consultation," I said.

"Of course. That makes it a lot easier sometimes, especially if the animal is poorly behaved. C'mon in. We'll sit in my office."

I thought back to the first visit to the veterinarian with Catsy, when she'd received her first kitten checkup. She went so wild that they had to subdue her in a net and then give her a mild tranquilizer before the vaccinations.

Dave led us to a small office, and along the way I caught sight of various rooms, dog snouts, and wagging tails, all held back by a maze of baby gates. The barking hit a crescendo as we passed by what looked like a puppy kindergarten filled with plush toys and tiny dogs.

"As you can see, my husband and I keep things quite secure here. We also have a fenced-in yard, and a doggie door. But we don't allow them to go outside unsupervised. We specialize in small dogs for boarding, but I train dogs of all sizes."

"Very nice," Jack said.

We went into a room with built-in floor-to-ceiling bookcases on two walls that were packed with books, and windows looking out at a tranquil rock garden and fountain. I nearly swooned. If I had a dog, I'd definitely bring it to Dave for daycare on the basis of his good taste in library decor.

"What a beautiful office. Love the bookcases." I eased onto a tufted brown leather sofa. Jack plopped next to me. My hand skimmed the cool leather, and Jack put his hand over mine.

Pleasurable prickles went up my arm.

Dave sat in a chair and reached for a notebook and a pen on a dark wood coffee table that matched the bookshelves.

"Thank you. So, tell me about your fur baby."

I cleared my throat. "Well, Catsy—"

"Is that her name? Catsy?" Dave wrote it at the top of the page.

"Yes."

"Actually, we wanted to chat with you about your credentials first," Jack said in a businesslike tone while squeezing my hand. I immediately imagined us naked.

"Oh, of course. I'm so sorry. I should've done that first." Dave stood and went to a messy desk and rifled through a stack of papers. After a few seconds he extracted a brochure, then walked back to us and handed the paper to me.

As Dave talked about his dog training and handling experience, I studied the glossy brochure. It had photos of a smiling Dave with various dogs. It also listed a short bio.

Dave is also an active member of the Wahoo community, and was elected to the town's city council, where he advocates for his constituents and for the environment.

This was our in. "Oh," I cried, pointing to the brochure. "You're on the city council! How awesome."

Dave, who had been telling Jack about the time he showed a Tibetan Spaniel at Westminster, looked to me and straightened his spine. The corners of his mouth turned down.

"Well, I was on the council. I lost during the November election. Lost by a hair. I campaigned so hard, spent tens of thousands of dollars. Now I'm in debt and the city is without a voice for the environment and the needy."

"Oh, that's a shame. I'm so sorry." My mouth twisted

to make a genuinely sad face. Dave seemed like a guy who truly cared, unlike Tyler, that useless ball of belly-button lint.

"Yes, that's too bad. I'm a firm believer that we need animal lovers in our local government," Jack said. "Are you planning to run again?"

Dave sighed. "I'm not sure. I felt like I was getting somewhere on the council, keeping development in check. I'm from South Florida and know how malls and subdivisions can get out of hand."

"I hear you on that. Lived in Miami for a while myself," Jack said in a folksy tone.

"I think there are plenty of people who agree with you on the development issue here," I said. It was true. My sister had a vast network of friends and acquaintances who rallied to protest every new condo building and housing tract. But in the end, the folks on the side of the environment always seemed to lose in Florida. I could never quite figure out why, but I had my eye on the usual suspects: corruption and greed.

They were the bread and butter of the Sunshine State.

Dave stared mournfully at his pad of paper. I got the sense that it really tore him up to lose the election. "I think you're right. But there are some well-financed candidates who will do anything to win."

I wanted to turn to Jack and give him a meaningful look, but kept my expression neutral.

"Really? In a small town like this? I'm pretty new here," Jack said. "Wahoo doesn't seem corrupt at all."

Dave tore a sheet out of his notebook and crumpled it

in one chubby hand. "The things I saw during the campaign would knock your socks off."

"Really?" I leaned forward in my seat. "Like what?"

"I probably shouldn't say."

"Oh, come on," Jack prodded chummily. "We won't tell anyone. We just want to know who to steer clear of."

A glimmer sparked in Dave's eyes. "My opponent, Tyler Carr, was sketchy as all get out."

Bingo!

"Hmm, I think I've heard of him." I put my finger on my chin. "Sketchy how?"

"I believe he, or one of his minions, paid a guy with my same name to run in the election. Tyler won by a hundred and twelve votes. The unknown David H. Smith received just enough votes to make me come in second place. If he hadn't been in the race, I would've won."

I allowed my jaw to drop, pretending to be shocked.

"No way, man. That's super messed-up." Jack frowned. "Have you told the authorities, or the news, or anyone?"

I marveled at how Jack was extremely conversational with everyone. It was truly a gift.

"I discussed it with the city manager and the city attorney, but they're pro-development and disliked me while I was on the council. So nothing happened on that front." Bitterness laced his tone. "I'm considering going to the police or filing a complaint with the ethics board. Thing is, I can't actually link Tyler to the *other* David H. Smith. I've tried asking around town and came up empty. He probably used a go-between is my guess, so that he stays clean."

My mind began to spin with possibilities. Could that go-between have been Gene?

"That's a lot of work just to be on the city council," Jack said.

"Sure is. But if you're also in bed with developers who will pay kickbacks, it could be very lucrative."

"I wonder which developers?" I mused aloud.

"Which ones *aren't* friends with Tyler?" He ticked off a few well-known housing construction builders in the region. "And he's also tight with that guy who bought the Covington property recently."

Prickles of awareness flowed through me. "The Covington property?"

He waved his hand in the air. "You probably wouldn't know the location, it's basically a swamp on the edge of town. But it's home to a lot of biodiversity. Well, it *was* home to biodiversity. Pretty soon, once the council takes its final vote, it's going to be a hundred and twenty-five three-bedroom, two-bath homes."

"Disgusting." I couldn't hide my ire.

Dave jabbed his index finger in my direction. "That's right, sister. The developer's a guy from New Jersey. Just moved down here with his family in one of those new houses. Several months ago, before the campaign, he flew down here and tried to bribe me to vote for the rezoning. When I didn't, it wasn't long before Tyler and David H. Smith got into the race. Rumor has it that he's tied up with the Mafia."

"What's his name?" Jack said.

Dave frowned. "It's unimportant. I didn't want to take up a bunch of your time. You're here for a dog consultation."

"It's totally fine," I piped up. "We love hearing local gossip. What did the developer look like, anyway?"

"Broad-shouldered, probably around forty-five or fifty. Had a thick accent. Oh, and he was bald."

My eyes widened. It sounded like the same guy who'd called me to catch that baby gator. What were the odds? "Oh my," I whispered.

Dave glanced at me in a funny way, probably wondering why I was muttering to myself. "Let's get back to your dog. That's more important, and it'll bring my blood pressure down. Don't want to have a heart attack." Dave chuckled sadly and clicked his pen twice. "I've been so stressed for months about all this."

"I'm sure. About that developer—" We needed Dave to tell us the name so I could confirm it was the same guy I'd visited the day of the gator call. But how? It had to be the same guy—it was just too coincidental in a town as small as Wahoo.

He cut me off. "So that's why I want to focus only on the positive. Tell me about your dog."

I looked to Jack helplessly. The amount of information in my brain made it impossible to think up a lie about a fake dog. "Catsy's not quite—"

"Well, she's not actually a dog," Jack stammered.

"Excuse me?" Dave looked to Jack, then to me. "What is she?"

"Catsy's a cat, and a girl. But we were hoping to take her out on a leash and were wondering if you trained cats." Jack winced.

I turned to him, while an image of trying to wrangle

Catsy into a harness popped into my head. If I tried that, my arms would look like ground chuck roast, and I laughed out loud. "Sweetie, I thought you told Dave on the phone that Catsy is a feline."

Jack scratched his cheek. "I swear I thought I did. You're sure I didn't mention that? It's a hard detail to overlook."

Dave pressed his hand to his chest. "You didn't tell me Catsy was a cat. I don't train cats. I despise felines. Dogs are obedient."

That was a strike against Dave, but I was hardly in a position to hold anything against him at this point.

"Oh," Jack and I said in tandem.

"She's a very smart kitten," I added. "You should see how she tears apart a catnip mouse."

"Sorry I can't help you." Dave stood up, a look of disgust on his face. "It was nice meeting you folks."

We stood, and I giggled because the situation was so awkward and absurd. "If we ever get a dog, we'll know who to come to, right, honey bun?"

Jack put his hand on the small of my back. "Absolutely, sweet cheeks."

I barked out a laugh, and Dave stared at me.

"She laughs when she's nervous," Jack said, sotto voce.

"Got it." By the tone of Dave's voice, I didn't think he actually did.

He led us out of the beautiful office, past the pack of barking dogs, and to the front door. Jack didn't move his hand from my back, and I didn't want him to either.

When we were safely at the porch and Dave was in the doorway, we turned to wave.

"Thanks again, sorry to take up your time," I said.

His mouth slanted downward. "I'm not sure what you two are up to, but I suspect you weren't here for training your cat. I can't trust anyone in this town."

He slammed the door. Jack and I walked to the car in silence, and quickly drove away.

I let out a long breath. "Yikes, that was super intense at the end."

"No kidding. But we got some amazing information."

"Yes," I cried. "So much information. I think I know the developer."

Jack took his eyes off the road and turned to me. "What?"

"Don't crash." I pointed at an upcoming stop sign. "Turn right and then left, and park on Main Street. Let's stop at the Crow's Nest for some coffee and I'll explain everything."

"Right, then left," he muttered.

"I'm going to make sure my sister hasn't texted me. Park anywhere on Main." I extracted my phone from my purse. I had no calls, and no texts from Vera.

My mind spun with possibilities. I tapped on my phone screen at my voicemail. I still had the call about the baby gator in the pool from the homeowner.

As Jack parallel-parked like a champ, I played the days-old message on speakerphone.

"Hi, uh, this is Bruce Doyle." He mumbled his name, but now that I listened to it a second time, I could under-stand what he was saying. "I'm at 760 Osprey Ridge

Parkway and I have an urgent situation here. There's a massive alligator in my pool. I've already called another trapper but it's been two hours and he hasn't called back. Can you come over and catch him? I'll pay extra. Thanks."

Jack killed the engine. "Who was that?"

I shot him a triumphant smile. "Let's get coffee. I'll tell you inside."

We charged into the Crow's Nest. Probably I should've felt a little ridiculous since it was my second time in the place today, but it didn't matter. I needed coffee to think.

The Crow's Nest was one of the oldest businesses in Wahoo, with lots of hanging ferns, a laid-back hippie vibe, and the best coffee in town. It was owned by the wife of my high school debate teacher, and she'd let us study there back in the day.

It wasn't packed, and I spotted a worn sofa in the corner. "Go grab that and I'll order. What would you like?"

Jack squinted at the menu. "A double espresso."

I went up to the counter, wondering if anyone I knew was working here. I was greeted by a fresh-faced teenage guy with a lip piercing.

"Didn't you come in a couple of hours ago?"

"Yeah," I said sheepishly.

It didn't take me long to order two double espressos, and with a squirmy, excited feeling I brought them to Jack. He accepted his cup and I sat next to him. Probably a little closer than I would normally, but a couple was at the next table, and I didn't want anyone to overhear what I was about to say.

Plus, I liked the way Jack smelled.

"OK, so that voicemail I played on speakerphone in the car? I think that's the developer Dave was talking about."

"Really?"

I nodded. "I went to a gator call at his house on Thursday. The same day I found Gene's body."

Jack frowned and I plowed on, holding up fingers as I ticked off details. "He was from New Jersey. He lives in Osprey Landing. He just moved here, into one of those new homes. It all matches with what Dave said."

"What does this have to do with Gene?"

I sighed, stumped. "I don't know. He's definitely tied to Tyler Carr and sketchy housing developments."

Jack sipped his coffee. "And possibly a stolen election."

I downed half of the little shot of espresso in one gulp and flicked my phone to life with my other hand. "Here's a photo of the gator in his house."

When the photos app opened, I paused on the picture that popped up. It was the one I'd taken at Barbie's house, of the picture of Tyler and Gene.

A flash of recognition lit up my brain and pinged around like a pinball in a machine, and I dropped my espresso from shock, splashing Jack's sneakers.

Chapter Fifteen

"**O**h my God, I'm so sorry," I yelped, setting my phone on the seat. "Let me grab you a cloth."

Jack reached for my arm. "It's OK, really. They're leather. They'll clean up just fine."

"No, let me get you a towel." I ran into the bathroom and pumped the dispenser, then hustled back and knelt at Jack's feet.

He chuckled and took the rough brown paper from me. "I've got it. Sit next to me."

After a minute of wiping his sneaker, he looked at me. "See? Like new."

"I'm so sorry."

He balled the paper up and set it in front of us, on a repurposed, worn trunk that served as a coffee table. "What startled you so much? You looked like you saw a ghost there."

I fished the phone out from under my butt and navigated to the photo. "This is Bruce," I hissed. "I didn't recognize him before but now I do."

He took the phone from me and held it close to his face. "Are you sure? It's really difficult to see the guy's face."

"I'm certain. Bruce is bald. And broad-shouldered like that."

Jack handed me the phone. "It's common for people to think they see parallels and patterns when it's really just coincidence."

"It's definitely him."

He leaned back and I did, too. Our thighs touched, but I was too amped up from making the connection between Gene, Tyler, and Bruce to pay any attention to my attraction to Jack.

"Maggie. Let's look at the facts. Dave said Tyler was tight with a developer from New Jersey. Tyler ran a third-party candidate with the same name to unseat Dave, so he could get kickbacks from the developer."

"Correct."

"OK, that's possible. Plausible, even. Now you're saying that Gene knew both men."

"They were in the photo together."

"Possibly, if you're identifying Bruce correctly. Let's say you're right. My question: why did Bruce call you to trap a gator, and not call Gene?"

My shoulders sagged. "That's a good question. Although remember, he did say that he called another trapper, but that person didn't call back. Gene's the only other trapper in town, so it was most likely him."

Jack massaged the back of his neck with his fingers. "This doesn't get us any closer to finding out who killed Gene."

"It doesn't. But it gives us two more potential suspects, in addition to his sketchy wife, the bartender he harassed, and the animal rights activist who hated him."

"And one of those five people is your sister's boyfriend."

I let my head flop onto the back of the sofa. "Don't remind me. What am I going to do about that? I don't want her anywhere near him."

Jack stared hard into the distance, toward the front door. His stare at the door was so intense that I wondered if he'd spotted someone he knew. My own gaze followed his, but there was no one. He apparently was merely lost in thought.

Then he turned to me and squeezed my knee with his big hand. "I've got an idea."

"What is it?"

"Your sister thinks we're dating, right?"

I tilted my head from side to side. "Pretty much. Maybe not dating, exactly, but on the road to dating. We're taking the onramp to the dating interstate. Why?"

He hung his head and laughed, while his hand still cupped my knee. Little zings of excitement crackled through me. I was starting to like this guy. He rolled with my humor, seemed to like it, even. He also appeared to be eager to try new things, however far-fetched they were.

My ex-boyfriend—Literary Fiction Larry—had been so serious and never went along with my spontaneous ideas. Like the time I suggested we drive to New Hampshire to pet llamas. He thought that was ridiculous.

"Here's the idea. We—well, you—propose a double date. That way we can spend uninterrupted time with Tyler in a casual setting. You can be incredibly sweet with him, and make your sister think you're really trying to get along with her new man."

My face lit up and I put my hand on his. "And you can play the bad cop and ask him lots of questions."

"Exactly."

My mouth dropped open. "Just this morning, in fact, my sister begged me to go out with her and Tyler, so I could get to know him. So this is perfect. You can come along, and voilà! Double date."

We stared at each other and grinned.

#

"This is so exciting," Vera squeaked from the back seat. "Do you know how long it's been since I've been on a double date with my sister?"

"How long?" Jack asked.

We were in his Prius, driving to our date. For a reason unknown to me—Vera had avoided my probing questions—Tyler was meeting us at the restaurant. Which happened to be in Fern City, in an entirely different county. It was a full half hour from Wahoo.

"Maggie and I were in college. We'd met twin guys at a club and went out with them."

I rolled my eyes. "We got stopped for speeding, and the driver, who happened to be my date, told me I should pay for the ticket because I'd distracted him."

Jack burst out laughing. "How did you distract him?"

Vera giggled. "He thought Maggie was just that hot."

"I feel that."

Vera's hand snaked around the right side of my seat and pinched my upper arm hard.

"Ow," I said. "Our dates were identical twins. I couldn't tell them apart. When we got to the restaurant, I think they switched because my date and I got pretty combative about the speeding ticket. Then one of them told us that he was a werewolf. And he was serious. We took a cab home."

Vera sighed. "The werewolf was my guy."

A comeback was on the tip of my tongue, but I refrained. Plus, we were pulling into the parking lot.

"Here we are," Jack said in a cheerful voice, reading from the sign out front. "Lord of the Wings."

Even though I wasn't looking forward to having dinner with Tyler, I was ridiculously excited to peruse the wing menu. There was nothing better than eating a pile of spicy, greasy chicken with your fingers.

We climbed out of the car and Vera walked a few feet in front of us, obviously eager to see her man.

"Nothing says a classy date like this place," I offered, while observing that it looked like a repurposed Taco Bell building. "Also, who has a romantic double date at a wing house?"

Vera was already through the door, and Jack held it open for me. "Us, apparently."

"My apologies for this night in advance."

Jack winked at me. Earlier, I'd told him all about Tyler Carr's nasty behavior in high school, and we'd mapped out a plan of questioning.

We sauntered into the restaurant. It was a sports-themed place, with a wall of televisions playing various ball games. Framed posters of women in bikinis were everywhere, and the entire room smelled of fried food. Something happened in one of the sports ball games and a gaggle of men at the bar cheered and hooted.

I hated it already. But if I had to endure a bunch of sports bros, I would in the name of wings. And defending my sister.

"He's back there," Vera said excitedly.

We wound our way around the bar, took a left, passed six booths, and at the very last one, near the restrooms, sat Tyler. It was hardly the best seat in the house, and I couldn't help but think he didn't want to be seen with us.

"Hey, baby," he said in a deep voice, standing up. "How's my best girl?"

Vera threw her arms around his neck and kissed his cheek. I nearly retched when I saw him smack her butt.

Jack must've sensed my annoyance because he put his hand on the small of my back and leaned into my ear. "Remember, good cop, bad cop."

I grunted in response, partially out of annoyance and also a bit out of pent-up lust. Jack's voice was low, growly, and held the promise of things I hadn't experienced in a very long time. It was like the audio version of salted caramel, and probably as bad for me.

"You remember my twin sister, Maggie, right?" With her arm still slung around Tyler's neck, she turned to me.

"Hey." I gave a little wave. "It's been a while."

"Maggie! It's great to see you."

"And this is Jack. He's Maggie's date."

The two men shook hands, and I noted with no small amount of satisfaction that Jack was far more muscular—and handsome—than the smarmy Tyler. Then I immediately felt guilty. This shouldn't be a competition between my sister and me. I was merely fishing for information. If Tyler was indeed free of political corruption and any involvement in Gene's death, and if he treated Vera well, I needed to accept their relationship.

Until those details were confirmed, though, he was guilty until proven innocent in my mind.

We all slid into the booth, Tyler and Vera on one side, and Jack and I on the other. I noticed that my sister sat incredibly close to Tyler, as if their hips were fused.

There was a foot of space between me and Jack, and I scooted away from the wall, a few inches closer to him. Had to make this look real.

"So, I hear this place has wings," I joked.

"Best wings in Florida," Tyler said. He slid a stack of menus to the three of us.

I pretended to study the laminated menu. "I guess that's why you wanted to come all the way here, instead of one of the nice restaurants in Wahoo."

Vera shot me a warning look over her menu. It was going to be difficult to keep my mouth shut and play the good cop. After all, Tyler was the one who stole my backpack freshman year and dunked it in the boys' bathroom toilet, then returned it to my locker.

We made small talk about the menu for about five minutes, then we all ordered.

Jack got the six-piece habanero mango wing combo. I ordered eight atomic wings, because Vera and I loved super-spicy food.

I thought she was going to order the spicy Cajun platter, but Tyler talked her into a double order of plain wings. No spice, no BBQ sauce, nothing.

"It sounds delicious," she squealed.

I narrowed my eyes at her. Normally she liked ghost-pepper hot. Melt-your-face-off scorching. Mouth-mangling fire.

Fortunately, the server brought our drinks—we all agreed on sweet tea, plus I needed to stay sober for the questions—and then we stared across the table at each other with tight, awkward smiles.

"So how does it feel to be back in Wahoo, Maggie?" I had to hand it to Tyler. He had a slick smile.

"It feels awesome. I'm happy to be home. Although it's a little weird because various high school memories keep popping up." I shot him a simpering smile.

He pointed at me. "You know, about that. I told your sister a while ago that I felt so bad for how I treated you both."

"You were kind of a bully, that's for sure."

Tyler chuckled, and I recalled how he'd laughed the same way when I'd walk into science class junior year. It was a menacing, snarky sound, and a warning chill actually went up my spine. "I was a bully. And I feel bad about it. My apologies. Dinner's on me."

"Well, that's very generous." I looked to Vera, who tilted her head and smiled, as if to say, *see, he's changed!*

"On to happier subjects. Where did you two meet? Boston?" Tyler motioned with his finger to me and Jack. Vera playfully smacked him on the arm.

"I told you, silly, he's our tenant. They met the other day and they've been inseparable."

Jack and I turned to each other. "Joined at the hip," I said, my voice dripping with a mix of sarcasm and desire. I felt like hot shit, but my bravado and my smirk faded quickly when I stared into his eyes.

One glance was all it took to set me ablaze. Prior to this moment, I'd never quite bought into the romance novel trope that a man's gaze could be so smoldering that it ignited a woman's soul on fire.

Obviously, I had to rethink my stance on this, because every inch of me felt like I could spontaneously combust.

Jack's eyes zeroed in on my lips, devouring them with a hunger akin to a famished man eyeing a plump, succulent drumstick. A teasing spark tugged at the corners of his mouth. It was an irresistible concoction of mischief and desire, and I was on board for literally anything he wanted right here in Lord of the Wings.

"Hey, you," he murmured huskily. God, his lashes were long. I was both envious and turned on.

I couldn't believe what we were about to do, right in front of my sister and Tyler and every patron of this fast-casual restaurant. Inhaling deeply, I braced myself for the impending collision of lips, knowing full well it was going to be amazing. OK, I also leaned in a few inches because I hadn't been this excited about a kiss in years and I didn't want him to think I was hesitating.

As our mouths met, time stood still, and my libido shot into overdrive like a racecar on steroids. In that moment, I couldn't have cared less about Vera and Tyler, or the fact that we were in a smelly wing joint.

I was ready to throw caution to the wind and indulge in some serious tonsil hockey with this man.

We finally broke apart, breathing heavy like marathon runners at the finish line. I stole a quick glance at Vera, whose beaming expression made it clear she approved of our lip-locking.

"Jack's even making her a bookcase," she burbled. "How's that going, anyway?"

"A new relationship. Sweet," Tyler said, turning to Jack. "You go, bro. A bookcase. That's serious."

Have I mentioned that I hate people who use the word "bro"? I took a long gulp of my tea, hoping it would quench both my lust and my ire. Jack sure knew how to kiss.

Damn.

"I'm working on a drawing first, to make sure Maggie likes my idea." Jack turned to me and grinned. "Then we'll go buy wood."

My heart went pitter-patter and I momentarily forgot why we were here.

I was definitely distracted by him and his wood. But no, we were on a mission. "What have you been up to since high school, Tyler?" I asked.

"Oh, a little of this, a little of that. I'm working for my old man."

"I hear you've been elected to the city council." I shifted away from the sexual force field of Jack's body.

"Yep, just last month. Really looking forward to making the town better. Wahoo's one of the top ten places in Florida where people are moving. That's according to the census. Did you know that?"

Vera looked at him with adoring eyes.

"I guess that must mean a lot of development," Jack said.

Tyler nodded. "We have to manage that growth, of course. But there's a lot of open land in Wahoo, and I think the environment and growth can coexist."

Ooh, I knew this guy was full of crap. "Like the Covington prop—"

My sister sensed exactly what I was about to say and kicked me under the table. "Jack, why don't you tell Tyler about your book? It's so fascinating."

I sipped my tea and listened, still salty about the Gator Heaven spot on the Covington property.

"I'm a criminology professor and writing a book on serial killers. Specifically, how to profile them. It's a book for investigators, not the public. It's pretty technical. I get into the weeds about how a detective can pick up on certain details to know if someone's a killer. A serial killer, that is," he chuckled.

"Well, that's something," Tyler said. "You ever talk with a serial killer yourself?"

"I have, actually. I've done some research and interviews in prison with killers. Since most are on death row or are serving a life term, they're eager to speak with anyone who shows up."

"That must've been creepy," my sister said. She had

a love-hate relationship with anything spooky or suspenseful.

"What's the difference between, say, a serial killer and a regular killer? For instance"—I tapped my finger-nails against the plastic iced-tea glass—"what's the difference between the person who killed Gator Gene, and say, Ted Bundy?"

Ugh. With that one question, I'd plowed over all of the questions Jack and I had planned. We were supposed to work up to the Gene discussion, not drop it into conver-sation like a bomb.

"Gosh, that Gator Gene situation is something else, isn't it?" Tyler's tone bordered on folksy.

"It sure is. What was up with him, anyway, Tyler? I know what I read in the papers, and from what Maggie and Vera told me." Jack entered the discussion smoothly, like he was sliding into the warm Gulf of Mexico on a summer day.

Tyler shrugged. "Gene was a piece of work."

"But who would've wanted him dead?" I asked. "And now my sister's a suspect in his murder."

Tyler visibly blanched and turned to Vera. "What?"

She shot daggers at me with her eyes while fiddling with her hair. "Oh, it's nothing, Ty."

Ty? She was at the nickname stage with him? Barf.

Tyler's face contorted in shock.

"What I can't understand," Jack mused aloud, obvi-ously rolling with what I'd started, "is why someone would want a gator trapper dead. What was he involved with?"

"Could've been anything. Gene knew a lot of people." Tyler had recovered and was back to grinning, yet the tops of his cheekbones were pink.

"How well did *you* know him?" I probed.

Another shrug. "He used to buy me and my friends beer in high school. And, oh, I went gator hunting with him once."

Aha! My mind flashed back to the photo.

"Catch anything?" Jack asked.

"Yeah, we got a twelve-footer. It was wild, put up quite a fight."

"Just you and Gene on that trip? Were you with anyone else?" I was probably going a bit too far with this question, but I had to ask.

"Yeah, just the two of us. We went south, near Lakeport."

"Lots of gators out there?" I asked. Lakeport was three counties away, on the edge of the Everglades.

"Tons. But hey, bro, what *is* the difference between a regular killer and a serial killer?" Tyler deftly steered the conversation away from Gene and back to Jack. I noted that Tyler scooted an inch away from my sister, and wondered why she hadn't told him about being questioned by the cops.

I'd also caught him in a lie. I gulped my tea, wondering what to say next.

"Mostly time and location. Serial killers don't usually kill without some premeditation. And they kill numerous people over time. Regular murderers kill only once, and their motives vary, but it's usually things like lust, revenge, or greed."

That last word hung in the air, and I noticed Vera was sweating despite the chilly air conditioner.

She flapped her hands in the air. "Let's not talk about such awful stuff. Oh! Our food's here."

The server appeared, setting our baskets of wings and fries in front of us. I was still turning over the possibilities of Tyler and Gene in my head, and picked up a drumstick and bit into it, thinking I'd be hit with an eye-watering, delicious spicy kick, one that might jog my brain into a creative way to press Tyler more.

Instead, I was met with a bland, sweet chicken taste. Weird. I took another bite.

As I swallowed, I looked over at Tyler. He'd bitten into a wing and his face was flaming red. His lips looked oddly puffy, even after that one bite. Eek. Apparently, our baskets of food had been switched, and spices didn't agree with him.

"You OK, baby?" my sister asked.

I had a fraction of a second to register my disgust at her calling him baby when he started to wheeze and clutch his chest. The red BBQ sauce stained his fingers and the collar of his white shirt.

"I'm . . . oh, God," he wheezed. "Call . . . an . . . ambulance."

Chapter Sixteen

A chaotic hour later, Jack and I sat in the waiting area of the regional hospital, while my sister talked with an orderly at a nearby nurses' station. Her face had been etched with a perpetual frown since we'd followed the ambulance out of the restaurant parking lot.

This was not the way I'd wanted to end the evening.

"I didn't know someone could be so allergic to spicy peppers. That chicken wing almost killed him," Jack said.

"I'm sure glad that server called 911 so quickly. I was certain Tyler was going to die there for a few minutes." I winced, thinking of his wheezing gasps at the table, then his shocking collapse onto the floor. "You really jumped in quickly with the Heimlich. Impressive."

Jack made a face. "I thought he was choking on a bone. Learned that in high school, when I worked as a lifeguard on South Beach."

When Jack had dragged Tyler to a sitting position, he'd wrapped his arms around him from the back and tried to dislodge what was in his throat by pressing into his solar plexus. My sister started to scream, and somehow Tyler—in between turning an odd shade of red and emitting a death rattle—had conveyed that he was allergic, not choking.

Fortunately, the ambulance service in Fern City was snappy, and had whisked Tyler out of the restaurant and to the hospital in what seemed like record time.

My sister walked over. Her face looked drawn and haggard. She sighed and sat next to me.

"How's Tyler doing?" I asked.

"He's going to be OK. They've stabilized him, but he'll have to be here overnight."

"Did you know he was that allergic to spicy peppers?"

She shook her head. "Nope."

"Well, he should've told you. Or worn some kind of medical alert bracelet."

Jack nodded along with my words, while Vera ignored me.

"I'll stay with him here at the hospital and get a ride back somehow. You two can leave."

"No, I can stay with you." The idea of my sister being here alone didn't sit well with me. "Why don't you come home with us, then you can drive out to see him tomorrow morning. Or how about this, I'll come with you tomorrow morning?"

She shook her head. "No, I don't mind staying. It's the least I can do, considering he was basically poisoned."

I rolled my eyes. "He wasn't poisoned. But he should've told the server about his allergy."

"This wasn't his fault," she said defensively.

A sigh escaped my lips. "I know it wasn't. But it wasn't my fault either."

"You were starting to question him about Gene." Vera folded her arms.

"Sure, but that has nothing to do with his severe spicy pepper allergy."

"Tyler isn't responsible for Gene's death."

I ran my tongue across my teeth, wondering if now was a good time to show her the photo of Tyler, Gene, and Bruce the developer. Given all of the heart-pounding drama at the restaurant, and the fact that Tyler would be staying in the hospital overnight, I figured that revealing my sleuthing wasn't the best idea.

"OK, we're going to drive back." I squeezed Vera's shoulder. "But call if you want me to come get you, OK? Even if it's in the middle of the night."

She mustered a watery smile. "Thank you."

We all stood and I hugged my sister.

"Tell Tyler we're sorry, and that we'll all go out again sometime," Jack said. He was so polite. It hadn't even crossed my mind to utter those words, because I still held a grudge against Tyler, despite his apology and near-death experience. If I never saw him again, it would be too soon.

As we walked through the sliding glass doors of the hospital, my stomach rumbled audibly. Jack gave me a sly side-eye. "Want to stop for a burger along the way?"

"Do I ever. I'm starving." I hadn't forgotten about that random, hot kiss we'd shared at the restaurant. But so much had happened since then, the kiss seemed like a fleeting dream.

We pulled into a fast-food chain across the street from the hospital and ordered some basic burgers, fries, and chocolate shakes.

Once at our table, we tucked into the food and ate in companionable silence. I inhaled half my burger and wiped my mouth.

"Want to go to Gene's funeral with me? It's the day after tomorrow." The minute the words came out of my mouth, I realized I was monopolizing Jack's time. "Sorry. You're probably writing."

He shook his head. "Don't worry about my book. I'd love to go."

I laughed, loud. "Right. Procrastinating."

"You know what I mean," he teased, grabbing a fry off my tray.

"He was lying, you know. Tyler lied about Bruce, when he said it was only him and Gene on the gator hunt."

Jack nodded slowly. "Lying or omitting the truth. He could've gone with Gene to Lakeport on a hunt. And then he could've also gone with Gene and the developer a second time."

"Either way, he was lying. Evading the truth. Omitting. Whatever you want to call it." I shoved a couple of fries in my mouth.

"Want my opinion?" Jack took a sip of soda.

"Of course."

"You're going to have to tell your sister about everything we've found. I think we need her help in trying to get to the bottom of this."

My stomach sank. He was right, but I wasn't looking forward to having that conversation with Vera.

I pondered this while we drove home. When we arrived, the night air had grown cooler. I shivered a little.

"You OK?" Jack asked.

"Yeah. I'm just worried, that's all."

"I get it. You and your sister have a lot at stake. But it's going to be OK. Really."

I glanced at his strong profile in the semi-darkness, appreciating his kind words. "Thanks. You really don't have to do all this with me. I'm sorry to drag you into our drama."

He opened his mouth, then closed it.

We stood at my door, the keys clutched in my hand, my gaze fixated on Jack. A twinge of curiosity tugged at me, urging me to unravel the truth behind our kiss in the restaurant. Had it been genuine or just an act?

Simultaneously, a wave of exhaustion threatened to engulf me, tempting me to surrender to the warm, inviting hug of my bed.

Words failed me as I stared into his dark eyes. All I managed to muster was a feeble "Um . . ." while swatting a mosquito off my tit. "Ow. I think I was bitten."

Yep. Smooth and seductive. That's me.

Jack, with his awkward smile, mirrored my uncertainty. His eyes dipped to my chest, then back to my face.

"I suppose this is, ah, goodnight," I stammered.

He nodded in agreement, and I'd be lying if I said that I wasn't disappointed. I expected him to say something funny about the evening, or something serious about our investigation.

But he stayed silent, and his hand rose to cup my jaw gently. As he leaned closer, his warm breath brushed against my skin, his voice a gentle whisper. "Goodnight," he murmured.

The soft tenderness of his lips on mine made me weak-kneed. I was awfully tempted to invite him into my bedroom.

But I didn't. Something about it didn't seem right just yet.

#

The next day, Vera and I were in the bookstore. It was beginning to come together; the shelves lining the walls were filled with shiny new books, and we'd arranged tables in the middle for special displays.

We had our favorite female-country-singer playlist on a portable speaker as we bopped around, arranging the store. It was exciting to be this close to opening, and both of us wore wide grins.

"I'm thinking spring-themed reads for this," Vera said, pointing at a rectangular table.

"Perfect. And over here at this smaller table, let's put the notebooks. These are adorable." I turned over a cute blank book covered in a cartoon llama print. "I actually think we have enough animal-themed notebooks to do a whole display."

"Awesomesauce."

Today, Vera seemed to be in a decent mood. Tyler had been released from the hospital that morning and was on his way to a full recovery. But I knew she wasn't entirely OK. She hadn't mentioned my kiss with Jack once. The old Vera wouldn't have wasted any time discussing *that*.

I paused to take a sip of water from my reusable bottle at the counter. Because things were going so smoothly today, I figured now would be a good time to bring up the results of my sleuthing. Better than if Vera was in a rotten mood, because then she'd just shut down and probably disappear for hours.

"How's Tyler doing?" I asked, hoping for an easy entrance to a difficult conversation.

She stacked five historical romance hardcovers together. "Much better. He's at his house, recuperating. The swelling in his face has gone down a bit. I think he's a little worried about missing the city council meeting this week. It's only his second meeting and they're supposed to talk about the rezoning of the Covington property."

I let out a noncommittal hum. There was no use putting off this discussion, so I grabbed my phone off the counter and walked over to her.

"About Tyler," I said in a hesitant voice.

"If you're going to tell me you hate him, spare me. He was nothing but nice to you, at least until he almost died. He even apologized for what he did in high school."

"I know. And I appreciated that. Truly. He wasn't so bad at dinner, and it's unfortunate it had to be cut short because he neglected to tell anyone of his spicy wing allergy. But you need to see something."

"I don't need to see anything. Maggie, I like Tyler. Please don't ruin it. He's the first man I've dated in a while who has accepted me for who I am. He doesn't even mind my skin."

Today she'd slathered on self-tanner, and smelled oddly yeasty.

I blew a breath out of my nose and probably looked a little like a bull. "He called you a Dalmatian in high school. You can do better."

"You think I can do better. And he's changed. You saw it yourself."

"I do think you can do way better. And don't give me this *I have vitiligo and my skin is all spotted* excuse. You're gorgeous. You're hilarious. You're brilliant. Any man would be lucky to have you. You don't need to date some dick." I stamped my foot on the terrazzo floor and felt a little like I was a child. This entire conversation felt like when we'd argued as kids—only back then, the arguments were about how she'd eaten the last Twinkie, not her dating a potential murderer.

"He's not a jerk," she insisted.

It was obvious that she was digging in her heels. Without saying anything more, I held up my phone and the photo of him, Gene, and the developer.

She leaned in. "So? He said he'd gone gator hunting with Gene."

"He also said he'd been alone with Gene. In this photo, he's with a third man. Don't you want to know who that is, and why he lied?"

"No and no. Where did you get that, anyway?"

I licked my lips. "I went to visit Barbie Robinson the other day."

"What? Why?"

"I've been looking into Gene's death." It sounded ridiculous to say that aloud.

"Who do you think you are? Agatha Christie? *The Rockford Files*? Mabel from *Only Murders in the Building*? You stole a photo."

I wanted to laugh, because we'd always teased Dad about his love for *The Rockford Files*. But I didn't, knowing even a grin would send Vera into yet more of a snit. "Jack's helping me. And no, I didn't steal it. I took a photo of a photo. Big difference."

She threw her hands in the air. "Oh, well, that's okay then. If some rando who just came to town five minutes ago is helping, then snooping around and conducting your own murder investigation is totally cool. Oh my goodness. Is that what you two have been doing together these past couple of days? You lied about going on a date and instead you're playing detective together? Was that kiss even real?"

That was the million-dollar question, wasn't it? "You were the one who wanted me to hook up with Jack."

"Unreal. I can't believe you've come home to do this. To do this to me. To sabotage my new relationship. Maggie, you know this is the first guy I've dated in a while." She was full-on whining now.

I resisted the urge to groan and shake her by the shoulders. "Vera, there's a lot you don't know about Tyler. A lot that Jack and I have found out over the last few days."

She snorted and began to walk away.

"No, you need to listen to me, Vera. I'm worried about you. I'm worried that Tyler is involved with some really sketchy stuff and maybe really is wrapped up in Gene's murder. Give me five minutes. If you don't want to listen after five minutes, I'll shut up."

Her nostrils flared and she flounced over to the floral-print loveseat, which was now flanked by a cool old lamp with a tulip shade and an intricately carved occasional table. She flung herself on a cushion, then tapped on her smartwatch and crossed her arms. "Five minutes."

Instead of sitting next to her, I paced as I talked. I disclosed everything, from what I'd overheard at Barbie's house to what Dave had told us, to the details about the election and the possible sham candidate.

Vera's hard gaze faltered, and she stared at my shoes. When I was done, I took a deep breath. "I'm sorry. I know you want it to work between the two of you. But you have to admit, there's a lot of smoke swirling around Tyler."

She swallowed once. Then twice. Then she blinked rapidly and I noticed a tear fall. I rushed to her side and sat next to her, putting my arm around her.

"Oh honey. I'm sorry."

She wiped the tear away. "I didn't tell you something. But now it kind of makes sense. Or maybe not."

"What happened?"

She gulped in a breath. "I was with Tyler the day Gene died."

"You were? When?" My heart surged to my throat.

"After we had lunch, I met him at the park. I did go

there, like I said. We walked for a little bit, and then I left my car there and went with him, back to his house."

"And that's when your gun was stolen. While you were at his house." I pressed the heels of my hands to my temples.

"Yes."

"Did you tell Alex Holt this?"

She nodded.

"You told him and you didn't tell me?" I was incredulous.

"I guess we both were lying to each other."

Her expression was probably as miserable as mine. "I don't know what it all means."

She shook her head. "I don't either."

I turned to look at her and took her shoulders in my hands. "Be honest with me. Do you think Tyler was trying to frame you for Gene's murder?"

Her eyes grew as wide as saucers. "No. No! Of course not. Why would he do that?"

"I . . . I don't know. But it all seems really strange and coincidental."

She wrenched out of my grip. "He wouldn't do that."

I wasn't so sure. "Has he said anything weird, done anything weird, in recent weeks? Think, Vera."

She shut her eyes. Shook her head. "I don't know. I don't think so. We don't usually talk about politics when we're together."

"Beyond politics. Think about whether he's acted strangely in any other way."

"I'll try," she said in a voice clogged with tears. Her

entire body crumpled into the sofa, as if my news had sucker-punched her.

"We need to clear your name, Vera. We can't have this cloud of suspicion hanging over you, or the store, as we're about to open."

"I know that." Tears streamed down her face. "But there is something else I didn't tell you."

I stroked her long, silky blonde hair. "What's that?"

"I accepted a personal loan from Tyler."

I let out a gasp. "You what? Why?"

"Because the bank would only give me so much, and we needed more."

"Oh shit. Why didn't you tell me this?" I was incredulous. It was as if the woman sitting next to me was someone I didn't know, and not someone I'd shared a womb with. "What's going on with you, Vera? Now I'm really worried."

She let out a snort and I jumped up to grab some tissues off the counter. She blew her nose with a honking sound and turned to me, her face blotchy and red.

"You're not angry?"

"I don't know enough to be angry. I'm shocked. Maybe I'll be angry later. How much money are we talking?"

"Twenty grand."

I huffed out a little sigh. It was awful, but not catastrophic. Maybe. It was an amount that we would almost certainly get once our father's estate was settled in probate court. But who knew when that would happen? "OK, we can work with that. It's not awful, unless the terms are. But honestly, now I really don't like Tyler and I question your sanity about mixing business with pleasure."

"It just sort of happened. He made it seem like it was the most natural thing in the world, like he wanted to help."

"Or he wanted you to not protest the zoning of the Covington property," I muttered.

"No. He wouldn't—" She stopped speaking.

"He wouldn't what?"

"He has made little comments about how I'm his activist girlfriend and has mentioned that if we were together long-term, things would have to be different. He has his eye on Congress, maybe even the Senate."

"Just what Florida needs. One more corrupt politician in DC."

"We don't know he's corrupt."

I rolled my eyes. "All signs are pointing to yes. And I really hate how he's gotten you into an ethical quandary, too. It'll be really difficult for you to have any credibility protesting any development now, if you took money from him. Did you ever think of that?"

She shook her head and let out a sob.

"OK. Look. We're going to pay the money back as soon as we can. Tonight, we're going to go over all the finances together, and I want you to explain everything that you've spent and borrowed so far."

She sniffled. "That will take so long. I'm terrible at math."

"Doesn't matter. In the meantime, Jack and I are going to keep sleuthing. We're going to Gene's funeral together tomorrow. Come with us."

"I refuse to go."

"Vera," I cried. "Come on."

She shook her head. "Everyone knows I hated him. I'd be a hypocrite if I went. Trust me, it will be strange if I show up to his funeral. I'll look guiltier if I'm there."

Maybe she had a point. "OK. Then I want you to try to get information from Tyler."

"He mentioned wanting to go to the funeral. I don't know if he'll be able to now, since he still hasn't recovered. He has these blisters on his face. What kind of information? I told him I'd visit him at his mom's today. I could casually ask some questions then."

I rubbed my lips together, wondering if this was safe. If Tyler did kill Gene for some reason, what would he do to my sister if she started poking around?

"Ask him if he knows a man named Bruce Doyle. He's a developer, but you can use the excuse that he was the man who called me about the baby gator. I'll text you a photo, and you can bring it up under the pretense of it being a funny story. See what he says, how he reacts. Can you do that?"

She shuddered in a deep breath and nodded, but I wasn't so sure.

Chapter Seventeen

Gator Gene had taken "rest in peace" to a whole new level, one that shocked even me, a native Floridian. Jack grabbed my hand and threaded it through the crook of his arm.

"Please tell me that's not a Pabst Blue Ribbon coffin," Jack whispered in my ear.

I blinked several times, not wanting to take off my sunglasses because I'd show my astonishment. I stared at the silver, white, red, and blue casket. Yes, indeedy. Gene was being buried in a beer can casket.

"I guess he's headed for that eternal happy hour in the sky." I took this opportunity to clutch Jack's bicep with my free hand, so I could feel his bulging muscle. I gave it a squeeze.

It was bigger than I thought. *Nice.*

"Are you copping a feel of my arm?" Jack murmured, without taking his mouth away from my ear or his eyes off the casket.

I fought back a grin. "Maybe."

Perhaps feeling up Jack's muscle was inappropriate in this venue, but I didn't think the deceased, or really anyone here, would give a crap.

Hell, they'd probably encourage this sort of thing.

The past day and a half—since my heart-to-heart conversation with Vera—had been a whirlwind. We'd wrangled the bookstore into decent shape, acquired one occupancy permit from City Hall, and Vera had walked me through the bookstore's ordering schedule from distributors.

Not counting that loan from Tyler and the unsolved murder, we were in pretty good shape.

I had to think of a plan to pay Tyler back quickly, but right now my attention was on Gene, and whatever clues I could glean from his funeral. This task wasn't easy because of the shockingly ridiculous casket that had turned everything into a farce.

Jack and I were rooted to the red-carpeted floor of the funeral home as we stared, open-mouthed. After I wiped the incredulous look off my face, I slid my sunglasses off and stuffed them in my bag.

The hundred or so other people in the room chatted amiably, as if the deceased wasn't lying feet away in a blue and white coffin crafted to look disturbingly like a giant tallboy of cheap beer.

Jack leaned into my ear. "Maggie, this is a really weird place."

"The funeral home?" I looked around and shook my head. "Nah. This looks like lots of other funeral homes I've been to over the years."

"No, I'm talking about Wahoo. It's a weird town."

He was just figuring this out now? I let out a small snort. "Look who's talking. You're the one who comes from Miami, is writing a book on serial killers, and doesn't wear shirts. Not to mention the lightning and shark attack."

He pressed his lips together, obviously trying not to laugh. He ran a hand over the buttons of his white business shirt. "It feels kind of funny to wear a suit. I'm not used to all these clothes."

I grinned at him. Jack was in a well-fitted, expensive-looking midnight-blue suit and a white shirt—no tie, open at the neck—and looked positively delicious. Probably an inappropriate thought on my part, considering where we were. Then again, all bets were off at a beer-themed memorial. I spotted a cooler in the corner filled with ice and cans of Pabst.

"At least it's a closed casket," I murmured.

We did a lap around the room and past the coffin. Vera had been correct; I noticed that several people stared at me as we meandered about. Most likely they were wondering where my sister was, or why I was there, considering my sister was a suspect.

We'd just finished our shuffle past the casket when I spotted Barbie. Today she was wearing a tasteful black jumpsuit, with clear Lucite heels. An interesting choice of footwear. She stood a few feet away and fluttered her fingers at me. Jack and I went to her, and she eyed him lustily. After a beat she turned to me and waggled her tongue. I ignored that.

"I'm so sorry, Barbie. My condolences." I reached out to her.

She held her hand toward Jack. "Why, hello there. I'm Barbie. Oh, and hi, Maggie. Is this your . . ."

She fluttered her long eyelashes. Jack shook her hand and introduced himself. "I'm Maggie's boyfriend."

A laugh burst from my lips. Barbie didn't notice.

"So that's why you weren't interested in that handsome officer. Now I understand," she purred, then looked across the room. "Oh, dear. The service is going to start in fifteen minutes. The funeral home gentleman is calling me over. Jack, please come visit at Big Sugar. It's on Main Street. You can try my cupcakes. I'll make you a pink velvet. It's my specialty."

She swept away.

"That's the widow? Why do I feel dirty, like I should take a shower?" A confused look was etched on Jack's handsome face. He'd shaved off his stubble, and I couldn't help but notice how soft the skin on his jaw looked.

"Yep. And there's the detective." My gaze lasered on Alex Holt, who was sitting in the last row, alone. There were at least ten rows of seats in this large room, and Holt was one of the only people sitting down. The rest mingled around the sides of the room and the casket. Probably everyone knew he was a cop, and since at least eighty percent of the people here likely had warrants or past brushes with the law, they were keeping a wide berth.

"You mean the handsome officer?" Jack teased.

"The officer who's in control of Vera's freedom. Let's go talk to him."

"Do you think that's a good—"

I pulled Jack along by the wrist and we wound our way around several people wearing camouflage hunting gear.

People had started to ignore the hushed, reverent atmosphere and were yukking it up, telling hilarious and bawdy stories about Gene. A few filtered words hit my ears.

He didn't know the gun was loaded!

That time we went to the Pink Pony in Tampa . . .

Gene sure loved cheap whiskey. That's why I brought a bottle.

I, too, needed a shower.

Alex was sitting in the middle of the empty row. Jack and I marched over and plopped down next to him.

He looked up from his phone. "Maggie Andrews, nice to see you again. Didn't really expect you here. Is your sister here as well?"

"No, she had some business to take care of at the store." It was the truth; Vera was waiting for our final book shipment.

Holt nodded and shifted his gaze to Jack.

"This is our tenant, Jack Bianchi. Jack, this is Alex Holt, the officer I was telling you about. I think both of you are the latest newcomers to town."

Not including Bruce Doyle, the developer, of course. As Jack and Alex leaned over my lap to shake hands, I scanned the room for Doyle. He wasn't here, as far as I could tell. It seemed unlikely that he would be, though. Other than the photo, there was no real connection between Doyle and Gene. Or perhaps there was, and I hadn't yet found the link.

"If you don't mind, Jack, I'd like to ask you a few questions about the day Gene died," Alex said in a low voice. "Shouldn't take long."

"Want to do it now? Or should I come by the station?"

Alex nodded curtly. "Sure. Why don't we go out in the hall? I'll just need a few minutes and this isn't going to start for a while, I don't think."

"I'll save our seats," I chirped, as if we were at a concert or something.

The two men rose and Jack slipped past me. Part of me was insanely curious about what Alex would ask, but I could guess. Another part of me was glad I was alone, because that meant I could sit quietly and observe people. It was something I'd perfected in my years at the zoo, those solitary moments while feeding the reptiles.

I watched Barbie gesture wildly to two men in suits and rectangular gold lapel pins. Probably they were funeral home employees. I also spotted a few people who knew Dad and had gone to his funeral, like Rodney from the chamber of commerce, the postmaster, and the woman who worked the night shift at the convenience store near the interstate, who insisted that aliens landed in Wahoo on the regular.

I was about to wave Rodney over when I spotted a familiar face: Diego Viernes. Goodness. That took some guts, coming here. An animal activist in a room full of hunters. He was in all black—shirt, pants, sneakers— and blended in with the funeral staff. For a second, I thought he might actually be employed by the funeral home.

He leaned against the far left wall and slowly shifted to stare at everyone. He'd started with his left shoulder against the wall, then he moved so his back was flat to the wall, then turned to his right shoulder. Our eyes locked and he quickly looked down.

I jumped up and went to him. He'd turned his back to me and was starting to walk away, but I blocked his path.

"Hey," I said. "Fancy seeing you here."

He mumbled a hello. "Could you please move out of the way?"

"Wait. Why are you here? Why are you acting so weird?" I hissed.

He shushed me loudly and pulled me into the back corner of the room. We were at least three feet from the nearest group of people, men who smelled like sweat. Gene sure knew some real prizes.

Diego stood in the corner, facing the crowd. He waved me to one side.

"I'm filming," he whispered. "My camera's in my messenger bag."

"What? Isn't that illegal?" I scanned the room for Alex Holt. He and Jack weren't back, and I noticed a few people sitting near where we'd just been.

"I'm collecting intel."

"Quite the amateur investigator, hunh?"

He scowled. "Look who's talking."

I inhaled. He had a point. "Have you found anything out? Anything good? About Gene's murder, I mean. Not about animals."

"No. I'm just filming to get a video record of who's here. I think there are a lot of poachers and exotic animal traffickers. Have you gotten any leads?"

While the idea of animal traffickers sounded a bit

far-fetched, it was entirely plausible with this crowd. "None lately. Hoping to get something today, but . . ." My voice faded as I saw a bald head enter the room.

Bruce Doyle.

I looked at the door Jack and Alex had gone through. Then I glanced to the seats, which were filling up. Then back at Doyle, who was taking a chair near the front. An idea came to me. I turned to Diego, my back to Doyle. "Does your camera record sound?"

He nodded.

"Want to team up?"

"Hunh?"

"There's a guy here who's suspicious. See the bald man? He's in the second row?"

"Black suit?"

"Yeah, him. He's a developer. I think he's up to something. You should sit near him during the service."

Diego squinted one eye. "I was hoping to stand back here and get a panorama of everyone."

"This guy hates the environment." It was a slight fib, but probably not far from the truth if Doyle wanted to build homes on Gator Heaven. "Trust me."

Diego nodded, the muscles of his jaw bunching.

"I want to see and hear the video. I'll come by later with my partner." Well, that sounded ridiculous. "I mean, my friend. Jack."

"Gotcha. Don't talk to me again today, I don't want to be seen together." With those words, he slipped past me.

Didn't want to be seen with me? Was I so awful? Did I smell? I tilted my head toward my right shoulder, hoping to catch a whiff of myself. All I could smell was my perfume. I'd worn my best black dress.

I pushed my way through the crowd and took my seat again. Apparently, people had noticed that Alex Holt—or I—had been sitting there and had left the three spots open. Where were Alex and Jack? How long did it take to ask questions? My heart started to pound.

When I saw Diego sit next to Doyle, I did a mental fist pump. At least that was going swimmingly. More people took their seats as strains of the Eagles' "Desperado" began to play at top volume.

It was a soft rock tribute to Gene's rebellious spirit. It was also tacky as hell.

I spotted Jack and Alex inching down the row toward me. Alex took his previous seat and Jack sat on my other side just as Don Henley was hitting the song's crescendo.

"How was it?" I angled my body and faced Jack.

"Went well. I'll tell you about it later. He's familiar with my work so we had a lot to discuss. He's a good guy. We might go fishing sometime."

I turned to face the front of the room, letting that information soak in.

Don Henley stopped crooning. A man I didn't recognize took the podium, and it turned out he was a lay minister from the funeral home. He read some generic Bible passages, quoted singer Willie Nelson, and motioned to the front row.

"Barbie Robinson, the deceased's widow, would like to say a few words."

She tottered up on heels. "Momma loves you," she said, patting the beer-themed casket.

I fought hard not to wince visibly.

Each moment was stranger than the last. She told the story about how she and Gene met—she'd been a bikini model at a boar hunting tournament—and she started to sob. I blinked several times, trying to square this sobbing woman with the cool and calculating one I'd talked with as she'd floated in the pool the other day.

As a funeral home employee escorted Barbie back to her seat, another man rose. I vaguely recognized him as the owner of a diner near the interstate. He launched into a story about how he and Gene used to drink beer together after high school and later shoot cans in the woods.

"One time we started a forest fire," the man said, chuckling. The crowd did, too.

I glanced to Jack, who wore a slightly baffled expression. I then snuck a gaze at Alex, whose face was like stone.

Speaker after speaker told stories about Gene. Most involved hunting, fishing, and bars. Some were bawdy, and the audience laughed at those parts. Honestly, that was possibly the strangest part about the service. Not the beer-can-shaped casket, or his widow's (possibly) fake tears.

It was that Gene seemed to have a lot of friends who would miss him.

This made me sad, and I became lost in my thoughts. Gene had been pretty terrible to my sister and me, and to other women, if the bartender was any indication. But to his guy friends, he'd been a great person. Well, if not a great one, an entertaining and adventurous one at least. Someone who always had beer, and who adored Johnny Cash during karaoke night.

Wait, was I sprouting sympathy for that pig? Gah.

A half hour later, people were still telling Gene stories. Jack jiggled his leg. Alex clicked his pen every thirty seconds. I knew this because I timed it with my watch. My eyes grew heavy and scratchy. I wished I'd drunk more coffee.

Then a man in a sharp-looking suit jacket took the lectern. By the looks of him, he wasn't part of Gene's good-old-boy inner circle, and his California drawl confirmed that.

"I only met Gene a short while ago. Six weeks. I'm an assistant director with a reality TV production company in Los Angeles, and I came out here to do some preproduction with him." He took a deep breath and gripped the sides of the lectern. "I was hoping to give you some good news today about Gene's show. After his death, we realized we'd filmed enough for a one-hour episode, and we were planning to release it as a special web series, as a tribute to Gene. Unfortunately, all of the footage has been stolen."

Gasps and murmurs filled the room. I snapped to attention, now fully awake. Why would someone steal the reality TV show footage of Gene? I turned my head to look at Alex, but he clicked his pen with his thumb and reached for the notebook in his chest pocket. He jotted a few notes but didn't meet my gaze.

When I looked at Jack, it was a different story. He raised his eyebrows and widened his eyes, and I mirrored him. He knew something was up.

The reality TV guy, who never gave his name, walked away from the lectern after saying a few kind and generic words about Gene's enthusiasm for hunting gators. I wanted to chat with him afterward, and my eyes followed him to his seat, which wasn't that far from where Diego was sitting near Doyle.

So much to keep track of.

I felt my phone vibrating with a message in my purse. As a man in a camouflage T-shirt told a painstakingly detailed story about how he and Gene once hunted a python in the Everglades while drinking an entire twenty-four-can case of beer, I leaned forward and opened my bag to check my text.

It was from my sister.

You are not going to believe this, but Tyler wants his money back. Says he needs it for his recovery because he's going to be out of work for a while. What are we going to do?

Chapter Eighteen

Multiple thoughts came to mind. The first, and most visceral, involved Tyler.

He wasn't only a jerk, but a scammer too. Why would he be out of work after a reaction to a bite of a spicy chicken wing? Why would he loan her money and then demand it back within a month?

He was clearly playing games with my sister, and I didn't appreciate it.

I tapped out a quick text to Vera. *Don't worry. We'll work it out. I'll be over after the funeral.*

I slipped the phone into my bag and tuned out the guy who was still telling the story of Gene's heroic capture of a python. Eventually, he ended his monologue, and the funeral home director took the lectern.

"It's clear that Gene was quite the colorful character. We should all be comforted to know that he's in a better place now. It was destiny."

An audible sob went up, and all heads swiveled toward Barbie, who stood and turned to look at the crowd. Her face was stained with mascara and tears. I wondered if she was drunk and emotional, or just putting on a show.

"It wasn't destiny. It was murder. And the police better find the person who did it," she cried.

I couldn't help but notice that she stared straight at me while saying that. A shiver flowed through me as a couple of people glanced over. Why was she acting this way, when she'd said the other day that she didn't think my sister or I had anything to do with Gene's death?

An awkward silence overtook the room, and then the funeral home employees ushered Barbie outside. Everyone else began to file out slowly. Jack, Alex, and I stood. The two men nodded at each other.

I turned to Alex and tried to appear cheery. "Good seeing you."

"I'll definitely be in touch with you and Vera." He walked off, without even a goodbye.

I leaned into Jack. "Let's go find that producer," I whispered. Even though my sister needed me, I couldn't pass up an opportunity to gather more information. There was also the matter of Diego and his clandestine video. I couldn't see him anywhere, but I figured we'd catch up with him later since we knew where he lived.

We made our way through the crowd. The producer was nowhere to be found, and I'd lost track of him when everyone cleared the room.

"I don't see him," Jack said.

"Maybe he's outside?"

We pushed through the double glass doors, into the muggy Florida winter. Immediately we were greeted with the smell of marijuana. Five of Gene's buddies were smoking pot. One called out to me and gestured to the joint in his hand.

"I'm good, thanks." Jack and I quickly passed the group

and headed into the parking lot. I instantly started sweating. It was midday, and by the moisture in the air and the blooming thunderclouds on the horizon, a storm was brewing.

I gently jabbed Jack in the side with my elbow. "Over there."

The producer, who wore a black jacket, black T-shirt, and jeans, was in the parking lot.

We took off at a fast-paced walk. The producer reached a red car at the far end of the lot and opened the driver's side door. Jack and I broke out into a run.

"Hey," I shouted, not caring if anyone heard me.

The guy, who was in his fifties, looked around, startled. Probably he was trying to get out of town with his wallet and dignity intact.

A few seconds later, we reached him. Sweat beaded on my forehead, and Jack's face was also shiny with perspiration.

"We wanted to ask you some questions," I wheezed.

"Who are you?" He lowered his black Ray-Ban sunglasses and looked at us with gray-blue eyes.

I swept a lock of hair off my sticky neck. "We're—"

"Podcasters," Jack said smoothly. "True-crime podcasters."

I nodded enthusiastically.

His look of skepticism turned into a broad smile. His teeth were so white I wondered if they were real. "Oh, great. Nice to meet you. I'm Chase Collins. I love podcasts. What's the name of yours?"

We told him our real names and explained that we

hadn't yet launched. "Gene's our first episode," I added.

"Gotcha. I'd love to help you with some sound for your production, but unfortunately, I've got nothing."

"Yeah, what happened? Someone stole the footage?" Jack asked.

The guy sighed. "Our editor was staying in a hotel here in town, and two days after Gene was found dead, someone broke into the editor's room and took it all."

"Don't you think that's a little strange?"

"Everything about Gene was strange." The guy smirked. "Everything about this damned place is strange. Florida makes California look like . . ."

He waved his hand helplessly in the air.

"Normal?" I offered.

"Amateurs?" Jack said.

The producer nodded. "Yeah. Both of those."

"What was on the footage that was so important?" I asked.

"Hard to say. It was mostly of Gene in the swamps, on boats, in his pool with his wife. But . . ." His voice trailed off and he looked down at his keys.

"But what?" I asked.

"Gene did talk about some local politics. A real convoluted story about the election. I didn't quite follow the whole thing, and let him yammer on. Figured it wouldn't make the show anyway, because who cares about a small-town city council race?"

"Did he happen to say something about Dave Smith? Or David H. Smith?" I was breathless now, but not from running.

Chase squinted one eye and tilted his head. "That rings a bell. He said he wasn't supposed to talk about it, but Gene didn't have a filter. Anyone who'd met him knew he couldn't keep a secret."

"What did he say?"

Chase shook his head. "I don't remember. I let the cameras roll when we were around Gene. We wanted the action scenes with the gators. And the scenes of Gene in his boat, of him making moonshine. Saying stupid southern stuff. Or sexist stuff. You know, clickbait."

Gah. Gross. I knew it.

"Gene made moonshine?" I wanted to retch.

"Yeah, he dabbled in it. I had a sip. I think my stomach no longer has a protective lining." He rubbed his belly.

"Yikes," Jack muttered under his breath.

"Well, thanks for the info. Do you have a card, in case we have more questions?"

Chase dug a thick white card out of his wallet and handed it to us. "I'm going back to LA today. No reason for me to hang around now. All this time in Wahoo, now for nothing." He sucked on his teeth.

Jack and I nodded and said goodbye. We walked slowly to our vehicle, and I showed him Vera's text.

"Things seem to be coming to a head, but I don't know what it all means." I flung myself into the passenger seat of Jack's car, just as fat raindrops began to fall.

We drove the five blocks to the bookstore, and Vera let us in. I could tell by her red-rimmed eyes that she'd been crying.

She locked the door behind us. "How was the funeral?" she asked.

Jack wandered over to the nearest table and picked up a book.

I took a deep breath. "Gene's buddies told stories about how he loved fishing, fighting, and, ah, fuc— . . . fornicating."

Jack looked up from the book and met my gaze. "They didn't use the word fornicating, though."

I fanned my face with my hand.

Vera smirked. "Classy."

"How's it going here? You OK?"

Her bottom lip quivered, and that's all it took for my sister to burst into tears. "I've messed this all up. I'm so sorry."

I folded her into a hug and led her over to the sofa. Jack followed and stood by while we sat.

"Tell me what Tyler said," I demanded.

She shuddered in a breath. "He's going to be out of work for a while and needs the money he loaned me. He was super nice and apologetic about it."

I scowled at her. "Now is not the time to defend that prick."

"I know," she wailed.

"Did you sign any formal loan paperwork with him?" Jack asked while pacing.

She shook her head. "It was only supposed to be until our father's estate was settled in court. It's not that we don't have the money, it's that Dad died and his estate's been tied up in court."

"Okay, well, why don't you just give Tyler his cash back and everything will be okay," Jack suggested.

"That's the problem. I spent most of it already. I have a little left and it was supposed to tide us over until we opened and started making sales."

Ack. Worst-case scenario. I rubbed my temples. Beyond my ire at Tyler, there was the matter of our real-life finances. We needed to eat and pay bills, and trapping reptiles wasn't going to cut it. There simply weren't that many nuisance gators in the area.

"Let me think. We could take out a second mortgage on the house."

She shook her head. "There's no equity. I checked."

I'd used most of my savings to help open the store and move home. "I do have a small retirement account. It won't cover the full twenty thousand, though."

Vera buried her face in her hands. "I don't want you to have to do that. We could try a couple more banks and take out another loan."

We'd already taken out one big loan, which was why I was so shocked when Vera said she'd borrowed money from Tyler. What a mess. "The other option is that you tell him you can't come up with the cash until we open."

But both Vera and I knew that making twenty grand in profit for a new bookstore was unlikely in the first six months, let alone the first few weeks.

"Let's call the attorney and ask him when Dad's estate will be settled. In the meantime, stall. Tell him you're working on getting him the money. Tell him you spent it."

Jack nodded. I nodded. Vera wiped her cheeks. "OK."

She sounded so miserable that my heart broke. I'd told Dad I'd look after Vera when he was gone, and I sure wasn't making good on that promise.

Chapter Nineteen

Jack left, and Vera and I spent the rest of the day at the store, trying to pretend everything was normal and happening on schedule. And on the surface, it was.

The store's decor was coming together, and with Vera's signature style, it looked like a pink, white, and silver book heaven. I was especially proud that we'd gotten in a wide selection of books in all romance sub-genres, and my sister had even lined up three well-known Florida authors for signing in the next two months.

We kept the conversation light as we shelved the books along one wall. We continued to make small talk in the car at the end of the day.

At home, I fed Catsy while Vera popped a frozen pizza in the oven. We ate in near silence, and I wasn't surprised that when we were finished, she asked if I could do the dishes because she felt a migraine coming on.

"Of course I'll clean up. You get some rest." I reached for her plate and saw she'd eaten only half a slice. "Don't worry, OK? We'll get through this."

She nodded and padded down the hall to her room. My chest felt heavy as I did the dishes and dodged Catsy as she wound her way around my legs. She seemed to think that whenever I was in the kitchen, it was a free food buffet.

Hoping to take my mind off the homicide investigation and our money woes, I grabbed a new romance novel and headed to the lanai. Vera had hung glass-bulb string lights around the perimeter, and I turned those on. It wasn't exactly light enough to read, but I loved the twinkling vibe so much that I sat on the daybed, holding the book in my hands and listening to the sound of the cicadas.

When I was about to flick on the lamp on the end table, I saw headlights to the right. The car parked, and I realized it was likely Jack. At least I hoped it was, since we weren't expecting anyone else.

My first instinct was to wander over and say hello, but I stopped myself. I'd bothered him enough in recent days. He'd been a near-constant companion, and he probably wanted space.

I pressed the heels of my hands into my eyes. Hell. I hadn't even been home two months and everything was a mess. Life in Boston had been orderly. Boring, but orderly. I'd had the same shift for two years, 7 a.m. until 3 p.m. My then-boyfriend and I would go out every Saturday night to listen to a band or see a movie. On Wednesdays we'd eat at our favorite restaurant in Little Italy, and occasionally we'd get a little wild and eat at an Ethiopian restaurant in Cambridge.

There was snow in the winter, and cherry trees in the spring. Ducks in Boston Common and the ebb and flow of college students. It was all nice, pleasant, and tidy.

Somehow, life had been turned upside down the moment I returned to Wahoo. The entire town seemed to be inhabited by chaos Muppets. Frankly, I felt a bit defeated, and had an urge to curl up in a ball on this daybed and never get up again.

There was a rap on the screen door. Jack was standing there, hands in pockets. Tonight, he wore a T-shirt, much to my disappointment.

He grinned. "Hey, you."

"Hi!" I jumped up and opened the door, acutely aware that he'd used the same two words before kissing me at the wing restaurant.

Catsy came darting in, and Jack walked through the door and reached for the kitten, scooping her up in one big hand.

I waved at the daybed. "Have a seat. Want some wine? Coffee?"

"Nah, I'm good, thanks. I had to run to the store for more printer paper, and when I got back I noticed the lights on and thought I'd come over and say hi. How's Vera?" He and Catsy sat next to me.

"She has a migraine. She's taking everything pretty hard. I feel terrible."

Jack nodded. "I admire how you stick up for your sister. I can't imagine my brother doing that for me."

"No?"

"He's ten years older. We're not that close."

I couldn't imagine life without Vera, and shot Jack a sad smile.

He stroked Catsy's back, and I wondered when the

kitten was going to unleash her tiny murder-mitten claws on his arm. Instead, Catsy reared up and nuzzled his chin with her face. Jack returned her affection with a kiss.

Meanwhile, my insides turned to goo.

"I've been thinking about your situation all day." Somehow, Jack was spared from Catsy's wrath. She leaped down and pranced away, her fluffy white tail high in the air.

"It's complicated, that's for sure."

"If you were an officer and had to make an arrest right now, who would be your prime suspect?" he asked.

"Oooh." I bit my lip. "Tough question. Let's assume the cops don't know any more than we do."

"I don't think they do, according to what Alex Holt told me at the funeral."

My eyes went wide. "Really?"

He hummed in affirmation.

I wanted to know more about their conversation, but the wheels in my mind turned, lining up all the potential killers. "Interesting. So here are the suspects, at least in my mind. One: Barbie. She's weird as hell, tried to divorce Gene at least once, and had a random, shirtless dude at her house not long after Gene died."

"Hey, don't knock the shirtless dudes."

I laughed. "Barbie stands to get a large life insurance payout and seems obsessed with owning the cupcake shop downtown."

"True."

"Two. There's Diego Viernes, the animal rights guy.

He was angry at Gene for destroying his video footage and for being an overall abusive jerk."

"We should check out his alibi with the grilled cheese restaurant."

I pointed at Jack. "We should. Hey, do you think Diego stole the footage from the producer?"

"Possibly. Although it would be pretty bold of him to kill Gene *and* steal the footage."

We mulled that in silence for a few seconds. "OK, we also know the bartender, Farah, hated him. But would she kill him?"

"Doubtful, so she's a weak suspect. We should take another run at her, though."

"There's also the most obvious suspects," I said, lowering my voice in case my sister was lurking.

"Tyler Carr and bald Bruce Doyle?"

I nodded. "I don't understand why Tyler would want Gene dead. Sure, they went hunting together, but that's meaningless. Lots of people go hunting together here."

"We know something happened during the election that Tyler won. That a candidate with the same name as the incumbent ran but had zero presence in any debate, forum, or newspaper article. But we have nothing linking Gene to this except that Hollywood producer's spotty memory of what was on the footage, which is mysteriously gone."

I snapped my fingers. "We need to try to talk to that other David Smith. The ghost candidate. See if he can tell us anything about Gene. Can you use your magical research powers to find out where he lives?"

"Of course. When do you want to take a run at him?"

"Tomorrow? I have to run a bunch of errands. The biggie is going to the motor vehicle department to get a new Florida license." I made a face, sticking out my tongue. "Vera knows that could take all day, so we can head out when I'm finished."

"Good deal. I'll find David H. Smith's address in the meantime. Text me when you're ready, I'll be here writing." Jack stood, as did I.

"Thanks again. You've really been helpful. I couldn't have done this without you."

There was a long, intense pause while Jack and I stared at each other. The wild part of me wanted to kiss him. The rational part screamed "he's rebounding!"

The wild part won out.

I scooted close to him. He inched nearer to me.

He closed his eyes. I closed mine.

We continued our slow, lusty path toward a kiss. I could smell his spicy, fresh-scented soap. I'd never been so eager to do this in my life. This was it, the night we'd hook up.

Yessss!

But our journey ended seconds later, not with our mouths fusing, but with our noses and faces colliding.

My eyes flew open, mortified. "Uh . . ."

His eyes did, too. "Hunh?"

We were close enough to feel each other's breath. Instead of kissing, we both laughed softly from our awkward attempts at making out.

"Sorry," I said.

"For what?" he murmured.

Then we did this thing where he went to kiss me just as I was pulling back. Then I went in for a smooch and he was rubbing his lips together. I planted a quick kiss on the corner of his mouth before retreating. I was a total klutz when it came to sex, apparently.

"Maggie, get the hell over here," he finally growled, wrapping his hand around the back of my neck. He pulled me close with just enough roughness that I squealed out of sheer delight and launched myself into his lap.

His touch was gentle yet electrifying. My heart thumped against my ribcage as his fingers caressed my cheeks with a delicate grace. In that moment, time ceased to exist, and our lips finally found one another's.

This time, there was no awkwardness. We melded together seamlessly, as if fate had orchestrated this perfect moment, just for us. Our tongues tangled, and he let out the sexiest groan.

"You're so damned beautiful, Maggie," he whispered against my mouth. "I've wanted to do this since the first moment I saw you."

He wrapped his arms around me and cupped my ass, drawing me closer to him. I was fully straddling him now. He seemed to like the flimsy shorts that didn't cover much, from the way he sucked in his breath as he squeezed my flesh.

He shut his eyes for a second.

"What?" I asked.

"Your ass feels perfect in my hands." He gave it another squeeze, then slapped it lightly.

I laughed and went in for another kiss. This was different from our moments in the wing restaurant. It was slow and dirty, intense and passionate.

"You're an incredible kisser," I told him, in between gasping for air and kissing him back.

He responded with a sexy growl.

I ground my hips into his, and within seconds he'd flipped me onto my back on the daybed. I immediately ran my hands under his T-shirt so I could feel his back muscles. They were even more glorious than in my fantasies.

I opened my legs and he settled between them. Now it was his turn to thrust as we kissed.

"Are we dry humping like teenagers?" I asked, then nibbled on his ear.

"We certainly are."

"I like it. A lot." The daybed, which wasn't new or well-constructed, shook and creaked under our weight and motion. Neither of us cared.

He thrust into me and lightly bit my neck. Oh yeah, this was getting good. Too bad we had our clothes on. I responded by pulling up his T-shirt, which he shed in record time. We resumed kissing. It was as if we were auditioning for a gum commercial, with our lips performing a perfectly choreographed routine. It was super hot.

Just as he was sliding his hand up my shirt, teasingly exploring my neck with his lips, the unexpected happened. He stiffened and abruptly raised his head, accidentally whacking me square in the chin. Ouch!

A symphony of startled cries ensued, echoing through the sunroom. I wriggled out from under him and promptly found myself sprawled face down on the floor. Super classy, I know.

"What the—" I began, trying to make sense of the chaos.

Jack sat up, confusion etched on his face, while Catsy, the feline mastermind behind this debacle, circled him, rubbing her face against his elbow while shooting me a nasty look, as if to say, *this man is mine, bitch.*

"She jumped on my butt," Jack explained, his voice a mixture of pain and amusement. "I was concerned she'd go for the exposed skin on my back. Are you OK? Sorry about my head."

"Yeah, I'm fine." I burst into laughter, unable to contain myself. "Foiled by a kitten. Now that's a new one."

However, as the laughter subsided, I looked at Jack. This kind of situation would have sent my ex spiraling into a foul mood, but here was Jack, grinning and shaking his head. His response was refreshing.

He extended his hand toward me, and I took it, rising with a grunt from my undignified position on the floor. I combed my fingers through my disheveled hair, while Jack retrieved his T-shirt and put it back on.

I couldn't help but let out a nervous laugh. Maybe he wasn't as good-natured about the interruption as I had initially thought.

"I'm truly sorry. Catsy's never pulled a stunt like that before," I apologized, feeling a pang of guilt.

The kitten stared at me, seemingly unfazed by the mayhem she'd caused or the lust she'd interrupted. She hopped down onto the cool tile floor, flopping onto her side and observing us with an air of self-satisfaction.

Jack took hold of my chin, gently tilting my head to meet his gaze. "No need to apologize," he murmured, his lips brushing against mine.

"You're leaving? Aww." I couldn't hide the disappointment in my voice. The thought of him walking out the door was disheartening. I wanted more. More kisses, more dry humping, more time with him.

He let out a sigh. "I don't want to, but I have to get a summary to my publisher by tomorrow morning. I didn't intend to stay long when I came here. I only meant to say hi."

He kissed me again, leaving a lingering sweetness in the air.

"Hi," I whispered, a hint of longing in my voice.

He groaned softly, torn between desire and obligation. "I've gotta go. But we'll resume this another time."

"Soon, I hope," I shamelessly admitted, my desires laid bare.

"Very soon," he assured me, sealing his words with one final kiss before reluctantly making his way to the exit, leaving me with Catsy as my sole companion.

As I watched him leave, a sense of anticipation settled within me. It seemed that even with Catsy's unexpected interference, there was promise of something more between me and Jack. I wasn't sure how I felt about that, since I didn't want a relationship. But I was certain that at the very least, we had a future between the sheets.

Catsy and I stared at each other, until I finally burst out laughing.

Chapter Twenty

Just as I expected, my errands lasted six long, boring hours. I had to open a new bank account, stop at the cell phone store to upgrade my phone, then wait a seemingly interminable time at the motor vehicle department. Once I'd changed my vehicle tags and gotten my new license, I was exhausted.

Thinking about Gene's murder made me even more tired, but curiosity won out. Plus Jack was doing all this work to help me and Vera, so I texted him when I arrived home.

Minutes later, there was a knock on the front door. I opened it to see Jack, who was in his usual outfit of jeans and a T-shirt.

My heart jumped into my throat. I'd been thinking about him nonstop since our interrupted hookup last night. Now that he was here in the flesh, a weird mix of lust and embarrassment hit me.

"Oh, hey," I said brightly, hoping he recalled the more sensual moments of last night, and not when I'd fallen onto the floor.

With a flourish, he handed me two printed papers. On one was an address, on the other a photo of a man who was fortyish and with a comb-over.

"David H. Smith. The ghost candidate. I found him."

I took the papers and studied them.

"Wow. Impressive. You're sure this is him?" The man in the black-and-white photo looked so generic that it could be anyone. A stock photo, even.

"Yep. Even a sham candidate had to file a few things with the Federal Election Commission."

I grabbed my bag and we were off. Dave the fake candidate lived at an apartment building on the edge of town, a new and sprawling complex with a bucolic view of the Interstate 75. It had a giant sign that said *If you lived here, you'd be home by now*, and all of the three-story buildings were painted the same wan yellow and clustered around a giant pool.

Fortunately, it wasn't gated, and Jack and I cruised on in. We drove in circles for a while, trying to make sense of the building numbers.

"This is Building H. No, wait," I said, leaning toward the windshield to squint. "Building Four. Unit H."

We were looking for Building Seven. We finally found it at the back of the complex and parked in one of the many empty spaces, one in the shade across the lot. A canal and a thicket of jungle-like scrub bordered this part of the complex.

"Are we podcasters today?" I asked.

"Seems to work well, don't you think?"

I nodded and we got out. I wished I'd chosen a sundress instead of a light cotton long-sleeve and khaki capris. "Good lord, it's warm."

We walked slowly, the humidity surrounding us like

invisible pea soup. David H. Smith's apartment was on the second floor, and it seemed as though it took a Herculean effort to drag ourselves up the stairs.

Jack knocked. And knocked again. There was no answer. We looked at each other and sighed.

"It's only four in the afternoon. Maybe he's working?" I said.

Jack knocked again. Just then, the door to the apartment to the left of Dave's swung open. A woman in a black sports bra, black spandex shorts, and hot pink shoes stood there. She nudged a small chihuahua back with her foot, came out into the hallway, and shut the door.

"Hey, y'all looking for Dave? I saw you through my peephole." Her eyes were wide, and dark brown in color.

"We are," Jack said.

"He moved about a week ago. Yes, exactly one week ago."

"Oh no," I cried.

"It's a real shame. I liked him a whole bunch. He walked my dog in the mornings when I worked. I'm a nurse, so I have some unusual hours. Real shame that Dave's gone." She looked to me, then to Jack. There was something odd in her expression, possibly because she hadn't blinked once. That made my eyes dry just thinking about it, and I blinked several times.

Jack stepped closer to her. "That's too bad. Do you know where he went?"

She shook her head, and her dark ponytail swung over her shoulder. "It was the weirdest thing. He was such a great neighbor to me and everyone else in this building—he used to help Lynne next door with her groceries, she's in her eighties—and then he just suddenly up and left. It was like he vanished. He basically ghosted the entire building."

"Weird," I said.

"The act of impulsive disappearing," Jack murmured, almost to himself.

"He seemed to care for all of us, was so friendly, but then vanished. I nearly called the cops, to be honest. I thought something might have happened to him, but the property manager told me that he moved out and didn't leave a forwarding address. Why are you looking for him?" She blinked once, slowly. "You don't look like cops."

Why did everyone keep saying that?

"We're podcasters. We're doing an episode on politics in Wahoo and wanted to talk with him," I said.

"Oh, cool," she chirped.

Jack reached into his back pocket and extracted the paper that he'd printed. "Just to make sure, are we talking about the same Mr. Smith? Was this your neighbor? It's such a common name."

He showed her the paper and she paused for a few seconds. "That's him. Not a great photo of him, he was better-looking in real life."

"Do you remember when he ran for city council?" I asked.

Her brows drew together, and she tapped her fingers on her lips a few times. "Dave ran for city council? When?"

I told her the dates of the recent election. She shook her head and her eyes grew wider. "Gosh, I didn't know that. I thought he was a computer programmer. He worked from home."

"Hmm. Did he have a lot of friends? Outside of the people in the building?" I asked.

"I would say so. He had people over all the time. Day and night. I even asked him when he got his computer work done, and he said he stayed up late. I'd see him at the pool with someone almost every other day. He loved the pool."

I took my cell out of my purse and flicked to my photos folder, to a picture of Gene. "Did you ever see this guy?" I held my phone out to her.

"Oh, yeah. Definitely. He asked me on a date. I just laughed it off, because he was kind of gross."

Bingo! Now we had a link between Gene and the sketchy council candidate. "And what about this guy?"

I tapped over to the Wahoo City Council page and a formal portrait of Tyler, wearing a blue blazer and a red-and-white-striped tie.

She squinted at it. "He definitely looks familiar. I didn't see anyone who wore that kind of suit here, though."

"How about . . ." I opened Tyler's Facebook page to a photo of him on a boat, shirtless and grinning. "Him?"

She shrugged. "Maybe? It's hard to tell. The other guy I recognized right away because of his hair. Big hair, like Elvis. You know." She made a motion with her hand from her forehead to her crown. "Um, like, I need to go. I teach an online fitness class and I have to get ready."

We thanked her for her time and she headed back inside. Feeling emboldened, I knocked on the other two doors on that floor in hopes of asking those neighbors questions about Dave, but no one was home.

Back in the car, I let out a groan as I put on my seat belt. "Obviously Gene had something to do with the election and Dave the sham candidate, but we can't exactly connect him to Tyler either."

"Police work is often frustrating. It's not as easy as it looks on TV." Jack paused and leaned forward. "Well, would you look at that."

I swiveled my head and followed his gaze. Since we were parked under a large tree at the far end of the lot— and since Jack had backed into the space—we had a bird's-eye view of the apartment. We watched as an electric-blue truck pulled in front of the building.

"That looks like Tyler's truck," I whispered.

"Sure does."

I held my breath as we waited for the driver to emerge. Sure enough, it was Tyler. And he didn't appear ill at all.

"Look at that jack-off," I hissed. "Is he carrying a bouquet of flowers? I swear to God, that man is like the human embodiment of period cramps."

I reached for the door handle, ready to confront Tyler and tell him off. Jack put a hand on my arm.

"Let's see where he goes."

"I think I know exactly where he's going."

He didn't notice us as he practically skipped up the stairs, which were open-air and visible to us. Sure enough, he knocked on the brunette neighbor's door. We watched as she hugged him, accepted the flowers, and kissed his cheek.

"Online fitness class my ass." I snorted aloud, thinking of poor Vera.

I raised my cell and attempted to take a photo, feeling like a private eye. They were too far away, and the hallway was a touch too dark, to make a good photo. I tried to zoom in by pinching the screen but that made the picture even worse.

Then she said something to him, gesturing to Dave's door. She used her hands for emphasis. "Uh, I think she's telling him about us," I said.

Jack pushed the start button on the car. Since it was an electric vehicle, we didn't roar—we glided.

"Do you think they saw us?" he asked.

"I don't care if they did. I can't wait to tell Vera." I texted her the photos.

I have no idea what that is. Are you on a gator call? she replied.

No. That's Tyler, YOUR Tyler, bringing flowers to another woman.

My phone rang a millisecond later, just as Jack drove out of the sprawling apartment complex.

"What are you doing stalking my boyfriend?" Vera's tone dripped with anger.

"I'm not stalking him. He showed up where we were."

"We?"

"Me and Jack. We were . . . sleuthing."

"Oh, for God's sake, Maggie, give it up."

My phone beeped with another call, a number I didn't

recognize. "We'll talk about this later. I need to get the other line, it might be a gator. Stay away from Tyler," I half shouted, then clicked over to the other call. "Gator Queen. Maggie speaking."

"Hi, uh, I saw your website and wondered if you handle all reptiles, or just gators." The male voice sounded shaky.

"I take care of all reptiles. What's going on?"

"There's a lizard in our toilet. We live in Wahoo Acres."

In the background, I heard a woman's moan. "We're moving back to Maine, do you hear me? This is the final straw in this godforsaken hellhole."

"Be quiet, Marge. I'm on the phone." The sound of a shuffling phone filled my ear. "Sorry. My wife's a little upset. She went in to use the facilities and found the, uh, creature."

I grinned. Northerners weren't used to the little gecko lizards that scurried everywhere in Florida. I imagined one of those two-inch lizards swimming in a toilet bowl, and pressed my lips together for a second so I wouldn't burst out laughing. This was a welcome diversion from that jerk Tyler.

"I can help you with a lizard. What's your address? My assistant and I will be right over. Oh, and give me your full name, too." I didn't want to make the same mistake as when I'd found Gene's body.

His name was Wayne Warren, and he gave me the address of an upscale condo complex on the edge of downtown. I hung up.

Jack shook with laughter as he drove.

"You ready for your first reptile call?" I asked. "This is going to be a good one."

Chapter Twenty-One

Wahoo Acres was the town's most upscale gated condo community, with a golf course, three pools, and its own shopping center. Only folks fifty-five and older lived here, which meant many were snowbirds from the north. Most of the residents used golf carts to get around, and the guard at the gate in front warned us to drive slow.

"We don't want any crashes with golf carts today," he chided. "That happened last Tuesday when Mrs. Field was listening to Frank Sinatra on blast and she didn't even see the two women in the golf cart pulling into the bingo parking lot."

Jack's expression turned to horror. "Is everyone OK?"

The guard waved his hand. "Meh. They were more upset about missing their bingo game."

We drove into the complex and pulled up outside a two-story, salmon-colored condo building. Two Mercedes, one black, one white, sat in the driveway. They both had Maine plates.

"Normally I'd go home to get my go bag, but I don't think I'll need it for a little lizard," I remarked to Jack as we walked up to the house.

The door opened before we even got a chance to knock.

"Thank God you're here." The woman, with short

brassy red hair and a thick Maine accent, wrung her hands. "I'm Marge Warren."

Wayne was inside. They looked like retirees out of central casting. He had on a light blue shirt printed with red hibiscus flowers, cargo shorts, black socks, and sandals. She wore a flaming red caftan and a matching turban. She was barefoot and smelled like vanilla cookies. I loved them immediately.

"It's pretty common to have lizards inside. Sometimes they find their way into some delicate places in the house." I smiled.

Marge fixed a steely gaze on me. "This is no common lizard, missy. This one's wicked large." She pronounced the word "laaaaage," and it made me miss Boston something fierce.

I followed her down the hall, trailed by Jack and Wayne. We passed through what was likely the master bedroom, decorated with seashell motifs on the bedspread, wall hangings, and throw pillows.

She pointed to the ensuite bathroom. "I went in to use the facilities and opened the lid and that . . . that thing was inside." She visibly shuddered. "Be careful when you open it. I'm afraid it will bite your face off."

I looked to Jack, who had a curiously amused expression on his face.

"Let's check this out," I said in a serious tone, and he nodded.

We crept into the bathroom, which had seashell-print wallpaper. Standing as far from the toilet as possible, I reached and opened the lid slowly.

"Holy shit," Jack shouted.

My eyes nearly popped out of their sockets and I closed the lid slowly. It was no small gecko.

It was a bright green iguana, coiled and chilling in the toilet bowl. Probably three or four pounds, and from its head to the tip of its thin tail, at least two feet long.

I heard a splash of water from inside the toilet.

"How in God's name did it get in there?" Wayne cried out. "What if it's someone's lost pet?"

I looked into the bedroom, where the couple stood with looks of horror on their faces.

"It's no pet. They run wild in a lot of places in Florida. Sometimes they make their way into the plumbing. They get into roof vents. I've heard of this happening before, but usually in South Florida, like the Keys. They're wily little creatures."

"We thought it was kind of weird this morning when the toilet wouldn't flush right," Wayne said, as he sank onto the bed. His shoulders rounded. Florida had defeated him.

Marge groaned. "I nearly had a heart attack when I saw it. What if it had bitten my derriere while I was trying to go to the bathroom?"

Jack and I looked at each other. His lips were pressed together and his cheeks were flushed pink, probably from trying not to laugh.

"OK, so here's what we're going to do. I'm going to open the lid and grab the iguana. We need a container to put it in. I'm sorry, but you caught us when we were out, and I wasn't fully prepared for this. I thought it was just a small lizard and I don't have my truck."

Wayne grunted as he climbed to his feet. "I have one of those large plastic containers."

"Perfect."

He wandered off, and Jack, Marge, and I made small talk as the splashing noise continued. We all stared at the toilet in horror.

"Wayne, hurry up," Marge hollered. "We don't want it to swim back down the pipes."

"I think you'd have to call a plumber in that case," Jack offered.

The woman swore under her breath and stalked out, her muumuu fluttering behind her.

"Bet you don't have days like this as a university professor," I said to Jack.

Wayne and Marge returned with a large plastic container with a lid. I instructed the couple to stay in the bedroom and close the bathroom door.

"In case it slips out of my hand. We don't want it running around."

"And to think I used to be worried about moose back in Portland," Marge grumbled, shutting the door.

I pushed the plastic bin so it sat flush with the toilet. "On the count of three, I'm going to open the lid and reach in. It might thrash around, so the minute I set it in the container, put the lid on."

"Got it."

"One. Two. Three."

I opened the lid and, in one swift motion, stuck my

hand into the toilet bowl. I gripped the scaly green creature's upper body and lifted it out of the bowl. Water dripped everywhere and its tail whipped at my bare arm.

I nestled it into the bin and Jack quickly closed the lid.

"Should we be worried it will suffocate?" he asked.

I wanted to hug him for that question. Men who thought about the welfare of animals were the hottest men of all. My ex hadn't been all that keen on animals, other than mallard ducks. He'd liked those, for some reason.

"It should be okay for a little while. Let's wash up and get out of here. When we're in the car I'll hold the bin and crack the lid so it gets air on the way home."

Jack nodded and opened the door.

"We got it," I called out.

Marge stood watching us, hands on hips, as we washed up in the sink. I couldn't help but notice our reflection in the wide bathroom mirror. I was much shorter than Jack, but we seemed to make a cute pair. I stopped myself from smiling. This fantasy of us as a couple really needed to end. So did our casual dry humping.

"What do we owe you?" Wayne poked his head in.

I shook my head. "This one's on the house."

After we reassured them that they probably would never encounter an iguana indoors again and that they were free to use the toilet, we left, with Jack carrying the container.

In the car, Jack set the container on my lap. "Where are we going to let it go?"

I cracked one edge about an inch. The creature was huddled in a corner of the container, probably scared. Poor little thing.

From the driver's side, Jack started the car.

"We can't just release it in the wild. It's illegal to do that with an invasive non-native species. That's why some places in Florida have so many problems with iguanas. And pythons in the Everglades."

"So what will you do with it?"

Maybe my uncle would want it. But he specialized in gators, and I wasn't sure if he even had proper accommodation for a smaller reptile.

I peered into the container at the critter. It really was rather beautiful, with skin the color of grass in the sunshine.

"Looks like Catsy will have a new friend, at least for now."

#

The arrival of the iguana in the house boosted Vera's mood. Wildlife always had, ever since we were kids. We both brought home stray animals, but she had a special love for ones that were unusual and slightly gross. For instance, I didn't mind snakes, but she adored them. The only reason she didn't keep them as pets was that she didn't think she had time to care for them, and because she thought having reptiles would turn off a potential partner.

So when Jack and I toted in the iguana, she cooed like it was the Gerber Baby in the flesh.

"Poor thing, in that toilet all alone," she said. "We have to keep it."

She dug out an old aquarium my dad had stashed in the garage, and Jack was kind enough to run to the pet store for a heat-emitting bulb, some food, and a fake tree branch it could climb in its spare time.

I suspected that within a few weeks, the iguana would have a larger enclosure. My sister squealed and clapped her hands as the creature climbed the branch. "Let's name it Harry! After Harry Styles!"

Jack and I looked at each other and shrugged. "Sure," I said. All I wanted was for Vera to be happy, and if naming the green creature after an international sex symbol made her heart sing, then I was all for it. We set Harry's tank on a table in the living room, so we could simultaneously keep an eye on him and watch TV.

The three of us sat, staring at Harry, who was hanging upside down on the fake branch. He seemed to be pleased with his new surroundings. Catsy walked in, gazed at the tank, then wandered off, unimpressed.

Vera shifted her body to look at us.

"Tell me about what you did today, and where you took those photos of Tyler. I thought you were going to get a new driver's license, not play detective." Her nostrils twitched and flared, and I worried she was going to lose her shit when she heard what we'd discovered about Tyler.

"I did, in fact, get a new license. Then Jack and I went to visit a city council candidate. Or tried to."

Jack filled her in on what we'd found. I clammed up and let him tell the story because somehow the recounting of seeing Tyler walk up to the woman's door with a bouquet of flowers seemed less offensive coming from him. Although I did pepper his story with the whispered words "prick" and "human ingrown toenail" a couple of times.

Vera's hardened expression crumpled into one of sadness. Her eyes welled with tears. "I don't know what to think."

I did, and was about to give her a piece of my mind when my cell rang. It was the regular ring, not the gator one. I answered.

"Maggie? Is that you?"

It was a male voice, and I said yes.

"It's Diego. From FETA. I think I have some footage you and your partner might want to see. It involves some pretty powerful people in town. Can we meet at a secure location?" His tone was serious.

A secure location? What was this? Watergate and Deep Throat? "Why don't you just come over to my house? My, uh, investigating partner is here, and so is my sister."

It was high time she got involved with our inquest. She needed to see and hear all evidence against her precious Tyler so she could quit him once and for all.

"OK, I can do that. But you don't live with any cops, do you? Or live next to them?"

"No cops here, just the three of us, a cat, and now an iguana named Harry that we rescued from a toilet today."

"You like reptiles? Cool," he said. "But you can't tell anyone I'm on my way."

"Your secret's safe with us. Come on over." I gave him

the address and hung up, rolling my eyes a little. Men could be so dramatic.

"Diego said he has some footage he wants us to see."

Jack raised an eyebrow. Vera threw up her hands. "Who is Diego?"

"He's an animal rights activist and a suspect in Gene's murder," Jack offered.

My sister looked at him like he had grown a second head, then scowled at me. "I can't believe you two. I thought you were dating."

"It's more like a fake relationship trope," Jack said, and I giggled.

Vera sat sulkily while Jack and I drank iced tea and chatted about reptiles for about fifteen minutes. Harry was happily munching on food pellets when there was a knock at the door.

"I guess this is my cue to go to bed," Vera said.

"Nope. You're staying and you're going to review this evidence with us," I retorted sharply.

Jack went to get the door, probably to allow Vera and me a few private moments to squabble.

"This is important. You can't be in denial about this situation. About the murder investigation or Tyler's sliminess. And they might be linked, so sit your ass down." I glared at her and she glared back.

"Fine." She crossed her arms. "Control freak."

Jack appeared with Diego, who today looked even more like an escapee from a boy band, albeit one who didn't own an iron. His button-down white-and-blue plaid shirt was rumpled, and his cargo shorts looked like they'd seen better days.

"This is my sister, Vera," I said.

She waved at him with a sour look on her face.

"You two really don't look alike." He took out a laptop from his bag. "Where do you want to watch this?"

I instructed him to sit in between Vera and me. Jack squeezed next to me, so the four of us perched, hip-to-hip, on the sofa. Catsy walked through, stopped when she saw Diego, then sprinted off.

"Is this the footage you got at the funeral today?" I asked.

Diego shook his head as he tapped on the computer.

"What's it from?"

"I got nothing from that guy you wanted me to sit next to." He cleared his throat. "You know how that producer said his footage had been stolen? Well . . ."

His index finger struck the space bar, and a video of Gene popped up. I leaned forward and tapped the space bar.

"Wait. Are you saying that you're the one who swiped the reality TV footage?"

Jack jumped to his feet and ran a hand through his hair. "You're showing us stolen material? Are you out of your mind?"

"Oh my God, we are all going to prison," moaned my sister. "Orange is not my color!"

"Let's not be dramatic," I said. "Can you elaborate on how you got this?"

Diego ran his tongue over his teeth. "Let's just say a

friend came into possession of all the footage. FETA thought it would show Gene abusing the gators."

Jack sat back down. "Does it?"

Diego shrugged. "I haven't watched all of it yet. There's hundreds of hours. Mostly it's of him boating, driving in his truck, and telling racist jokes. He didn't seem to be that great of a gator trapper, because the one scene with an actual gator, it swam away and Gene almost fell in the water."

"That's because he sucked as a trapper," I said. "Anyway. Is this even legal for us to watch?"

Jack scratched his head. "It's a legal gray area. But—"

"Look," broke in Diego, "I made a copy of this for you. I figured you'd want to give it to your cop friend because it's important. But you can't tell him where you got it."

"If it's that important, why don't *you* give it to the cops?" Vera asked. It was a logical question.

"I hate the police," Diego replied. "And since you're all hot to trot about finding Gene's murderer, then I figured this was a pretty big clue."

I sighed. "OK, show us the footage and we'll evaluate."

"I need to keep my identity secret," Diego said.

"Fine," Jack and I said simultaneously. I could tell by the way he jiggled his knee that he was just as curious to see the footage as I was.

Diego tapped the space bar again. The laptop screen filled with the image of Gene, on a boat.

"Tell us about Wahoo," a female voice said. *"What's it like? Politically, socially, that kind of thing."*

"That's the producer's voice," Diego added.

"Wahoo? Wahoo is like a Wild West for fishin' fanatics and brawlin' enthusiasts. It's the true epitome of freedom," Gene opined. *"Throw in the best-looking chicks in Florida and you've got paradise."*

"Why didn't he run the Wahoo chamber of commerce?" Vera said dryly, and I snickered. This was an improvement. A wise-cracking Vera was better than a sad Vera.

"Politically, it's starting to heat up. The things I know about this town would knock your socks off," Gene continued.

"Like what?" the off-camera producer said.

"Well, for starters, I helped fix an election."

I gasped and squeezed Jack's knee.

"Huh? How'd you do that?" the woman said.

"There was one candidate who really wanted to win. I don't know why he wanted that crap job so bad, probably because he was getting kickbacks from someone. I didn't ask. But he came to me, wanting to know if I knew anyone with the same name as his opponent. Turns out I did, and I connected the two. Sure enough, the candidate won."

"Hunh? I'm confused. I don't get how that works?" the producer cut in.

"You're not too bright, are you? That's OK, you're pretty. Here's how it went. My acquaintance was running for office. He wanted to win. His opponent was a guy with a generic name. Very generic. So I knew a guy with pretty much the same name, and asked him if he'd run for the seat. So there were three people in the race. Two with almost the same name, and my acquaintance."

"Holy crap," I whispered.

"What an idiot," Jack said, capturing my hand in his.

"*Ohh, I see. So voters would be confused and possibly vote for the wrong person.*" The producer was starting to catch on. As was Vera, because she sat, wide-eyed, as if in shock. Tyler's race had been the only city council contest on the ballot. It had to be him.

"*Exactamundo,*" Gene said. "*Pretty brilliant, if you ask me.*"

"*Uh, isn't that illegal? Why are you telling me these things?*" the producer asked.

"Because he's not that bright," I muttered.

"*It ain't a crime to ask a friend to run for office,*" Gene said.

The conversation turned to turtles, and the producer asked Gene if he'd ever tried turtle soup. Diego clicked off the video and stood up.

Jack stood as well. He paced while Diego peered into the iguana's tank.

"That's Harry," I said helpfully. "The critter I was telling you about."

"Whoa, awesome," Diego replied.

"What are we going to do about this video?" Vera asked, her voice notching up an octave. "We are harboring stolen property!"

I drained my tea, feeling a little guilty that I hadn't offered any to Diego. Where were my southern manners? I climbed to my feet.

"We're going to give it to the police, and we'll keep Diego's name out of it. That's what we're going to do," I said. "Now, who wants sweet tea?"

Chapter Twenty-Two

The next morning, I confidently marched into the police station and asked for Detective Alex Holt. The receptionist asked me to wait, so I sat in a hard blue plastic seat that was bolted to the floor. I'd only been inside the main Wahoo police station once in my life. It was in sixth grade and we were on a class field trip. The only thing I remember about that day was when they wanted to fingerprint us for fun.

Vera had refused because she didn't want to get her fingers dirty. I'd refused in solidarity. Dad had praised us both, telling us that it had been an excuse to keep our prints on file in case we committed crimes as adults.

"Don't want to get too chummy with the law," he'd said, then he'd taken us out for ice cream to reward us for our "street smarts."

Man, I missed Dad something fierce. Tears pricked at my eyes and I rubbed the wetness away.

Five minutes later, Alex poked his head through a door. "Ms. Andrews, come with me."

I followed him down a hall and into a spacious office.

"I see you've gotten an upgrade," I said, looking around. It was a definite improvement in his surroundings; there was a new wooden desk, an office chair that looked aerodynamic, and two other comfy seats. There was also a floor-to-ceiling bookshelf, filled with legal titles and spines that said FLORIDA STATUTES.

I expected to see a few framed personal photos. A wife, kids, maybe a dog. But there were no intimate touches of decor here. However, he did have a few tasteful prints on the wall, including a map of Spanish Florida.

I stood staring at the map for a second.

"That's an original," he said. "I bought it in St. Augustine."

"It's wonderful." Vera would adore this print. She loved Old Florida stuff.

He moved behind his desk and sat in the sleek chair. Today his stubble was a little longer, and with that strong jaw, he looked like he could play a cop in a Hollywood movie.

"So, what have you got for me? I don't think you came by to check out my new office."

I sank into one of the leather chairs on the other side of the desk and fished out the thumb drive that Diego had given me. The previous night, Jack and I had combed through it to make sure there was no other evidence or documents on it. We'd heard plenty of foul, racist, and sexist things from Gene, but didn't seem to find any further illegal activities.

With a flourish, I handed it to Alex, reciting what Jack had coached me to say. "This came into my possession. I thought you might be interested in the contents."

Alex scowled at me as he took the device. "What is it?"

"Watch it. There's only one file on the drive. Don't

worry, there are no viruses. If you want, we can play it on my laptop." I patted my messenger bag.

He looked at me, then at the thumb drive, then sighed.

"No, I'll use my computer."

He opened a laptop and plugged the drive into the side—I noted that he didn't insert it into his desktop—and leaned back as he watched with the sound up all the way. Gene's gravelly, phlegmy voice bounced around the room, inspiring an instinctive nausea in my stomach. Even in death, Gene was revolting.

"I'd start at about three minutes thirty seconds."

Alex tapped on the keyboard and played the clip. When it ended, Alex played it a second time. Then a third. I sat silently with my hands folded in my lap and watched his bright blue eyes scan the laptop screen.

He tapped on the keyboard and removed the device, then snapped the laptop shut. "Where did you get this?"

"Someone gave it to me. It's interesting, isn't it?"

He scratched his jaw. "It is indeed. Who gave it to you?"

I swallowed hard. "I'd rather not say."

"This doesn't have anything to do with the stolen videos from the reality TV people, does it?"

I shrugged and widened my eyes. "I'm not really sure."

He studied me, most likely assuming (correctly) that I was lying.

I leaned forward. "Want to know what I think?"

"You're going to tell me anyway, so lay it on me."

I smirked. "I think Gene helped Tyler Carr fix the election in Tyler's favor. Then Tyler killed Gene because he was blabbing about his corruption. So you can take my sister's name off your suspect list."

Alex stroked his chin for a second. "OK, let's think about your theory. It makes sense, sort of. But the fact remains that your sister's gun and bullet were used to kill Gene. How do you explain that?"

I took a deep breath to steel myself. "Her weapon was stolen. You haven't found the gun, have you?"

That loser took her gun to frame her, but we didn't have evidence of that yet. A chill went through me. "She reported it stolen almost immediately. Why would she shoot someone and then report a stolen gun? Makes no sense."

Alex leaned forward and propped his chin in his hand. "No. We haven't recovered the weapon. I appreciate you sharing this video with me, and I'll take it under advisement."

I wondered if that was cop speak for *get lost*. "So does that mean my sister's no longer a suspect?"

He stood up, which meant it was my cue to leave. "Everything's still on the table, Ms. Andrews. But this video does provide some interesting evidence about an election. We're going to have to analyze it for authenticity, of course."

"Of course. But listen, you have to know something. My sister's not capable of killing any living creature. Christ, she adopted an iguana that I fished out of a toilet yesterday. She hated Gene, but she'd never hurt him." I took a deep breath. "She, well, we, are about to open the bookstore. We don't want murder rumors to tank our business. I'm urging you to make an arrest or clear her name. Or something."

I wasn't above begging at this point, and looked at Alex with a pleading expression.

"Justice is sometimes slow. If there was election tampering, we might have to call in additional resources, like the feds. This could complicate the murder case." He reached for his pen and clicked.

The realization that this could take months to resolve made my heart plummet to my feet. I nodded slowly and walked out, wondering if I should've had Jack deliver the video instead. Would Alex have taken him more seriously?

I sighed as I trudged to my car. This wasn't the instant resolution I'd hoped for.

#

The next couple of days crawled by. Much to my dismay, on Friday morning, Jack had to make a quick overnight trip to Miami for an in-person faculty meeting and to check on the tenant renting his home. It was a bit shocking to realize that I actually missed him.

I didn't tell Vera any of this, of course. It seemed supremely unfair that I'd found someone interesting right as her relationship was breaking apart. Plus, I wasn't sure what was going on with Jack. Were we friends with benefits? Would we eventually end up in bed? Or would our relationship fizzle once our investigation ended (whenever that was, hopefully sooner rather than later).

So we focused on work and avoided all topics involving Tyler, relationships, or men. We kept our viewing to bad reality TV while drinking box wine.

We also managed to get the proper permits for serving food and beverages at the bookstore, and we were exactly one week from opening. I could tell by the frequency of Vera's migraines that she was getting more and more nervous.

On Friday evening, I even brought her a smoothie in bed. Because it was oppressively and uncharacteristically hot for January in Florida, I'd made blenderfuls of various fruit concoctions. They were tasty and healthy, and I whipped one up into a smoothie bowl, topped with fruit, nuts, and granola. I figured I might have to spoon-feed it to Vera, who lay in her darkened bedroom after a long day of paperwork and last-minute preparations. I left the door cracked a bit so the hall light spilled inside just enough that I could make my way to her bedside.

"Please eat a little," I begged.

She sighed and sat up against her pristine white tufted headboard. When the curtains weren't drawn and the room wasn't shrouded in darkness, Vera's bedroom looked a lot like the store, with lots of pastel florals, worn white furniture, and soft pillows.

"It's going to be OK." I spoke soothingly, as if I were trying to coax Catsy into her carrying case. "We've gotten so much done these past few days. We're ready to open. You've been amazing."

"I'm still thinking about Tyler. He texted me five times today."

I stirred the smoothie bowl. "Try some. Lots of healthy nutrients."

She opened her mouth and I fed her a spoonful. "That is tasty," she murmured, taking the spoon and bowl from me.

At least she was eating. "What did you tell Tyler?"

"I said what you told me to say. That I'd get him the cash by the end of the week."

Even though it was technically the end of the week, I wanted to stall. I was prepared to take out a loan from my 401k to pay off Tyler, but that would take time. Part of me kept hoping the probate judge would rule in our father's estate, and we'd have access to our inheritance. Who had known that the court would take months with Dad's estate?

"Good job," I said to Vera. "Has he asked to see you?"

"No, probably because he's with that brunette." Her tone was bitter. "But whatever. I'm over him. I should've known when he told me he didn't read books."

I fought the urge to roll my eyes and say, *well, duh.* "Weeding out men based on reading material is a good litmus test. Remember what John Waters once said: if you go home with somebody and they don't have books, don't screw 'em."

"Why do you have to be so crude?" She finished the smoothie and handed me the bowl and spoon. "Thanks for the dinner. Did you bring some to Jack?"

I shook my head. "I made it for you, not for him. And anyway, he's in Miami on a quick trip."

Vera managed a weak smile. "You're the best. You

know that? Even if you've been pretending to be a detective for the last couple of weeks and have a mouth that's fouler than a trucker's during rush hour on a Monday morning."

I grinned and squeezed her knee under the covers. "Get some sleep. Things will be OK. I got a good vibe from Alex Holt the other day."

It was kind of a little white lie, but one I wanted her to believe. Heck, I wanted to believe it as well. "You need to have faith in the universe, Vera. Or a higher power. Or the power of your romance bookstore idea. Have faith in us. Twin power."

She let out a cute little squeak and snuggled back into her plush bed, covering herself with a couple of pillows.

As I walked out and closed the door, I wished I could believe my own words. I wasn't normally a risk-taker, and here I was, two months after quitting a stable job to open a new business and start fresh.

We had practically no savings, and who knew if we'd even have customers—or if Vera would be cleared of murder after all.

Chapter Twenty-Three

The next day was Saturday. I awoke with the sound of the doorbell in my ears. I turned my head to look at my phone.

It was five thirty in the morning.

A surge of panic went through me. Didn't cops usually make arrests at this hour? Hadn't I seen a number of early-morning raids on television over the years?

The pounding on the front door echoed again through the house. Wearing only my sleep tank top and shorts, I ran out. My room was closer to the front door than Vera's, so I wasn't sure if she could even hear the banging.

I flung the door open and exhaled. It was Jack, with rumpled hair, a wild expression, and (of course) no shirt. He held an IPad in his hand.

"What's going on? Is everything OK? Is something on fire? It's five thirty," I grumbled, then turned to go inside. "I'm not a morning person. Obviously, you are."

Jack charged past me. "Just drove back from Miami. Left three hours ago, then saw this when I got here and checked my phone. I couldn't wait any longer. You need to check this out."

He pushed the iPad into my hands, and a little thrill of satisfaction went through me when I saw his gaze sweep down my body. While rubbing sleep out of my eye, I sank onto the sofa and spotted the website. It was the *Orlando Sentinel*, the biggest local daily newspaper.

WAHOO CITY COUNCILMAN ARRESTED ON FEDERAL ELECTION CHARGES

I gasped and a slightly colorful swear word slipped out of my mouth. Jack sat in the reclining chair.

"Tyler Carr, a newly elected Wahoo City Council member, was arrested and charged with planting and funding a fake candidate, manipulating results from the May local elections, and illegal campaign finance contributions," I read aloud. "What a shit stain. I'm going to wake my sister up for this."

The paper had a photo of Tyler getting into what looked like an unmarked police car. In handcuffs. In the corner of the photo was Alex Holt's telltale broad frame.

It was probably terrible of me, but I couldn't help but cackle. I stood and handed Jack the tablet, then ran up the stairs and burst into my sister's room.

"Get up! You need to read something!" I cried, then tempered my enthusiasm. She probably wouldn't appreciate me celebrating the fact that her boyfriend (a term I used loosely) had been charged with multiple federal crimes and hauled away by the feds in handcuffs. "Vera, honey, something big has happened. Jack's here."

She threw off the covers and looked to the cute white retro-themed clock on her nightstand. "It's five thirty in the morning. Why is Jack here? What's wrong? Is it Catsy?"

"Just come out to the living room. We need to show you something."

She mumbled something about using the bathroom and I swept out of the room, wanting to read more of the story.

From the hall, I could hear Catsy in the living room, yowling. Her schedule was thrown off, and she demanded treats.

"Girl, what do you want?" I heard Jack ask her. "Talk to me."

I turned the corner to see Catsy in the middle of the room, squaring off with Jack.

"She wants to eat," I said. "Otherwise she won't shut up. Hang on for a quick second."

In the kitchen, I fed Catsy her special feline breakfast food—"Morning Meals," with seafood and egg, which smelled a little like ocean-tinged puke—and put on a pot of coffee.

We'd need fortification to get through the next hour or so. How would Vera take this news? I clenched and unclenched my fingers out of nervousness as I waited for the coffee to brew. Frankly, I was glad to have a few minutes alone to compose myself, because I knew my sister would be upset by this news.

I walked back into the living room carrying two mugs of coffee. I handed one to Jack and set the other on the coffee table in front of my sister.

Vera, with her mussed blonde hair, sat on the sofa in her pajamas with a grumpy frown.

"Did you show her?" I asked Jack.

He handed her the iPad. "I was waiting for you."

She scowled at the screen, then her eyes widened. "Oh my God," she whispered.

She read part of the story aloud.

"The charges, which were filed in federal court in Orlando, accuse Tyler Carr of paying David H. Smith $10,000 to run as an independent in Wahoo's city council race.

"The goal of the payoff, prosecutors allege, was to 'confuse voters and influence the outcome' of the race.

"Under state law, those charges carry sentences of up to five years in prison if convicted.

"Authorities are still seeking Smith. His neighbors at an apartment complex told the Sentinel that he recently—and abruptly—moved out of his unit two weeks ago."

Vera let the tablet rest on her lap. Her head flopped back. "Well, now I know why Tyler wanted me to return that money so bad. He probably knew that he'd need it to pay his lawyer."

I folded my arms. "Here's what I don't get. Why did he go to all this trouble to win the race? It's not like the Wahoo City Council pays a salary and it's not a full-time job. And he might have won fair and square, given who his father is."

Jack nodded slowly. "Someone's probably behind this. Likely someone who had financial interests in getting Tyler on the commission. A lobbyist, perhaps. Someone who needs the commission to vote a certain way, someone unethical."

"That sure narrows it down in Florida," Vera said, her

voice dripping with sarcasm. "I can't believe how gullible I was. I believed all his crap, everything he said about the environment and wanting to do right by the town. And here he was, paying a guy to be a sham candidate. I still want to give him the money back soon. I don't want any ties to him at all."

I sat next to her, thrilled that she'd finally gotten the message about Tyler's sleaziness. "Of course we'll pay him back, every penny. But please don't blame yourself. He sounds like a class A manipulator who took advantage of you."

She snorted. "Yeah, because I'm single and obviously desperate, so he picked me as a prime example of a loser."

I lightly tapped her knee. "Wrong. He picked you because you're gorgeous and smart and he probably wanted people to think that one of the town's leading voices for the environment was in favor of his stupid candidacy."

"Maybe," she muttered.

"We have to just keep our focus on the bookstore."

"But, Maggie?" She set the tablet on the coffee table and reached for her mug.

"Yeah?"

"This doesn't clear me as a suspect in Gene's murder. We have that hanging over us. I'm still worried how that will affect the opening."

I released a thin breath and looked over at Jack. By the way he was stroking his stubble, I could tell that he was probably wondering the same thing I was.

Was Tyler's election fraud somehow linked to Gene's murder? The timing of it all seemed too coincidental for my taste.

#

News that Tyler had been arrested spread around town like an oil spill in the Gulf of Mexico. Everyone was talking about the case, from Rodney at the chamber of commerce to the tourists in line at Cheesy Does It to the employees at the post office.

Everyone seemingly had something to say about Tyler. They talked about his many girlfriends, his underhanded business dealings, his nonpayment of debt. How his rich father had bailed him out of all sorts of scrapes, including, but not limited to, a DUI in another county, a fist fight at a strip club, and fishing without a license.

He was worse than even I imagined, which was no small feat.

All of this, of course, was difficult for Vera, who worked on bookstore stuff from home for the rest of the weekend. She practically barricaded herself in her room and refused my offer of picking up burritos at her favorite spot.

On Monday morning, she asked if we could drive into the bookstore together.

A good sign, I hoped.

After I finished my coffee, I quickly showered, changed into a cute dress, and we headed to the bookstore. Vera locked the door behind us and switched on a single floor lamp. For some reason, she didn't turn on the overhead lights and, because we had brown paper over the windows, it was like a cave inside. It took a few seconds for my eyes to adjust to the darkness after being in the bright Florida sunshine.

Vera immediately went to work reshelving a column of books while I watched, bemused.

"You don't want the historicals closer to the door?" I asked.

"No, I want to switch out with paranormal."

"OK, up to you, of course. Vera, weren't we going to take the brown paper down from the windows today, so people can see your beautiful display?"

"I think we should wait until the night of our party." She pushed a book onto the shelf and didn't look at me.

"But we were going to create buzz before the soft opening."

She lifted a shoulder and straightened two books. "Do you like five books and then a stack of books facing out, or should it be six? Maybe we should postpone the opening."

"Hey. Look at me. Why don't you want to show off the window? It's gorgeous."

The window space in this store was one of the largest on the block, and the display she'd created was exquisite. It showcased a two-cubby bookshelf she'd painted herself in the perfect shade of distressed white. It was stuffed with hardcover books, with two titles displayed on top. There was also a comfy-looking wingback chair in gold, and a small matching white table. On top of the table was a rose-patterned teapot, cup, and saucer.

We'd had a local florist deliver a stunning bouquet of pink roses that almost perfectly matched the teapot, but they sat on the counter, near the cash-register-slash-computer.

Vera turned to face me. "I don't want people staring at me. What if they know about me and Tyler?"

I threw my hands in the air and paced. I didn't want to remind her that no one knew she and Tyler had been dating, since he hadn't taken her out anywhere in town. That was exactly the wrong thing to say, so I tried something different. "We're opening the store in days. People are going to come in and they're going to look at you. You're going to have to put on your big girl panties and deal. I'm sorry."

"I know, but right now I feel awkward. Embarrassed."

"You have nothing to be embarrassed about. Tyler should be embarrassed and ashamed for what he did to you and this entire town. Let that douchenozzle stew in prison. We need to put all of this behind us and concentrate on the future."

"But how can I when I'm still a suspect?"

I stopped pacing and gnawed on my lip, wondering if I should pay Alex Holt a visit. "No news is good news. And I assume that if they thought they had enough evidence on you, they would have arrested you by now. Right now, you need to focus on opening the store."

She swallowed hard, and I knew she was on the verge of tears.

"C'mon, Vera. Let's take the paper down from the

window and put the flowers out. People will love it, and their reaction will cheer you up. You'll see."

"OK. I can do this." She shuddered in a breath.

"Yes, you can."

I carefully stepped onto the raised platform in front of the window, trying not to disturb anything. Vera stood with her hands on her hips, watching me, as I gingerly removed the tape from the brown paper that covered the windows.

Once the paper was down, a bright ray of sun flooded the store. She handed me the vase of flowers, and I set it on top of the bookcase, next to a beautiful hardcover copy of *Pride and Prejudice*—the one that Vera and I had read when we were teens. The book was nestled safely under a glass display dome.

It had been our mother's book, and through it she was guarding the store.

And hopefully, us. We needed all the help we could get, from both this world and any other.

Chapter Twenty-Four

A few hours later, in the early afternoon, Vera and I drove home. We discussed stopping at Blue Orchid, Wahoo's only Thai place, for a late lunch. Vera loved the restaurant for two reasons. One was the kind couple who owned it, the other was the spicy shrimp soup that could peel paint off walls with its fire. It was even too much for me.

As we were about to turn down the road to the restaurant, the news came on the radio. Wahoo had a local station that mostly played seventies and eighties pop tunes, but it also kept the town abreast of current events. The announcer had been on air for seemingly my entire life, and when I heard the jazzy intro jingle, I instinctively turned it up.

"Ladies and gentlemen, boys and girls, and all you delightful gators and flamingos out there, welcome to Wacky Waves 101.5 FM, your home for news that's wilder than a Florida Man and hotter than a pelican wearing sunglasses! In today's top stories, a January heatwave sweeps the Sunshine State, a Wahoo man discovers a secret mermaid hideout, and a local city councilor charged with corruption is released with an ankle monitor. But first, a word from our sponsor, Cheesy Does It!"

I reached to tune the knob to another station, but Vera stopped me. "I need to hear this," she hissed.

Our Thai meal was about to be in jeopardy. I could sense it. I slowed the car and made a right toward the restaurant as the announcer came back on. My stomach started to rumble at the thought of pad thai.

"A federal judge has released a Wahoo city councilman and ordered him to house arrest pending trial. Twenty-seven-year-old Tyler Carr, who was arrested recently on election tampering and fraud charges, was released on bail this afternoon. Florida's governor has also removed Carr from office. Today, Judge Marvin Brown ordered Carr to wear an ankle monitor and to have no contact with anyone at City Hall. He was released to the custody of his parents . . ."

"At least he spent the weekend in jail," I muttered. "Wonder how that went for him."

"Go home," Vera commanded.

"What? What about Thai soup?"

"Since Tyler's home, I need to bring him some things that he gave me. I don't want them in the house."

I gripped the steering wheel so hard that my fingers left imprints, as if I were trying to squeeze out every last drop of stress like toothpaste from a tube nearing its end.

"We should probably eat first." The last thing we needed was Vera going to Tyler's house and causing a scene.

"I'm not hungry. Go home." She pointed toward the windshield.

With a sigh, I steered the car home and didn't say

another word. Once inside, I played with Catsy and checked on Harry while Vera disappeared into her room. Twenty minutes later, she came out with a tote bag bursting at the seams.

"Goodness, how much stuff of his do you have?" I asked from my perch on the sofa, where I was tickling Catsy's soft belly.

She patted the bag. "Mostly books on business motivation and ethics, junk like that. Books he obviously didn't read."

Obviously. "Are you sure you want to do this?"

She nodded and made her way to the door. "I'll be back in a while."

"There's no way I'm letting you go alone. I don't trust that man." I scrambled to my feet and grabbed my keys and purse.

# # #

Tyler and his parents lived in one of the giant Mediterranean Revival homes that circled a small, historic downtown park. The houses there were historic and gorgeous, all pink stucco and barrel-tile roofs. Beautiful old mango and avocado trees dotted the yards.

As a teenager, I'd always looked at this neighborhood warily, as if the sheer beauty of the homes might contain some sort of evil. To me, they'd looked like haunted houses, something I'd see on TV. Maybe I'd been right, I thought, as we walked up the perfectly manicured walkway of Tyler's family home.

Vera raised her fist to knock, then turned to me. "You don't have to come in."

"Oh, I'm coming in." I didn't trust Tyler one bit.

She rapped on the door, then pressed the doorbell. Her face was pinched and hard and I could tell this took a lot of courage.

Footsteps came into earshot, then the door swung open.

It was Tyler. Gone was the cocky smirk and the knowing gaze. Today he looked like a broken man. A haunted expression clouded his eyes. He hadn't shaved in days, and his shoulders drooped. His mouth looked like it had been stung by bees.

My sympathy remained unmoved. I glanced to my sister, worried that she'd lose her resolve and have sympathy for the jerk.

"Vera, sweetie," he whispered.

I snorted and rolled my eyes.

"This is yours." She thrust the bag into his arms. "All the books you gave me. And your sweatshirt."

He stared down at the bag, his chin quivering. I wanted to tell him to cut the theatrics but remained calm. I folded my arms and he glanced at me, then quickly looked to Vera.

"I'm glad you came over. I was thinking of you," he said. "Can you please come inside? I'd like to talk with you in private. I tried calling you."

"Only if my sister can join us." Vera's nostrils twitched.

His mouth formed a hard line for a split second, then he nodded and stepped aside.

"Let's go into the living room. I don't want to disturb my parents. They're out by the pool. They're not happy with me now so it's best that I don't introduce you today." We followed Tyler through the mazelike historic home. I'd have been impressed by all the antiques and art if it weren't for the fact that the place was tied to him.

The fact that he hadn't introduced Vera to his folks made me irrationally angry. I shook my head and sighed.

Once in the living room, Tyler set the bag in a corner then turned to us. "Can I get you some coffee? A drink? Iced tea? My mom just made a pitcher and it's really good. I have no idea what she does, but it's delicious."

"Iced tea would be wonderful, thanks," Vera said.

"Nothing for me," I replied in a sour tone. Why were we hanging around?

Nodding, he walked out of the room. I turned to Vera. "You were seriously considering a future with a man who is baffled by an iced tea recipe?"

"I don't want you to say a word while we're here," Vera said.

"OK." This was her mess. I was here only to lend emotional support.

We sat in uncomfortable silence, with her sitting in a leather wing chair, checking her phone. I remained standing and studied a portrait above a stone fireplace. It depicted a bucolic scene of the Everglades at dawn, which raised my annoyance level to new heights, since Tyler's developer father never met a swamp he didn't want to pave over.

My thoughts turned to the Covington property and

Gator Heaven, and by the time Tyler came back in, I was good and worked up in my mind.

He handed Vera a tall glass of tea. It appeared that he'd washed his face, since his hair and the collar of his shirt were wet. He also smelled as though he'd doused himself in cologne, and the odor of frat party mixed with dashed dreams filled the air as he sank onto the end of the sofa.

I took a seat on the edge of an ottoman and my eyes ping-ponged from Tyler to Vera.

"I'm sorry," he started, and I had to stop myself from laughing.

Vera, against all odds, maintained a stone-cold expression. "Did you kill Gene?"

Even I was floored by her blunt question. Leaning forward, my eyes bulged in disbelief.

Tyler buried his face in his hands. "No," he whimpered. "I didn't do it. I swear."

He lifted his head to meet Vera's gaze. Part of me almost felt sorry for the guy, with his flushed cheeks, teary eyes, and swollen lips. Then I remembered the time he stuck maxi pads to the outside of my high school locker, and any trace of sympathy evaporated.

"But you're somehow tangled up in his death." She crossed her arms and fixed him with a steely stare. I suspected she used that same look on rowdy kids at the library.

"Yeah, and I'm sorry for dragging you into this. The whole plan wasn't supposed to end like this, but Gene—"

"Hold on," I interjected. "You purposely involved my sister without telling her?"

Finally, Tyler glanced at me sheepishly. "It's a long story. I've been thinking about telling you."

"Oh, a thought crossed your mind? Must've been a lonely journey." I crossed my arms. I wasn't leaving here until Tyler explained himself. He owed Vera that much, at the least. Prick. "We've got all night."

"We sure do," Vera chimed in. "What the fluff, Tyler?"

He let out a strangled sob, then swallowed. "I'm going to cooperate with the prosecutors. I've a meeting later this week to tell them everything, although my parents want me to keep quiet. My lawyer says we need a few days to gather additional evidence and paperwork but might as well spill the beans now. You have to promise not to breathe a word to anyone, OK?"

Vera and I both nodded, but deep down, I thought, *fat chance, buddy*. I'd sing like a songbird to Alex Holt the second I walked out of here.

"It all began during my political campaign. I met this guy named Bruce Doyle at one of my fundraisers. At first, I didn't think much of him, but then he suggested we go fishing, with a professional guide and all. So I contacted Gene since he knows all the primo fishing spots. The three of us went out on Gene's boat, and Bruce and I got to talking about the campaign and development. Turns out, he had bought the Covington property."

"Gator Heaven," I muttered with distaste.

"What?" Tyler asked, confused.

"Never mind. Continue."

"Bruce wanted to know my chances of winning, and I told him it'd be a close call. The real Dave Smith, my opponent, had a strong following and was the incumbent. That's when Gene butted in on our conversation. He mentioned this news story he'd read out of Miami about 'ghost candidates.' You know, running a third person with the same name as your opponent, to siphon votes away. Gene claimed he knew someone with the same name, a guy he met at a bar. And wouldn't you know it, Bruce loved the idea."

"Shocking," I deadpanned. "I didn't know Gene could read."

"The plan went pretty smoothly from there. The three of us agreed that Bruce would pay Gene to convince his friend to run for office. David H. Smith, the impostor candidate, would also get a cut. In return, I promised to vote in favor of Bruce's development if I won."

"Which you did," Vera interrupted.

"I won the election, but the rezoning vote hasn't happened yet. And now that I've been removed from office, I won't be casting a vote."

"Such a shame," I remarked. Vera shot me a wicked look, but I brushed it off. "I still don't get how all this led to Gene's demise. It sounds like you and Bruce had everything under control."

Tyler shifted his gaze to me, a hint of arrogance shining through his smirk. "Things were going smoothly until Gene started to blab. He couldn't keep his mouth shut, first blabbing to some hot bartender at the Shady Lady. He told people he knew some secret about the election. Bruce was getting anxious because Gene was also going on that reality show, and the last thing he wanted was Gene telling the world about the election. This all went down in November and early December. Then Vera and her group started protesting the property sale, and that made Bruce even more jumpy."

Poor Bruce. I shot Tyler a sickeningly sweet expression.

"And then you thought dating me would halt my protests," Vera stated.

Tyler exhaled sharply through his nose. "Sort of. I feel guilty about that. And downright awful about what happened next."

My eyes couldn't resist rolling like marbles. "Sure you do."

"What happened?" Vera inquired.

"Bruce wanted Gene gone, but he didn't want the evidence to point back to him, or me, or the David guy. He wanted to pin it on someone else. And that's when you and I went for that walk in the park, and your car got broken into."

A sickening realization washed over me. "You allowed Bruce to break into my sister's car, steal her gun, and then kill Gene, all while knowing my sister would be accused of murder?" I sprang to my feet, yelling. "Vera, let's get out of here. I've had enough of this skeevy pond scum."

"Wait," Vera whispered softly. "You actually gave Bruce permission to use my gun in a crime?"

Tears streamed down Tyler's flushed cheeks. "I'm sorry. I thought he was just going to scare Gene. I realized what I had done later that day and had a panic attack. That's why I turned myself in, why I wanted to apologize, why I asked you here today."

"You're a real piece of work." I paced the room, seething.

"You were willing to throw me in prison to save your butt?" Vera struggled to comprehend Tyler's actions.

"I'm sorry," he wailed. "That's why I'm telling you now and am going to tell the feds. I don't want this pinned on you. It's my way of making amends. Can you forgive me? Please?"

A suffocating silence enveloped the room, though if glares could make a sound, Tyler would be deaf from the way I was piercing him with my eyes. Finally, Vera rose, her head held high.

"Let's go," she whispered to me.

As we walked out, Vera paused by the sofa and stared down at Tyler. "You're a burden to humanity."

Maybe it wasn't the most creative insult, and not one I would've used, but it suited me just fine. We left the house, leaving behind the sounds of Tyler's sobs.

On the short drive home, we didn't speak of the conversation at Tyler's house. We rolled down the windows and cranked the radio, singing at the top of our lungs to Tina Turner's "Better Be Good to Me."

It was just like old times, except today was a little sweeter, because Vera was about to be exonerated from a crime she didn't commit.

Chapter Twenty-Five

Once we were home, Vera started pacing the living room. I flung myself on the sofa, pressing my hand to my forehead. Now that everything had sunk in, I wasn't convinced that Tyler was being above board. Questions swirled in my mind.

"That was wild," I muttered.

At that moment, Catsy came careening in. She took one look at Vera, jumped up on the sofa, ran the length of it (trampling my lap with her tiny paws), then flew down and attacked at a catnip mouse with her back feet.

"Can you believe that guy?" Vera fumed.

"Actually—"

My sister interrupted and held up a hand. "Don't say I told you so."

I was going to say something about how shocking it was that the guy who used to fart loudly in algebra and blame it on others would find himself in trouble with the law, but I refrained. No, Vera didn't need my snark right now. She needed logic.

"Do you think Tyler is actually going to tell everything to the authorities? It puts him in a pretty bad light. I'm sure he'll cut some deal to try and avoid prison time, but still."

Vera stopped pacing and gaped at me. "Well, he said he would."

I scrunched my eyes shut, exasperated. "You need to stop being so naive. Why hasn't he told anyone yet? Is he even telling the truth? And he said his parents didn't want him to talk."

A pained look crossed her face. "Do you think we should let someone in on Tyler's secrets now? Before his parents get to him?"

I opened my eyes. "Uh, yeah. I think we should call Detective Holt pronto. That information can't wait."

Vera stepped over a sprawled Catsy to take her cell out of her bag. She handed it to me. "You talk. I'm way too nervous. He's saved in my contacts."

I scrolled to Holt's number and pressed the call button. It rang and rang, until his message played. I hung up. "I'm getting voicemail. What time is it? Maybe he's gone home."

Vera checked her watch. "Oh, fluff. It's three thirty."

"Well, he should be working for another hour or two, right?"

She shook her head. "Sometimes city workers don't stay past three if there's no essential work. That includes the police."

Apparently, this was some sort of new town rule that I'd missed while being gone for so long. "Isn't policing considered essential?" Something told me that Alex Holt was not the kind of man to knock off work at three thirty in the afternoon.

She shrugged. "Let's drive to the police station and see if he's on duty."

"Sounds good." I rose from the sofa.

"Let's give Catsy a treat before we go." Vera scooped up the kitten and pressed a kiss to the top of her head. "Look at this little pudding cup."

"That little pudding cup is becoming a chonk." She was also hampering my sex life. But no need to tell Vera that right now.

"She's fluffy, not fat, Maggie."

We gave Catsy a few salmon snacks and left the house. On our way to the car, we spotted Jack in the doorway of the cabin, waving to us.

"Oh, let's tell Jack what we heard. He'll be interested," I said, turning to walk in his direction.

"I'll wait in the car," Vera called out.

Today, Jack was wearing a Miami Heat T-shirt, jeans, and flip-flops. He beamed adorably as I approached.

"Hey there, tater tot," he said.

I paused to grin. He was giving me a nickname already?

"You're not going to believe this." I proceeded to tell him the abridged version of Tyler's confession in one long sentence. I was breathless when I finished.

The shock on Jack's face grew. "That's a whole ride, that story. What a snake. Is Vera OK?"

"Yeah, she's angry, which is progress. We're on our way to tell Detective Holt everything. Want to join us?"

His expression fell. "I wish I could, but I have a call with my publisher about the book. We're discussing covers so I can't miss it."

"Aww, it's okay." I waved him off, not wanting him to

see how disappointed I was. He'd helped so much in our sleuthing, and I wished he could see the case through.

"How about I come over with some prosecco and pasta later?" he said. "A little celebration."

"That would be amazing."

He raised his hand for a high five, and I slapped his palm. But instead of me pulling my arm back, I kept my hand pressed against his. He didn't move either, and we stood there, staring at each other, grinning. I was thinking about the other night when we were horizontal, and I'd bet he was too.

"See you tonight," I said, and bounced off.

Fifteen minutes later, Vera and I marched into the police station. We stopped at a window, where a bored-looking man shifted his eyes from a computer.

"How can I help you?" he asked.

"We're looking for Detective Holt. We have some important information about a case he's working on," I said.

"Crucial information," Vera added.

The man, who was about sixty with gray hair, a pink button-down shirt, and a purple bow tie, nodded and tapped a few keys on his computer.

"The detective is out for the afternoon. According to this"—he tapped a few more keys—"his calendar says he's at a monthly meeting of Central Florida detectives. It's in town, though."

Vera and I looked at each other, stumped.

"When will he be back?" I asked.

"Tomorrow morning. Usually gets here around eight."

"Where is he in town?" Vera asked.

The man stared at us, stone-faced. "I can't tell you that."

After I thanked him, I pulled Vera into a corner, out of earshot of the dapper dispatcher guy. "Let's just leave him a detailed voicemail."

"And a text."

I nodded and we went back to the car, where I left a long and rambling message for Alex Holt. It was so long that I had to call back three times and leave additional messages. Then, instead of trying to type it all out in a text, I sent him a message in all caps.

LISTEN TO YOUR VOICEMAIL. URGENT. WE CAN'T MESS THIS UP. BIG NEWS, AMIGO.

Sighing, I turned to Vera, who was sitting in the passenger seat. "Well, that's done."

"What should we do now? I'm too keyed up to feel hungry."

I chewed on my bottom lip for a beat. "How about we drive by Bruce's house? To make sure he's still there and all. Just out of curiosity."

"Yeah, that seems like a plan. It seems difficult to believe that he'd stay in town after Tyler's arrest. He's probably already gone."

I pulled out of the parking lot and pointed the car in the direction of Doyle's house. "Criminals aren't known for being smart."

Then again, I thought, *are amateur sleuths?*

#

"Wasn't this where you fell off the bike and skinned your knee so bad that I was convinced you were going to lose a leg?" I asked as we drove into the Osprey Landing subdivision.

"I'd forgotten about that," Vera said. "I really thought I'd be an amputee."

I turned down Bruce's street. "In retrospect, you were a dramatic child."

Vera's laughter was swiftly hushed by my gesture. I pointed to my right as I drove.

"Just up ahead, on the right. Can't miss it. Salmon-colored house," I whispered, intending to maintain a discreet vibe.

"What's the plan when we get there?" Vera inquired.

"We don't have one."

As I crawled along the road, I couldn't help but regret bringing my red F-150 and its throaty muffler instead of Vera's silver sedan. My truck was hardly inconspicuous.

"There's some activity at the back of the house." Vera strained her neck toward the window, urging me to circle back for a better view.

I drove down the street, took a right, and then promptly got lost. As we rolled through the suburban landscape of Osprey Landing, the streets unfolded like neatly woven ribbons, lined with white picket fences and manicured lawns. Picture-perfect houses in pastel hues and lone palm trees dotted the landscape. It all looked the same.

Letting out a string of swear words while navigating the perplexing suburban labyrinth, I muttered, "How does anyone find their way here without getting lost on the regular?"

Eventually, we stumbled upon Bruce's street again and passed by a second time. I failed to spot anything suspicious, but Vera insisted she glimpsed a box truck lurking in the rear.

"It's hard to say for sure, but what if he's moving something out?" she pondered.

"Not exactly a crime," I countered. "Wish we could get a clearer look."

"We can," Vera chirped. "Remember the path near the canal? Where we used to race bikes with Donnie Stillman? I'll bet it's still there, and it goes past all these homes."

"Oh, right! I haven't thought about that in years." I made a clicking noise with my tongue. "Where should we park? And whatever happened to Donnie?"

Vera twisted in her seat. "A couple of years ago, Donnie lost three fingers to fireworks on the Fourth. Last I heard, he was on disability. Oh, it's on the main road, there's a turnoff to the canal."

"If we can find our way out of here."

We managed to leave Osprey Landing, and just as Vera said, there was a small unpaved road off the main street. I drove in slowly, the jungle-like scrub almost swallowing the truck. It was so thick that the strong Florida sunshine couldn't penetrate the foliage.

"Keep going," Vera urged, pointing straight ahead.

After a couple of minutes of driving, we came to a clearing in the brush. I parked, and we sat staring at the murky greenish-brown water of the canal. In Florida, a canal could mean many things—in Fort Lauderdale, for instance, it meant waterfront property complete with docks and million-dollar yachts.

Here, canals were for drainage and flood protection for the Snake River. There were no docks or yachts, but folks often found good fishing on the banks. This particular canal split two subdivisions—Osprey Landing and Osprey Landing II.

Strips of heavy scrub foliage buffered the water from the homes.

"If we follow the canal a few hundred feet that way, we should be able to walk into the woods and see the back of Bruce's home." She motioned with her hand. "It's a short walk, no biggie."

I glanced at my sister. She was wearing tan capris, a lemon-yellow button-down blouse, and a matching headband. And dainty tan ballet flats. Also, it looked like she'd taken time to straighten her hair today. She was going to be a mess if she went into those woods.

"You can stay here. I don't want you to ruin your shoes." In contrast, I was in jeans, a long-sleeved gray cotton top, and sneakers that had seen better days.

"These old things? Nah. I'll go." She climbed out of the car, and I followed.

"Let's put on some bug spray first. I've got some in the back."

"Good idea."

I rooted around my go bag and found the spray. We doused each other front and back, like we used to before going on an expedition with Dad. I pointed at my bag. "I have an extra hat. Do you want it?"

Vera wrinkled her nose. "Fine. But my hair will get messed up."

"I don't think we'll run into any Italian male models while out here, so you can risk it."

We donned our hats. Vera looked sporty. I tucked my hair underneath and probably looked like a teen boy. I didn't give a crap, though. At least that way there was a chance my neck might sweat less.

I locked the truck and pinned our location on a map on my phone so we'd be able to find our way back. Then I slipped the straps of my backpack over my shoulders—I never went into the woods without a few key items—and we set off.

"This isn't bad at all," Vera said as we walked.

It wasn't. There was a small worn footpath that paralleled the canal. Since the water was about five feet from the path, I wasn't concerned about gators or other critters. They were easily spotted out here in the open.

I was more concerned about the woods, but felt pretty confident that I had the tools and reptile expertise to handle anything.

We slowed about three hundred yards into our walk. Vera put her hands on her hips and looked toward the woods, to her left. "The house should be right about here."

Vera took the lead as we filed into the woods. It wasn't

like the cool, damp forests of New England that I'd explored over the past several years.

We stepped into the thicket gingerly and picked our way through. I'd been worried the ground would be wet, muddy even, but thankfully it was solid and dry. That was the only blessing, however.

The air was thick with the pungent yet familiar scent of both Florida flora and decomposing vegetation. Palmetto fronds, armed with their spiky edges, threatened to shred our skin like cheese graters. I became tangled in a vine and flailed to extricate myself.

"Shitfire," I said.

Shafts of sunlight, playing peek-a-boo through the tangled mess of branches, highlighted the wild chaos surrounding me. I felt moist everywhere, and I hated both the word and the sensation. Birds, hidden among the foliage, chirped and squawked, mocking our journey.

Still, this felt undeniably like home. My mind began to drift to all the times I'd accompanied Dad on hikes like this.

"You getting bitten?" my sister called out.

"Nope," I replied. "We might want to keep it down. I think I can see a house up ahead."

Vera stopped and we peered through the foliage. Mosquitoes immediately swarmed us but kept a respectful distance because of the spray. From experience, I knew that wouldn't last long, and we'd be attacked sooner rather than later.

"Is that his place?" she hissed.

"Let's get a smidge closer. Can't make it out from this angle."

We tiptoed in tandem, inching our way until we arrived at a ginormous boulder. We squatted behind it, but I suspected it wasn't concealing our presence at all.

"Yup, that's the one," I said, slipping my backpack off. I unzipped the top and fished out a water bottle. "Here. Take a swig."

Vera cracked it open, took a long sip, then handed it back to me. I took a sip and screwed the cap back on, placing it on the ground near the rock.

We draped ourselves over the boulder, gazing intently at the house. No doubt about it, we had hit the bull's-eye. I recognized the pool, the shed, and the rear of the house.

I extracted a pair of binoculars from my bag and peered through them. "I don't see Bruce or his son."

"I swear I saw movement when we drove by. Someone's here," Vera insisted.

I handed her the binoculars, and she held them to her eyes.

Unlike my previous visit to Bruce's, there was an enormous dumpster out back. It was almost as large as the shed.

I mentioned this to Vera, and she nodded. "Maybe he's tossing out some junk before getting out of town."

"Do criminals bother with thorough cleaning before going on the lam?" I joked.

"This one does."

The deep male baritone jolted me, causing Vera to

drop the binoculars. They landed with a muted thud on the forest floor. We swiftly turned around, leaning on the rock for support.

There, standing between us and the canal, was Bruce.

Chapter Twenty-Six

Vera and I gasped at the same time, only hers was like a high-pitched squeal.

"Is that him? Bruce?" she asked. "What. The. Fluff?"

"That's me all right," he said, a sinister smirk on his face. "I don't think we've met. I'm Bruce Doyle. Maggie, this must be that twin sister you were talking about. You don't look anything alike. No offense, but she's prettier."

"Fraternal twins," I muttered. "And I know."

Bruce waved his beefy hand in the air, indicating that he truly wasn't interested in my answer. Today he wore a sleeveless white tank top with sweat stains, and cargo shorts. Sweat mingled with the thick hair on his shoulders.

"It's nice seeing you again, Bruce," I said briskly, hoping that I could bluff my way out of this. "We were back here tracking a gator and didn't anticipate we'd end up behind your house. Imagine my surprise when I saw your—"

"Save the explanation for someone who cares. I know you were casing my house then came back here to spy on me."

Vera shook her head. "Not at all. We were—"

Again, Bruce interrupted. "I was following you the entire way from the police station. Don't lie."

"What? Why? How dare you?" I couldn't hold my shock or anger in any longer. "You happened to see us downtown and decided to follow us? What's wrong with you?"

"Creep," Vera added.

Bruce shook his head and chuckled. It was a low, menacing sound. "I was following you on purpose. You see, a little birdie told me that Tyler spilled his guts to you."

The background hum of the forest—the insects buzzing, the birds chirping, the occasional rustling of leaves—fell silent. I opened and closed my mouth, not quite believing his words. My eyes drifted to my backpack. Did I have enough time to reach for my gun . . . no, I didn't.

Because the cops still had my gun for the ballistics tests. Hell.

I started to snicker from nerves, then forced myself to shut up. "Who told you what Tyler said to us?" I asked.

"Tyler. He called me after you two left. He was crying and everything, wanted forgiveness and money for a new lawyer. He told me what he said to you, and I put two and two together that you'd go straight to the cops." Bruce lifted a shoulder. "That guy Tyler can't keep a secret. He was like that other one. Gene. Can't believe I came down here to this godforsaken place and did business with two snitches. Idiots. Gene and Tyler were the sorriest excuses for men I've ever met."

Tyler! What a worm. No, that was an insult to worms.

I edged closer to my sister, until our shoulders touched. "Well, that's unfortunate for you. Sorry your

Florida dream didn't pan out. We'll let you . . . do whatever it is you were doing, while we go home, okay?"

I grabbed Vera's wrist and was about to pull her away when Bruce took a step toward us.

"I don't think so. You ladies are coming with me."

I cleared my throat. How were we getting out of this? Bruce loomed large and was blocking us from the path to the car. "I'm sorry, but we have some things to do at the bookstore. We really need to be moving on."

Vera wrenched her wrist out of my grip and folded her arms. She glared at Bruce. Hoo boy. The last thing I wanted was an angry Vera.

"Bye now," I said, taking a step forward. Maybe if I ignored Bruce and showed bravado, he'd let us go.

"Nope." Bruce said. His hand slithered to his back and came up with a gun. "You two know way too much. I'm not feeling charitable because I've had the worst time in this stupid town and I think I'm gonna take it out on the two of you. Since you two wrecked my real estate deal."

I held my hands up, palms facing him. My heart wasn't just racing, it was like a hummingbird's wings against my chest. "We don't know anything. And what we do know, we've forgotten. Or will forget. So, no harm no foul." At this point, I wasn't above begging for my life. "Please, just let us go. You don't need to kill two innocent women . . ."

"But there is harm, and there is a foul. Two of them. You—" Bruce pointed at me, then at my sister. "And you. You both know that I stole blondie's gun to kill Gene. And because of that little slime puppy Tyler, you know that

I helped fix the election too. You're not above going to the cops, since I saw you there earlier. I can't let you two go."

"At least we can all agree that Tyler's a slime puppy," Vera said. I almost laughed because it was funny. And true.

"We were at the police department inviting people to the bookstore opening," I lied. Inside, my stomach sank. We'd worked so hard on the bookstore. Were we going to even make it to the opening? Waves of adrenaline and fear flowed through my body, and everything around me seemed sharper.

This wasn't what I'd had in mind when I left Boston two short months ago.

Vera stepped forward, her eyes shooting daggers at Bruce. "You wanted to develop the Covington property, which to me is a bigger crime than killing Gene or fixing the election. Fluff you. You deserve to be in prison."

She pointed in his direction.

"Vera, come on," I groaned under my breath. "Work with me here."

Bruce gaped at her, probably incredulous that she was challenging him. I probably would be staring at her, too.

Except my focus was elsewhere. Like on the alligator immediately behind Bruce.

The creature silently loomed in the scrub brush. It hadn't been there a moment before, but it had stealthily crept up on us, almost camouflaged by the brush. It must've come from the canal, because its rough black skin seemed extra shiny from water in the late-day sun.

"Um. Don't anybody move," I said in a steady voice. My eyes felt like they were popping out of my head. The gator wasn't the biggest I'd ever seen, but it was formidable. Probably a six-footer that weighed more than Vera and me combined.

"I think you're getting your roles reversed, missy. I'm supposed to say that. Now here's what we're gonna do. We're all gonna walk back to your car, so the three of us can drive somewhere real private together and . . . what the hell?" Bruce had turned his head slightly and spotted the gator.

"Seriously. Don't move," I warned. "I'm not joking."

Bruce let out a long string of swear words. "I'm gonna shoot it."

"I wouldn't do that," I said. "If you miss, we're screwed."

The gator was about ten feet from Bruce. It lay on its belly, staring at him with vacant glassy eyes. It was possible it was merely curious and could turn tail at any second. Or it could be hungry, and Bruce looked like a hairy five-course meal.

"How come?" Bruce's voice quivered.

"Sudden movements will likely provoke it. Gators can reach speeds of up to thirty miles per hour in short bursts. It'll be on you before you know it."

Our only chance to get away from this lunatic was to play on his fear of reptiles. In reality, the gator was probably more afraid of us. Maybe. I didn't want to risk it.

"Then you trap it, or whatever you do. Go on." Bruce urged me with his eyes.

Vera snorted a little laugh, then began to chuckle

softly. "You think we can just wrangle a gator like that? Are you off your rocker?"

"Isn't that what you do? Trap gators? Come on. Do something!" Sweat wasn't just beading on Bruce's face, it was cascading like a waterfall. He raised the hand that wasn't holding the gun to swipe the perspiration out of his eyes, and the gator moved a foot forward. "Aw, hell, look at how fast it moves. Like a freakin' snake, crawling like that. I'm gonna shoot you two if you don't make it go away."

"Hope you're a good shot," I said.

Since Bruce was in between us and the gator—and since Vera and I were near a rock that we could hide behind—I felt a bit emboldened. The critter was easily twenty feet from us. Close enough to put a little fear in me, but since Bruce was nearer to the gator, I wasn't extremely worried about Vera and me.

While alligators could run fast in short bursts, they tended to run in a straight line, and weren't very bright. Come to think of it, Bruce wasn't that bright either.

If Vera and I were alone and ambushed by only the gator, we'd hide in silence behind the rock until it moved on. With Bruce and the gun, though, all bets were off.

"Here's one thing I don't understand, Bruce: why did you call me to trap a gator in your pool? Why didn't you call your buddy Gene? You could've saved some money."

He stammered for a bit. "I . . . I wanted the thing out of my pool. Your number was the first that came up online. So I called. Boy, was Gene angry when I told him I'd called you. That's how we got to talking about you two, and when I found out Vera was involved in the protest group. Later I came up with the plan to put both of you out of business by stealing Vera's gun and using it on Gene. Then I called and sent you to the place you'd discover Gene's body. Did that gator get closer?"

It hadn't, but I wouldn't tell Bruce that. "It definitely did."

"What are we gonna do here? Wait for it to eat us?"

"Yep," I said. There was no way I'd tell him that if we stayed silent and unmoving, the gator would get bored and walk away.

"Screw this." Bruce pointed the gun at the gator. That simple movement of raising his arm inspired the gator to open its jaws and hiss. It was a primal sound that even made the hair on my arms stand up.

Bruce whimpered and pulled the trigger. Either he was a bad shot or he was too terrified by the alligator, because he missed the reptile by a mile. Because the gator wasn't pleased—who could blame it—it took a few menacing steps toward Bruce.

He fired a second, and a third time. Probably he missed because of all the sweat in his eyes. Or perhaps those were tears.

As he aimed the handgun again, Vera turned to me. "That's my gun. Jerk."

She calmly walked over to Bruce. "Hey."

He turned to her. My heart was in my throat because the gun was pointed directly at her. Was she nuts? What was she doing?

I tried to keep track of the gator, but I couldn't rip my

eyes off Vera, who grabbed the barrel of the gun and Bruce's wrist and twisted.

"GO FLUFF YOURSELF," she hollered.

The gator hissed. Bruce let out an inglorious grunt. For a half second, I was paralyzed with fear. Should I subdue the gator or help Vera?

Neither was a good choice. But since the gator was still fifteen feet away, and because the creature wasn't maliciously evil like Bruce, I made my choice.

I ran to Bruce and kicked him squarely in the dick while he fought with my sister over the gun. My foot hit the right spongy spot, because he doubled over with a yell that echoed through the woods.

"Ass clown," I muttered, giving his junk an extra kick for good measure.

Vera wrestled the gun out of his grip. The gator paused and hissed. It was louder, which meant it was closer.

"C'mon," I cried. "Let's go!"

Vera and I tore out of the scrub, running in a zigzag pattern around trees and through the woods.

We burst into Bruce's manicured backyard. We didn't stop at the shed, or the patio table, or the pool. We hauled butt faster than a caffeinated squirrel on roller skates and kept going until we were in the middle of the empty suburban street, smack in front of Bruce's house.

We doubled over, hands on knees, panting. After a few seconds, we straightened to stand and looked around. There was no Bruce and no gator.

Vera still appeared pristine, with only a little mud on

her flats, but somehow I looked like I'd just spent a week on the war front. I had streaks of dirt and a few leaves stuck to me. My pants were ripped. I took off my hat and shook out my hair. A twig fell to the ground.

In the distance, police sirens wailed, and they seemed to be nearby.

Vera and I glanced around. As far as the eye could see there were dozens of identical new stucco homes, palm trees that swayed gently in the breeze, and lawns so picture-perfect and green that they didn't seem real. No people anywhere.

It seemed incomprehensible that we'd just been in a brawl with a gator and a murderer.

A police car turned onto the street, its wheels and siren screaming.

Vera scrunched up her face. "Can you believe they tore out all those incredible orange groves for this?"

Epilogue

It was the night before the bookstore's official first day, and Vera and I stood in the store, beside ourselves with excitement. In less than fifteen minutes, our guests would start arriving for our pre-opening bash. We'd invited the other business owners on Main Street, some acquaintances we knew from high school, the staff of the local library, and, of course, Jack.

Straight From the Heart looked out-of-this-world perfect. We had tall vases of white and pink roses placed around the store, tables stacked with romance novels and blank notebooks, a display of bookmarks and book lights, and, most importantly, floor-to-ceiling shelves that were packed with new, glorious books.

The entire place smelled like lavender and paper, roses and joy, and I inhaled a happy breath. My gaze landed on the counter, where we had a silver-framed photo of Dad, Mom, Vera, and me, from twenty years ago. We were on the bank of the Snake River, kneeling next to a medium-sized gator with rope securing its feet. Dad held its jaws shut. We figured it would be a great conversation piece while people were paying for their books.

My heart swelled with emotion.

If only Dad was alive to see this. We'd told him so many times over the years how we were going to open a bookstore together someday. And we finally had. We'd also continued his legacy with the trapping business.

"It looks so beautiful. The decorations are perfect. You did it," I gushed to my sister. "This is going to be the most popular store in all of Wahoo. You wait and see."

"*We* did it. I couldn't have done it without you. You prodded me to take the chance and open this, and you kept me on track. And you helped clear my name from a murder charge. Isn't that wild to even say aloud? We got our happy-ever-after."

And we had. Moments after Vera and I ran into the street outside of Bruce's home, Alex Holt and a platoon of cops came roaring up. Alex had listened to my voice-mail and then called Tyler, who continued to spill the beans about what he knew. Tyler simply couldn't make up his mind on who to trust and what to confess, so he gave up and told Holt everything.

"It was a little dicey there for a day or two. But we make the best team. Always have, always will."

Vera threw her arms around me and a sob escaped from her mouth. "I'm so sorry."

I patted her back. "It's OK. You don't have to keep saying that."

"No, it was my stupidity and terrible taste in men that led to all this."

"It was not. It was greed and paranoia and a bunch of guys who were trying to bend the rules to get ahead. I'm just glad that in the end, Tyler did the right thing by telling Holt everything."

"He was such a pile of old garbage," she whispered into my hair. "Tyler, I mean. Not Alex Holt. He seems quite wonderful."

Now both Tyler and Bruce were awaiting trial without bail. Tyler on election fraud charges and Bruce on a homicide charge. Even Chad, the boy toy in Barbie's house, was caught up in the arrests; he'd been friends with Tyler, Bruce, and Gene, and was charged with obstruction of justice and a handful of other petty crimes. Somehow, Barbie remained unscathed. I'd like to think she was innocent, but no one knew. Plenty of folks were gossiping, though.

And yes, Bruce had survived. The alligator never attacked him. As I always tell people, gators are more afraid of us than we are of them, and that gator in the scrub was no different. Bruce later told the authorities that it had run off after the scuffle with me and Vera. He'd been so frightened that he'd curled up in a ball and waited to die. He'd also pissed himself.

Holt had found him like that and arrested him without a fuss. He was now in the county jail, along with Tyler.

There was a possibility that Tyler would be charged with being an accessory to murder. The governor had removed him from office, and a special election had been called. Dave, the dog trainer, had jumped into the race.

I'd sent him twenty-five bucks for his campaign, mostly because he seemed like a good guy, and I felt bad about deceiving him that day at his house.

My concern wasn't with politics, though. It was with my sister.

"You sure you're OK?" I broke apart from her and wiped my thumb across her tear-stained cheek.

She nodded. "Now that I have some space from Tyler, I realize he wasn't good for me at all. Or for our business."

That was the other unexpected positive thing to have come from all of this. Because Tyler's assets were frozen, we didn't have to pay back the money he'd loaned to Vera immediately. We would absolutely do so, because I didn't want the karma of keeping Tyler's dirty cash. But we just weren't under extreme pressure to come up with it right away.

"You need to let me pick your next boyfriend, OK?"

She laughed and sniffled, dabbing her eyes with a napkin. "You're probably a better judge of men than I am, I guess."

"Dunno about that. But I know I have your best interests at heart, and I can see right through people who don't." I took a deep breath. "Are you ready for the party?"

It was five minutes to seven, and there were several people standing outside our door.

"Let's open up," Vera cried, and I unlocked the door.

Our fellow business owners, followed by some folks we knew from high school, streamed in. Vera and I chattered excitedly about the shop, and a few people took us aside separately, wanting to know more details about Tyler, Bruce, and Gene.

A tall, white-haired man pushing a stroller walked in. I recognized him immediately.

"Dave! Thank you for coming." I'd sent an invite to Dave Smith, the wronged city council candidate. Never did I expect him to come, but here he was with a tiny dog in a stroller.

He opened his arms for a hug, which was surprising, considering how angry he'd been the last time I saw him.

"I couldn't resist seeing your store. Also, I wanted to apologize for being snippy that day you came to the house."

"Really, I should apologize. Jack and I were fishing for information and we used a ridiculous excuse to come talk with you. Of course cats can't be trained."

Dave chortled.

"I don't know, kids. Catsy's pretty smart. We could try." The male baritone and the presence of a hand on my back sent electricity through my body.

It was Jack.

I beamed at him. "When did you get here? I didn't see you walk in."

He and Dave shook hands and chatted about the store. I soaked it in, drinking my glass of champagne. Pink, of course. Vera came over with a fresh bottle and topped off our drinks, then set the bottle on one of the many silver carts we'd rented so people wouldn't leave glasses on the tables near the books.

I introduced her to Dave, and she cooed over his dog.

"This is Chanel the Chiweenie." He pointed to the puppy, who was about the size of Catsy the kitten. Then Dave appraised my sister, who was wearing a white 1960s-style shift dress embroidered with pink flowers. "That is an adorable dress, girlfriend."

Thrilled by his compliment, my sister informed Dave that we had a new romantic mystery novel involving dogs and led him over to the far end of the room.

Jack and I stared into each other's eyes. "Hey," he said softly.

"Hey back. Glad you're here. Doesn't it all look amazing? Look at those bookcases."

Nodding, he scratched the back of his neck. "About that bookcase that I owe you."

I laughed and waved my free hand in the air. "You don't have to build it. We don't have to pretend anymore."

"I bought all of the materials and really did sketch out a blueprint. And maybe I'm not pretending. Don't want to pretend. I mean, I know that things are a little, ah, new, with me and my dating life, and you're just getting out of a relationship. But I was wondering if we could take things slow and, yikes. I'm too old for relationship games. I don't know what I'm doing." He laughed. "I like you, Maggie Andrews."

"Yes." I wanted to squeal from joy but controlled myself.

"What?"

"I'd like to take things slow. I'd like to not pretend. I like you too."

We stood there in the middle of the crowd, grinning at each other like horny dorks. OK, we were horny dorks.

From the warmth of my face, I suspected I was an unflattering shade of pink, but didn't care. Probably I would have stayed like that all night, staring into Jack's sexy dark-brown eyes, if I didn't spot Alex Holt coming into the store, looking like an extremely uncomfortable bull in a china shop.

"Guess who just walked in? Our favorite cop," I said. My stomach instinctively tightened, because every interaction I'd had with the man had involved a homicide case. Why was he here?

"Oh, cool. I invited him. Your sister said I should. We met up yesterday for coffee. I think he's going to read my book before I send it to the publisher. He had a lot of experience with a serial killer up in Tallahassee and I'm looking forward to his input." Jack waved and Holt ambled through the crowd toward us, narrowly avoiding knocking over a rack of bookmarks.

Holt was casual tonight, in jeans and a blue plaid button-down shirt that enhanced his broad frame. He looked like a former football player or something.

The two men clapped each other on the shoulders.

"Everything okay?" I asked. "You're not here to give us any bad news, are you?"

Holt laughed. "Nope. Just here to wish Vera well in her new endeavor. And you, too."

My stomach relaxed. "Thanks. If you get any gator complaints, you know who to call. Champagne?"

Alex nodded, and I walked away in search of a fresh bottle. When I found it, I filled a glass for Jack and waved at Rodney from the chamber of commerce, who was talking with the owner of Cheesy Does It near the werewolf romance section. Nearby, I spotted Diego Viernes, the animal rights hacker guy, checking out the science fiction shelf while nibbling on a carrot stick.

Even Barbie was here, wearing a white jumpsuit and tall white heels. Tonight, she resembled a Dolly Parton impersonator. She'd brought her pink velvet cupcakes, and they were out-of-this-world delicious. That woman could bake.

I blew her a kiss, and she blew one back.

When I delivered the champagne to Alex, Jack was nowhere to be found.

"Where'd he go?" I asked.

"He went to use the facilities. And uh, I'm glad we're alone because I wanted to ask you something personal."

My heart sped up. The way Alex kept swallowing, and his goofy little smile, told me that he was going to ask me out. Oh, dear. This would be awkward. I liked Alex, but not in that way.

Plus, Jack. They had such a good bromance going. It was kind of shocking that Alex hadn't noticed the attraction between the two of us.

Alex cleared his throat. "The place looks great," he said.

"Thanks. It does. Vera worked so hard."

We both nodded.

"What did you want to ask me?" I prodded, wanting to get this over with.

"Oh, right. Um." He paused and ran a hand over his dirty-blond beard. He was handsome, but not at all my type.

"Keep this between us, please."

"Of course."

"Do you think your sister might want to hang out? With me? Maybe for coffee or something? I know she was dating Tyler and all, but I didn't get the impression they'd been together long. Or that she was that into him."

I gasped, then exploded in laughter. Alex looked horrified.

"Sorry, sorry." I gulped down the rest of my champagne as relief flowed through me like the alcohol's bubbles. "I'm not laughing at you. I do this when I'm nervous. I apologize. My sister is not in love with Tyler, and she's very much single. I think she'd enjoy going on a date with you."

"You wouldn't mind? I know that we had our differences there, for a little while."

"Are you kidding? It's a great idea." I beamed. "The two of you make a great match. You should ask her out right this second. Seriously. I think it's cute that you even wanted my opinion."

"I wanted to broach the topic with you, because you know her best. And you seem so protective of her. I've never met anyone who wanted to prove someone innocent like you did."

"She's my twin. My best friend. My everything." Tears came to my eyes, and through the blur I saw Jack near the counter, laughing with Vera. She was showing him the photo of us and our parents. "C'mon. Let's go chat with her."

We walked over to the counter and I slipped my hand through Jack's arm. He smiled at me, and I beamed at my sister. She looked up shyly at Alex, who seemed adorably nervous around her as he gripped his champagne and cleared his throat.

"Is that the two of you?" He pointed to the framed photo.

"This is us when we were five, with our dad. Even back then we were trapping gators. My sister and I are fierce. You should come with us on a trapping call sometime," she said to Jack and Alex, but mostly to Alex.

"I'd like that," he said.

She twirled a lock of her hair. It was hilarious how she loved to flirt and watching her brought a wide smile to my face. Tonight, she was fizzing away like a bottle of pink champagne.

To be honest, I was too.

"A toast," Jack said, holding up his champagne. The three of us did as well.

"To the Gator Queens," he said. "May they trap alligators, sell books, and solve crimes."

We all took long sips of our bubbly and chatted. Eventually, Vera and Alex drifted away. She claimed she wanted to show him her favorite romance novel.

I turned to Jack. "What are you doing later?"

He lifted an eyebrow. "Dunno. What are you doing?"

"Hopefully more of this."

I leaned over and kissed him softly on the lips. It was time to rethink the concept of happy-ever-after.

— THE END —

Acknowledgments

Thank you to my agent, Jill Marsal, for not giving up on this book, and to Katherine Pelz, for wanting to edit another one of my bonkers stories.

About the Author

Tara Lush is a Florida-based author and journalist. She's an RWA Rita finalist, an Amtrak writing fellow, and the winner of the George C. Polk award for environmental journalism. She was a reporter with The Associated Press in Florida, covering crime, alligators, natural disasters, and politics. She also writes contemporary romance set in tropical locations under the name Tamara Lush. Tara is a fan of vintage pulp-fiction book covers, Sinatra-era jazz, 1980s fashion, tropical chill, kombucha, gin, tonic, seashells, iPhones, Art Deco, telenovelas, street art, coconut anything, strong coffee, and newspapers. She lives on the Gulf Coast with her husband and their dog.